SILVER

SILVER

PARIS WILLIAMS

atmosphere press

To my mom and dad.

Thank you for the never-ending stream
of unconditional love and support.

CHAPTER 1

Lucy arrived at the office to start her shift to find that the door had yet to be unlocked. "Typical," she said to herself. "Why would we be open at almost two in the afternoon?" She reached into her purse and began the search for her keys. Every day, Lucy told herself that she should have her keys out and ready when she got to the door, and every day she stood on the street rummaging through her bag. Maybe she was hoping that one day she would get there and wouldn't need them, but so much for wishful thinking. Finally, she found her keys in their usual spot, at the bottom of her purse, and unlocked the door. She walked up the single flight of stairs, thinking that it would be a good idea for her to give the hallway a deep cleaning. There was a musty smell, and her hand was covered in dust when she touched the railing. At the top of the stairs, there was a single door that read "CLI FO D SI VER, P.I." She looked on the ground and found the "L" from "Silver" by her foot. She bent down and picked it up so that she could add it to the letter graveyard she had started on her desk, and then she tried to press the peeling "D" and "V" back against the window. Once satisfied that she had bought at least one more day for those two letters, she unlocked the door and entered the office.

She hit the lights and walked across the room to her desk, well, her table that was masquerading as a desk. Everything was as she left it the night before, showing her that he did not take her threat of physical violence lightly. It wasn't the fanciest reception area, but Lucy took a lot of pride in it. The room wasn't very large, and none of the furniture matched, but she kept things spotless. They couldn't fit much into the room but wanted it to look as much like a waiting area as possible, so he made sure to provide her with a desk in front of his office door. On both sides of the room, there were two chairs with a small end table in between them covered in out-of-date magazines. No two chairs were alike, and whenever she told him to update the magazines, he told her it was point-less, considering that no one was reading them. Her desk was pretty bare except for an office phone, a cup full of pens, and the other letters that had fallen off the door. She didn't have her own computer, but when she worked, she would set up her laptop and work on her homework whenever there were no clients, which was most of the time. She dropped her purse on her desk chair and placed the "L" with the "F" and "R," then turned to open the office door behind her. She started to turn the door lever but then remembered the time she opened it to find him lying on his couch ass-naked and thought it would be better to knock.

She rapped her knuckles against the door loudly three times, then put her ear to the door to see if she could hear a response. "Are you in there, Silver?" she shouted through the door, and the only answer she received was an angry grunt. "Are you dressed?" Again, another grunt. "Ready or not, I'm coming in," she shouted as she turned the lever and entered the room.

She hit the light switch next to the door and was thankful

that at least he had his pants on this time, but that was the only nice thing she could think of to say about the current state of Clifford Silver. His office was not much smaller than the reception area, and his desk sat in the middle of the room with nothing on it except a computer and a phone. Along the wall on the left-hand side of his office was a small couch, and next to it was the door to the only bathroom in the office. Lucy often complained about how inconvenient it was that anyone who had to use the bathroom had to go through his office, but he always joked that he did not want anyone shitting in his bathroom anyway. In the corner of his office was a coat rack that held a few small jackets and his gun holster.

All six foot four inches of Clifford Silver were sprawled out along the couch, which wasn't long enough for him, so his ankles and feet hung over the arm. His drool dripped down the seat of the couch, creating a small puddle on the floor and adding to the rest of the drool stains. He tried to shield his eyes from the new light that had been introduced into the room, but Lucy wasn't going to let him off that easily and walked over to him to shake him awake.

"Why do you hate me?" he mumbled to her, and Lucy nearly passed out from the fumes coming from his breath.

"If I hated you, I wouldn't be waking you up to tell you that you're about to be late picking up Chrissy again," she said as she walked over to his desk to throw away the empty bottle of Jack Daniels that was left there the night before. Silver jumped out of his daze, feeling around himself for his phone, which Lucy was already holding to hand him. "It's 2:05."

"Fuck!" he shouted as he sprang to his feet. He ran to his desk and opened the second drawer on the left, which doubled as a bathroom closet, to grab his toothbrush and toothpaste that he keeps in the office with the rest of his toiletries.

"That's a good idea. Your breath smells like shit," said Lucy. She casually reached into another desk drawer, where he kept clothes on top of client files, and pulled out a clean shirt for him to change into, or at least a cleaner shirt than the one he was currently wearing.

"Fuck you," he mumbled with his toothbrush in his mouth. He rinsed his mouth out and came back into the room. Lucy was opening the shades to the window opposite his couch.

"Don't get me wrong. I'll take shitty breath over walking in and seeing your dick again."

"Whatever; you know you liked what you saw." He snatched the shirt she was holding out for him. "You stared just a little too long before you covered your eyes."

He wasn't wrong. When he interviewed Lucy to be his assistant, she was so distracted by looking at him that she could barely answer his questions. She had always thought private detectives were fat and balding slobs with food stains on their shirts from late-night stakeouts, but Clifford Silver was tall, handsome, had a head full of hair, and was in excellent shape. He pulled off the shirt he was wearing, revealing his toned chest and abs. If he hadn't told her himself, she would have never guessed he was biracial, with his complexion. His skin was a lighter shade of brown, but not as light as you would typically expect from a person with mixed parents. He had hazel eyes and very thick and curly hair when he went a while without cutting it, which was currently the case. Lucy cut her eyes away after he finished putting on the new shirt, hoping he didn't catch her staring. He might have if he wasn't busily scratching at a stain on his shirt. At least she got the food stains part right.

"I took this job to observe and learn from you, and that's not what I thought I would be observing," she said.

"Well, you have to observe something. It's not like we have clients beating down the door," he said while he looked for where he had sat his phone down.

Again, Lucy picked up his phone and held it out for him as she said, "How many clients do you think you miss when you sleep past noon with the door locked and they can't get in?"

"If you really cared that much, you would drop out of school and work here full-time, so we won't miss those clients," he said, snatching the phone from her.

"Yeah, devoting my life to waking your drunk ass up every day isn't as appealing as you think."

"Wow, you would rather get a proper education than take care of me?" He pretended to be shocked. "I wish you would've put 'selfish' on your résumé so I wouldn't have hired your ass."

Lucy chuckled. "Please, I doubt anyone else would've taken this job for what you pay me. I could've put that I was a serial killer on there, and you would've still hired me."

"Touché." Silver laughed as he threw his toothbrush back into its drawer and grabbed his keys off his desk.

"What's the point of showering and brushing your teeth here if you're still going to be late every day?"

"You know I hate my bathroom at home. I can't even open the door all the way because the toilet is behind it."

"Then why would you rent it?"

"Because I'm broke, and it's all I could afford."

"If you're so broke, why don't you just give up the apartment? You sleep, shit, and shower here anyways."

"I can't live in my office, Lucy; that's unprofessional. Call me if you need me." He ran out the door as Lucy shouted back at him, but he couldn't hear her response. He had to get from Bridgeview to Matteson in fifteen minutes. Leave it to Tonya to move Chrissy to the suburbs. If he didn't know any better, Silver would have sworn she did it to make him put more miles on his car when he wanted to see his daughter. She always said he loved that car more than her, and towards the end of their marriage, he started to agree with her, but how could she blame him? A '65 Shelby Mustang and the second most precious thing in his life, his daughter Chrissy being the first.

He jumped in the car and pulled into traffic, praying that Cicero wouldn't be backed up today, which wasn't likely. On days like this, he wished he still drove a car with a siren so that he could breeze through traffic. The last thing Silver needed was to be late again and have his ex-wife threaten to not let him see his daughter for the twentieth time that week, as if it wasn't bad enough that she divorced him while his life was in turmoil. He knew he wasn't the most pleasant guy to be around after he was forced to retire, but she knew it wouldn't last forever. So now he spends every night on a couch in his office, and the only time he gets to see his daughter is in the fifteen minutes it takes to drive her home from school. He had to beg Tonya to even allow that privilege, and he knows that she has teachers spying for her at the school, calling her when he's late. As he turned on to Cicero, he thought that traffic wasn't as bad as he thought it would be when his phone rang.

"Hi, sweetheart! How is Daddy's princess?"

"You're running late again, aren't you, Daddy?" Chrissy's little six-year-old voice said through the phone.

"Just a little bit, baby, but I promise I'm almost there."

"Ok, but you know Mommy's going to be mad again."

"Remember when I told you Mommy doesn't need to know everything?"

"Yes ..."

"This is one of those things Mommy doesn't need to know."

"We could tell Mommy we stopped for ice cream before you took me home."

"That's an excellent idea."

"But I'll need to have ice cream when I go home, so she'll believe it."

"Baby, are you blackmailing me?"

"What's blackmailing?"

"I'll explain it to you while we get ice cream."

"Yay! Ok, Daddy, I'll see you when you get here."

"Ok, baby." Silver laughed to himself as he hung up the phone. She had definitely learned that from her mother.

Silver checked the clock as he pulled up to the school. Only twenty minutes late, not bad, he thought to himself. However, he could see his daughter standing with her teacher; from the look on Mrs. Drisdell's face, she was not impressed.

Chrissy ran to the car's passenger door as soon as the wheels stopped moving, while Mrs. Drisdell took a couple of steps toward the car with her arms folded. As soon as she was within shouting distance, she said, "Mr. Silver, you're late again."

"Sorry, there was traffic, and you know I'm coming from the city," said Silver as he tried to hurry and get Chrissy's seat belt done so they could shut the door as soon as possible.

"Might I suggest you leave out earlier? That way, traffic wouldn't be a factor."

"Wow, Mrs. Drisdell, what a wonderful suggestion," he said to Mrs. Drisdell before he whispered to Chrissy, "Baby, close the door." And gave Mrs. Drisdell a wave goodbye before she could give him detention.

"She really doesn't like you," said Chrissy as he pulled away from the school.

"What!? Of course, she likes me. Everyone likes your dad."

"Not Mrs. Drisdell. Her and Mommy talk about how they don't like you on the phone all the time," she said, confirming to Silver there was a snitch at the school. "Mommy told her that no one likes you. Is that true, Daddy?"

Silver looked at his daughter in her big, light brown eyes and could see the concern on her face. It really pissed him off that Tonya would say something like that while Chrissy was in earshot of the conversation. Their marriage didn't end on good terms, so there was no love lost that she had a low opinion of him, but he would never talk down about her and let Chrissy hear him. It wasn't his place to change her view of her mother.

He smiled at Chrissy and ran his fingers through her curly brown hair. "Do you like me?"

"Of course, Daddy."

"Are you someone?"

"Yes," Chrissy said, with a confused look on her face.

"Well then, how can no one like me when you are someone, and you like me?"

"But, Dad, I'm just one person."

"You're the only person that matters, princess," said Silver as he gave her the most reassuring smile he could manage. It was sweet that she was so concerned for her old man. "So, how was school? Did you learn anything today?" he asked to change the subject. Chrissy began to describe her entire day, and Silver listened intently. He loved these moments with her and thought it was vital for her to know that, although he no longer lived in the same house as her, he still wanted to know everything going on in her life and that when she talked, he would always be listening. She was telling him about what she had for lunch when his phone started ringing. "Hey, Lucy. You're on speaker, and Chrissy is in the car, so watch your mouth," he said when he picked up.

"How soon can you make it back to the office?" Lucy asked on the other end.

"We're getting ice cream, then I'll be dropping her off, so maybe an hour. Why?"

"We have a potential client who would like to speak to you."

"That's fantastic! I'll be there as soon as I can. Lucy, please don't let them leave."

"Handcuff them to the radiator. Got it," Lucy said as she hung up the phone. Silver laughed at the thought and then hoped to himself that Lucy wouldn't literally handcuff whoever was waiting for him. It had been a couple of weeks since his last client, but kidnapping was a level of desperation he hadn't reached yet.

Silver got Chrissy a vanilla cone and watched her struggle

to keep it from dripping all over her hand while he drove her home. When he pulled into the driveway, Tonya was waiting on her front step with her arms folded.

"Oooh, you're in trouble," Chrissy sang out while licking her fingers.

"Just remember Dad wasn't late. We went for ice cream." Chrissy nodded to let him know they were on the same page, then they both jumped out of the car to face the music.

"You're late," Tonya said calmly as soon as he could hear her.

"Look, Ma, Daddy got me ice cream," Chrissy shouted at her as she ran into the house.

"Finish your ice cream and get started on your homework. I'll be there in a minute after I talk to your dad." Tonya turned towards Silver just as he was trying to creep away. "Where do you think you're going?"

"I figured I would get out of your hair. Plus, I have a client waiting for me back at the office." Silver took another step towards his car.

"If you're going to be late, you need to call."

"I wasn't late. We just stopped for ice cream."

"Then you should've called and asked if it were ok to do so."

"I didn't know I needed permission to get ice cream with my daughter."

"You're not the one that has to deal with her once she's on a sugar high."

"Well, in that case, how about you let me spend more time with her besides just picking her up from school? I would happily deal with her sugar high."

"Have you stopped drinking?"

"I've stopped drinking during the day."

Tonya had to stop herself from laughing. He always had a way of disarming her when she was trying to have a serious conversation. "Well, until you stop drinking altogether, this is all you get."

Silver paused for a moment. He wanted to promise her that he would, but he knew it would be a lie; after all, what else would help him to sleep at night? "You look more and more beautiful every time I see you, T."

He said that to change the subject, but that didn't mean it wasn't true. Silver still had some hard feelings about the divorce, but every time he laid eyes on her with her long legs, full lips, and beautifully smooth chocolate skin, his heart thawed just a little. "Compliments won't get you out of everything," she said as she smiled at him.

"Really? That's my go-to move," he said with a sly grin. "It always worked in the past."

"Well, lucky for me, this isn't the past." Silver could see the concern grow on her face. "I worry about you, Cliff."

"I know, T, and I'm working on it, I promise." He reached out and grabbed her hand. "But in the meantime, can you not let Chrissy hear you tell her teacher that you hate me?"

She pulled her hand away. "I never said that. I said that no one likes you; there's a difference."

"Mhmm, well, I don't think she knows the difference, and it's confusing for her."

"Ok, I get your point," she said as she rolled her eyes.

"I do have to go. I wasn't lying about that client waiting for me."

"You actually have a client?"

"Wow, that was mean. Just for that, the next time you want some of this." Silver twirled in a circle. "I'll give you some, but I won't be happy about it."

"I wouldn't hold my breath if I were you." She turned to go inside. "Don't be late tomorrow."

He watched her close the door, then got in the car and started the engine. Before he drove off, he looked at the house. "She know she want some of this."

CHAPTER 2

Silver was able to make it back to the office pretty quickly. On the way back, he called Lucy to make sure the client was still there, and Lucy let him know that she was willing to wait. He parked in his usual spot and headed upstairs. When Silver entered the office, Lucy was at her desk, and the client was sitting in a chair to her left, thumbing her way through a magazine. He walked over to introduce himself and tried to take in as much about her as possible. She was white and looked to be about mid-fifties from the gray hairs that were starting to peek through the blonde. She was a good-looking woman, although she seemed pretty tired, or maybe it was stress. His eyes fell to her hands, perfectly manicured with a wedding ring on her left ring finger. Did marital problems bring her to his door? She sat with excellent posture, and she wore a red blazer, black slacks, and those heels with the red bottoms that he could never remember the name of, which meant he probably couldn't afford them. Overall, she was not from this part of town.

"Hi, my name is Cliff Silver," he said, holding out his hand. "And you are?"

"Sara Lindsey," she said as she shook his hand.

"It's very nice to meet you, Mrs. Lindsey. Thank you so much for your patience. If you give me just one moment to get settled, then we'll get started." Silver started walking towards his office. "Lucy, can I borrow you for a moment?" Lucy followed him into his office and shut the door behind her. "You get any info from her while you were waiting?"

"Nope. She only wants to speak with you, but she definitely comes from money. That outfit, shoes, and purse cost a couple of grand, easy."

"Yes, she definitely stands out on this side of town." That worried Silver. Why would she come to him? She must have the numbers of plenty of investigators that cater to people of means. So how did she even hear of him?

Lucy could see the confused look on his face. "Is something wrong?"

"No, bring her in." Silver had questions, but was in no position to turn down money. While Lucy was grabbing Mrs. Lindsey, he reached into his desk and grabbed his bottle of aspirin; his head was ringing from the night before. "Please have a seat, Mrs. Lindsey," said Silver when Lucy reemerged with the client.

"Thank you for seeing me without an appointment," said Sara Lindsey as she sat across from him. "Your associate told me you were with your daughter. I hope I didn't interrupt your time with her."

"No worries, Mrs. Lindsey. I was just dropping her off at home. Please tell me what I can do for you?"

Mrs. Lindsey glanced over at Lucy. "Would you mind if we talked privately?"

"Mrs. Lindsey ..."

"Please call me Sara."

"Sara, Lucy is my apprentice, which means she's here

to learn and observe. So, I can vouch for her discretion, and having her involved also means that I can provide around-the-clock service subbing her in when I have other obligations."

Sara thought for a moment, then nodded a silent approval. "I want you to follow my husband, Richard."

"That's something we can definitely do for you," said Silver. "Is there something in particular you're hoping for us to find?"

"I'm hoping you do not find anything," said Sara sharply.

"Look, Sara, I understand how difficult it must have been for you to have to come to someone in my profession, but whether you're hoping to catch him doing something or not, I need to know what I'm looking for in order to do my job." Silver paused to let that sink in. "Why don't you start by telling me about your husband?"

"Richard and I have been married for the last six years," she began. "For the first five years, we were very happy, but recently things have changed."

"Things like what?"

"He used to be very romantic and attentive, but now he's barely home, and when he is, we may as well be strangers."

"Do you have reason to believe he's cheating on you? Have you overheard any conversations or seen any suspicious messages on his phone?"

"No. It's just that everyone told me that I was a fool for marrying Richard because he just wanted my money. Now that he's acting this way, I'm beginning to suspect it's true."

"What does he do for a living?"

"He works for a law firm that's based downtown."

"Does this law firm pay him well?"

"Very well."

"So why would anyone think he was after you for your money?"

Sara's eyes fell to her lap, and when she looked up again, they were brimming with tears. "You have to understand he's a few years younger than me."

"How many years is a few?" asked Silver.

"Twenty-two years." Sara searched Silver's face for a reaction, but he didn't give her one.

"Does he work long hours?"

"Very long hours."

"That would explain why he's barely home, and I'm sorry he doesn't show you much attention, but if he comes home every night, when would he have time for an affair?"

"He does not come home every night." Silver urged her to continue with his eyes. "He hates commuting from our home outside of the city, so he keeps an apartment downtown where he sleeps during the week. He only comes home on weekends."

"And you believe that he's using that apartment to see other women," said Silver as more of a statement than a question.

"Yes," said Sara, finally letting a tear fall from her eyes.

"I still don't see why you believe money is his motivation."

"Does it matter?" She was almost shouting. "Do you want my money or not?"

"I'm sorry for all of the questions, Sara. I was a former cop, and we're trained to ask a lot of questions," he said softly.

"Bottom line is I do not care why he is having an affair. I just want to know if he's having one."

Lucy spoke for the first time, "If he's cheating, we can get the proof you need. Our rate is two hundred dollars per hour plus expenses, and we require two thousand upfront."

Silver tried to catch Lucy's eye to signal her to cut it out. Charging her that much could run her out the door, but before he could make eye contact with Lucy, Sara reached for her purse. "That won't be a problem."

She reached in, pulled out exactly two thousand dollars in cash, and handed it to Silver along with a picture of her husband as she stood to leave. "We'll be in touch," said Silver as he grabbed the money. "Before you leave, would you mind telling me how you found out about me?"

"I was referred to you," she said quickly, then she turned

and tried to hurry out the door.

"Referred by who?" he asked before she could escape.

She stopped with her hand on the door lever; after a moment, she turned her head back towards him. "I'd rather not say, and quite frankly, I don't think it's important. My money is good, no matter how I made my way to your door."

Silver didn't respond; he just gave her a nod. Seeing that her answer was satisfactory, Sara opened the door and exited, leaving Silver and Lucy to get started on her case.

"That was risky going for that much money," Silver said as soon as he was sure he wouldn't be heard. "What if she would've walked out?"

"Yeah, but not as risky as asking so many questions," Lucy responded.

"Something about her story doesn't sit right with me," said Silver as he leaned back into his chair. "It doesn't add up."

"Does her money add up?" asked Lucy sarcastically.

"Money isn't worth it if you end up in some shit."

"You're a PI. Your entire job description is dealing with people's shit. Part of what people pay you for is discretion."

"Discretion means that I won't discuss their business. It doesn't mean that I don't get the entire story."

"You're not a detective anymore. It isn't your job to find all of the answers."

Silver rolled his eyes and turned his chair away from her. He hated when she threw his current job status in his face.

"I'm just saying, you can get answers, or you could get paid," she said.

"I guess you're right," he responded, admitting defeat, although there was definitely something still nagging him. For the moment, he would let it rest. "Still a bold move, going after that much money."

"I figured she wouldn't mind. She's clearly desperate, and something tells me that she would pay anything to avoid what she would have to give him in a divorce," said Lucy as she shrugged her shoulders.

"Ok, I'm starting to see why I hired you."

"And if we do a really good job, maybe she'll refer us to some of her rich friends."

"Well, we better do a really fucking good job."

"Where should we start?"

"I'm going to go to the precinct and get them to pull Richard Lindsey's sheet. I want to make sure he's not some con man. I know it's unlikely, but it's possible he's been playing her all of this time."

"You think he could go all of these years without her knowing the real him?" asked Lucy.

"Like I said, it's unlikely, but love is blind. You'd be surprised what someone can get away with when you don't want to see the truth."

"Couldn't we pull his sheet ourselves?"

"Theirs would be more extensive, and if he is a con man, he must be pretty good at hiding his tracks. I'm assuming her lawyers would've had him thoroughly checked before she married him."

"You sure you don't just want to see Rita?"

"Rita was just my partner, nothing more," Silver said, rolling his eyes. "And now she's just a friend."

"I don't know about you, but I don't look at my friends the way you look at her." Silver started to walk away from Lucy, but she followed him. "And also, friends don't turn friends in."

Silver stopped in his tracks and turned to face her. "I told you not to bring that up."

"I'm just saying, be careful. Ford wants to lock you up, and you know she doesn't have your back."

"I'm going to leave now and try to forget this conversation ever happened so that I won't have to fire you. Get in touch with Sara and get her husband's schedule and where we can pick up his trail. She left so quickly I didn't get the chance to get that info from her." He turned again and started walking towards the door.

"Will do, and just so you know, you would be lost without me," she shouted at him as the door closed behind him.

―――――――――――――――――――――――――――――

Silver walked into the bullpen, scanning the room to ensure Captain Ford was nowhere to be found. Ford wasn't his biggest fan and would probably have him forcibly removed. His office was on the other side of the room and resembled a giant fishbowl, so Silver could see right into it. The lights were off, so Silver assumed that no one was home, but he still gave the room one more scan to be sure. Once he knew the coast was clear, he made his way to Rita Kaye's desk. She was sitting there doing paperwork, but damn, did she make even that look good. You could see her curves even while she sat, and her brown skin actually glistened. She had dark brown eyes that he often found himself getting lost in, and Silver always joked that the only reason she got confessions was because of the hypnotic effect she had on men; with a face that beautiful, who wouldn't tell her anything she wanted to know? He watched her for a moment while she twirled one of her braids around her finger, something she did when she was deep in thought. It was a shame he had to interrupt this picturesque moment.

"How's the best detective in Chicago?" he shouted, breaking her attention from her work.

"What do you want, Silver?" She crossed her arms as she turned to look at him.

"I just wanted to come see you."

"Usually, when you want to see me, we get lunch or dinner. You only risk being seen by Cap when you need something. So, spit it out."

"Well, since you insist, I have a new case and ..."

"And you were hoping I could run the person you're investigating's name."

"Wow, Kaye, you know me so well." Silver flashed her a smile, hoping his charm would get this favor done for him.

Rita turned her chair around so he wouldn't see her blush. "I told you no more using police resources for personal favors."

"Come on, Kaye, this client is paying a lot of money, and I wanna make sure this guy isn't violent before I have my assistant tail him."

"You shouldn't have that little white girl tailing anyone. You're gonna get her hurt." Rita stood from her desk and walked towards the break room.

"Lucy can handle herself, but if the guy has a violent past, then I won't let her go near him." Silver chased after her but made sure to stay behind and enjoy the view.

"Staring at my ass won't get me to change my mind."

"What if I did some other things to your—"

"You finish that sentence, and I'll break your jaw." She walked into the break room and over to the fresh pot of coffee.

"Come on, Kaye, all you have to do is type his name into the computer and let it do the work for you." He leaned onto the counter next to her. "Come on, partner, help a brotha out."

"We're not partners anymore, and you're barely a brotha."

"Damn, just going to rub my white side in my face." Silver faked like he was offended. "When I get pulled over, I'm black, and that's all that matters."

Someone that they hadn't noticed before laughed from the other side of the breakroom. They both turned and looked at the man standing in the corner, and when he saw their eyes on him, he stopped. He was a young Hispanic man dressed in plain clothes, which meant he must've been a detective. He was a squatty guy, and his haircut suggested that he was former military.

"Silver, this is my new partner, Javier Estrada."

Javier walked over to the two of them and held out his hand. Silver studied him for a moment before reaching out and shaking it. "Nice to meet you. You can call me Silver."

"You're her old partner?" asked Javier.

"The one and only."

"You're the one they accused of ..."

"Accused of what?" Silver asked, as he took a step toward Javier.

Javier stepped back as his eyes roamed to Rita, begging for help. He could see her behind Silver, shaking her head to let him know he was in danger. He looked back at Silver and stammered, "Accused of being a great detective."

Silver stared at him for what felt like an eternity for Javier. "Why, thank you, Jose. I really appreciate it."

"Uh, it's Javier," he said, correcting him, but Silver had already focused his attention back on Rita.

"So, you really aren't going to run that name for me, partner?"

"Nope, I'm really not."

"I can run it for you," Javier said enthusiastically.

"Wow, Jose, you would really do that for me?"

"It's Javier, and yeah, just give me the name."

"His name is Richard Lindsey. Here's his picture for you to match with his DMV photo. Look at that, Rita, you just might be replaced." Silver put his arm around Javier.

"You wouldn't replace me."

"And how come I wouldn't?"

Rita turned toward Silver and seductively walked to him. "Because if you do," she said as she moved in closer. "You'll miss your chance." She was so close Silver could smell the shampoo in her hair. "To continue to fantasize about something you'll never have," she whispered softly in his ear. Then she turned and walked out of the break room, leaving Silver and Javier wondering what had just happened.

"We should pull that sheet," Silver said to break the tension.

"Umm, yeah, follow me to my desk," Javier led Silver out of the break room and back into the bullpen. He sat at his computer, and Silver sat in a chair to the side of the desk.

The chair had wheels on it, so Silver rolled over to Rita while he waited for Javier to sign in. "So, Kaye, how often do you fantasize about me?"

"Who the fuck said that I ever fantasize about you?"

"Isn't that what you said in the breakroom?" Silver said, pretending to be confused.

"I've always admired your ability to hear whatever you want, no matter what was said."

Silver leaned in closer, getting a whiff of her shampoo again. "You know your fantasies can become a reality," he said softly.

Rita looked him in the eye. "And how would Tonya feel about that?"

"I'm divorced, remember."

"Only on paper." They held eye contact with each other, neither breaking the tension between them.

"I have that info for you," Javier said, breaking the trance they were in. "You just want to know his criminal history, right?"

Silver smiled at Rita before breaking eye contact to look at Javier. "Yes, specifically anything violent."

"Nothing violent, just some parking tickets and traffic violations."

Silver stood up. "Well, thank you so much, Jose. Kaye, it was lovely to see you, as always, but I really should leave before—"

"Who let this trash in here?" a deep voice shouted from across the bullpen.

Rita jumped up from her desk. "Sir, he was just leaving."

Silver turned to get a look at Captain Arthur Ford, a short, fat white man whose mustache was so thick Silver often wondered if the man glued hair from the top of his head to his upper lip.

"It's nice to see you too, Captain. Have you gotten taller since last time?" said Silver. Javier stifled a chuckle but became very interested in his computer screen when he felt Ford's eyes burning a hole in the side of his head.

"Get the fuck out of my precinct before I lock you up with the rest of the criminals." Ford began to walk towards Silver.

"Like I said, sir, he's on his way out," Kaye said, stepping between the two of them.

"Yeah, I was just stopping by to see if Rita here wanted to get some dinner, but she's busy, so I'm leaving." Silver kissed her on the cheek. "Until next time, and it was very nice to meet you, Estrada."

"Next time I catch you in here, I'll lock you up where you belong," said Ford as Silver made his way to the elevator.

"You make it a habit of locking up innocent men?" Silver asked without breaking his stride.

"Do you actually catch husbands cheating on their wives, or do you just plant that evidence too?"

This made Silver stop. He could feel his body temperature rise with his anger. "It was nice to see you, Captain," he said as he stepped onto the elevator and pressed the button for the ground floor. For once, he and Ford agreed on something, but with one slight difference: if they see each other again, Ford won't lock him up for no reason. Silver will give him one.

CHAPTER 3

Silver drove back to his office, gripping his steering wheel so tightly he could leave an impression of his hand on it. Every time he came face to face with Ford, this is how it would end. Ford purposely pushed Silver's buttons to try to provoke him, and the captain knew just what buttons to push. Nothing would make Silver happier than to knock that ugly-ass mustache right off Ford's face, but he knew that's exactly what Ford wanted. An assaulting-an-officer charge would be the perfect reason to lock Silver away.

Not long after he left the precinct, Rita sent him a text asking if he was ok. He shot her a text back saying he was fine, but Silver knew he wasn't fooling her. She asked if he wanted to get dinner once her shift was over, but he declined. He wasn't in the mood to talk about how his life was going or to get a pep talk about how he shouldn't let Ford get to him. The worst was when she complained about work. He could always tell that it was her attempt to make him not miss the job as much. It was very sweet of her to do so, but it never worked. He was made to be a cop, and it just reminded him that he was no longer one.

When he returned to the office, he sat in his car for a while. It was a point of pride for him that no one ever saw him down and that he looked invincible to the never-ending stream of bullshit that his life had become. He often found himself sitting in his car and practicing his poker face before he faced someone. Whether it was Chrissy, Lucy, Tonya, or Rita, nothing was more important to him than everyone seeing him be his usual self. After he felt like he had himself together for this particular situation, he got out of his car and headed upstairs. He thought that maybe he would send Lucy home early. That way, he could get started on his nightly therapy.

"Did you find out anything?" asked Lucy when he walked into the office.

"Yeah, nothing popped on our guy except for some tickets," Silver responded as he walked past her into his office. "Did Sara give you his schedule?"

"I wrote it down and left it on your desk."

Silver walked over to his desk and sat down. He scanned the schedule Lucy jotted down for him. "Ok, I'll watch him all day tomorrow, just to be extremely sure I'm not putting you in harm's way. Then from there, I'll work out a schedule for us."

"Who's going to pick up Chrissy tomorrow?" asked Lucy.

"I still will. According to this, Lindsey will still be at work, so I shouldn't miss much."

"Ok, boss. Sounds like a plan." Lucy picked up the picture of Richard Lindsey sitting on Silver's desk. "Good-looking and a lawyer. If Sara doesn't want him, I'll take him."

"Why wait? That would make this a quick and easy job."

"Have we reached the point where you're pimping me out for clients?"

"Not until I buy my purple suit and cane," said Silver with a chuckle. "Why don't you cut out early today? Now that we have a case, you may be working some long hours for the next couple of days, so you should get some rest."

"Don't have to tell me twice." Lucy stepped out of his office to gather her things. "Do you have any plans tonight?" she shouted from the other room.

"No, I was going to see if Rita wanted to grab some dinner, but Ford caught me there and asked me to leave."

"He asked?"

"Now that you mention it, it was more of a demand. He shouted something about, 'If I see you again, I'll throw you in a cell.' "

"And you still think it's a good idea to keep showing your face there."

"Ford is all talk," said Silver dismissively. "He can't lock me up unless I give him a reason to."

"Keep playing with fire, and I'm sure he'll find one." Lucy turned to leave but doubled back. "What are you going to eat for dinner?"

"I don't know. I'll probably order in."

"You're not going to have another liquid dinner, are you?" she asked with a hint of worry.

"I promise I'll try solid foods today," he said with a wink.

Lucy hesitated for a moment and contemplated whether or not she should buy him food and force-feed him herself but decided to trust him. "Ok. Well, I'll head home. Talk to you tomorrow."

"Text me when you've made it home," he shouted at her before the door could close. He saw her hand reach back in and give him a thumbs-up before the door closed fully.

As soon as she was gone, Silver opened the drawer with his spare clothes and client files. He lifted everything out of it to get to his whiskey stash. There was one bottle left at the bottom of the drawer. He pulled it out and saw enough to pour himself one drink. He reached back into the drawer and grabbed his favorite glass. He sat it on top of his desk and emptied the whiskey into it, making sure to get every last drop. He took a sip and slouched in his chair as his eyes rolled to the back of his head.

Silver sat there staring at the glass in his hand. He thought about what Tonya had said to him earlier. In the back of his mind, Silver wondered if she blamed herself for the drinking. Thinking that maybe if she would've stayed, he wouldn't be staring at the bottom of an empty bottle every night; the truth is it had nothing to do with her. Yes, it sucked that she filed for divorce, but he checked out on her after he lost his job. Tonya had tried to stick by him and help him through that dark time, hell, she still was, but he didn't make it easy. Then there was Chrissy to think about. Neither of them wanted her to see her father become a shell of himself, so yes, it sucked, but he understood. Maybe he should put her out of her misery and tell her that he drank to ease the guilt, that William Hargrave came to him whenever he closed his eyes, and the whiskey kept him away.

Silver sat there in his silent office, letting his thoughts roam. When he looked back at his glass, it was empty. He hadn't realized he had finished it. He picked up the empty bottle on his desk, which happened to be the last bottle he had in the office. Looks like tonight he would be saved from himself. Although he had promised Lucy he would eat, and bars have food. Before he could talk himself out of it, he patted his pocket to make sure he still had Sara's two thousand dollars, and he was out the door.

Rita walked into the bar and scanned the room, looking for Silver. She had just arrived home when she got the call to come to pick him up. They used to go to Sean's whenever they closed a case to celebrate, but now she was usually only there to babysit him.

"Hey, Sean," she said to the guy standing behind the bar.

He smiled when he saw her. "Hey, Rita, it's been a while."

"Been putting in some long hours. Where is he?"

"His usual spot." He side-stepped and pointed to Silver, who was nursing a drink at the end of the bar.

"Thanks for calling me, Sean."

"No problem." Sean looked up to see another customer trying to get his attention. "It's the only time I get to see you these days." He flashed her a flirty smile and then went to take care of his customer.

Rita took a deep breath, then walked towards Silver. From what she could tell by looking at him, he wasn't belligerent. He was just sitting, staring straight ahead with a drink in front of him. It looked as if he was staring at his own reflection in the mirror of the bar display. She almost wished he was belligerent. Seeing him like this really scared her. It made her feel like the demons in his head were beginning to win.

"Come on, Cliff, it's time to go," she said when she was next to him.

He looked up at her with bloodshot eyes. "Oh hey, Rita. You come to join me?"

"No, I've come to take you home."

He scoffed and looked back at his reflection. "I'm not ready to go home."

"I think you've had enough."

"Look, Rita," said Silver with slurred words. "You can have a seat, or you can get the fuck out."

"Whatever." Rita started to walk away, but she couldn't leave him like this. "How about we make a deal?"

"I'm listening."

"I'll sit with you for a little while, but you're done drinking."

Silver gulped down the last of his drink and slid the glass to the other side of the bar. "You have a deal," he stammered.

Rita took off her jacket and draped it over the chair next to him, then she pulled it out and took a seat.

"So, Rita, what brings you here? You close a case today?" he asked.

"Sean called. He thought you might need a ride home."

"Sean!" he shouted. "You snitched?"

Sean walked over to the two of them. "Yeah, man, can't have you hurting yourself."

"Bullshit," Silver fired back. "You just wanted to see Rita."

"I want my friend to make it home safely," said Sean as he took Silver's empty glass and walked away.

"Come on, Cliff, let me take you home," Rita pleaded with him.

"What's the rush?" asked Silver.

"I want to get home to my bed."

"Well, that's boring."

"I'm sorry, but you have already caused me enough grief today," she said, annoyed. "Ford handed my ass to me after you left."

"I didn't mean to get you in trouble."

Rita looked at Silver, and even through the drunken haze, she could see the sincerity. "It's ok. You know Ford; if he isn't mad about one thing, he'll find another."

"That's because he's so short."

"Yeah, maybe," Rita chuckled. "So, are you going to tell me what's on your mind?"

"I don't have anything on my mind."

"You sure?" She caught his eye through the mirror. "It seems like you're trying to drown something."

Silver stared back at her through that mirror as if he were contemplating something. "No, I'm just celebrating having a new client."

Rita didn't believe him but decided not to press too much. "Tell me about your new client."

"She's an older lady who thinks her younger husband is going to leave her and take her money."

"How much older is she to him?"

"She old as fuck," he exclaimed, reminding Rita that she was talking to a drunk person.

"Let me guess; he's a struggling artist."

"Nope, he's a lawyer."

"That's weird."

"That's what I said," he said excitedly. "But Lucy told me to stop asking questions and just do what she wants."

"Lucy, with great advice as usual," said Rita sarcastically.

"We need the money. We're this close to losing the office." Silver tried to hold his thumb and index finger close to each other without touching them, but he was so drunk he kept tapping them against each other.

"Maybe you don't need the office. You can do your job from anywhere."

"Yes, but where would I sleep?"

"You lost your apartment?"

"No."

"Then why don't you sleep there, stupid?"

Silver went silent for a moment. Even drunk, his first instinct was to protect what he was truly feeling and thinking. "I like the couch in my office."

"Well, how about I take you to that couch now?" Rita stood from the barstool to signal that it was time to leave.

"Ok, fine," said Silver begrudgingly. He stood from his barstool and stumbled when he went to take a step. Rita caught him before he could fall and threw his arm across her shoulders so that she could help him keep his balance.

"I'll see you later, Sean," she shouted as she snatched her jacket from the back of her seat.

Sean looked up from the drink he was pouring. "See you guys later. Please get home safe."

"We will. Thanks again for calling," said Rita while she strained to hold up Silver's weight.

Once she felt like he had his equilibrium back, she let him stand on his own, making sure to stay close just in case he stumbled again. He took a couple of wobbly steps, but for the most part, he seemed sturdy, so she let him walk on his own. They ambled across the room towards the exit. Rita walked behind him with her hands up, ready to catch him. It felt as if she were helping a baby take its first steps. It took them forever to reach the exit as Silver walked at a snail's pace, occasionally stopping and teetering when the room was spinning too fast. Rita was willing to walk as slowly as necessary so that his big ass wouldn't fall backward and flatten her.

When they finally made it, Rita stepped ahead of him to open the door and usher him through. She had made sure to park as close to the door as possible, figuring a long walk would be a struggle for him. They walked up to the car, then she balanced him next to the curb so that she could get the car door open. Now came the hard part, maneuvering all six foot four inches of Silver into the car. Luckily, he has recently given her a lot of practice with this move. She turned him around so his back was facing the car, then bent him at his waist. She gingerly sat him down as far back on the seat as she could, and once he was seated, she bent down to lift his legs into the car. After ensuring every part of his body was in, she closed the door and lightly jogged to the driver's side. Silver was trying and failing to put on his seatbelt when she got in. He must have been seeing double because he kept missing the clasp. Rita grabbed his hand and helped guide it to the right place, then she put on her own and started the engine.

"I'm assuming you want to go to your office?" she asked before she pulled away from the curb.

"Yeah," he mumbled in return.

Rita looked over, and his head was pressed against the window with his eyes closed. She reached both hands over and grabbed his head to lean it away from the window. Rita didn't want to go over a bump and have his head slam against it. The headache he will have in the morning will be bad enough without any help. When he appeared to be comfortable, she pulled off to take him to his office.

Like clockwork, Silver began to snore about five minutes into the drive. Rita laughed to herself; his snoring used to be annoying, but it was white noise at this point. She wished he would've had dinner with her like she suggested so that she could've made sure he wouldn't overdo it. Rita tried to have dinner with him as often as possible. In her head, she told herself it was because she missed her friend, but deep down, she knew it was so she could slow his drinking. It was hard to see him like this. When they had met, he was so full of life. She never saw him without a smile on his face, and his presence could light any room, but now so much had changed. For the most part, he did a pretty good job at hiding it, but she often would look at him when he wasn't paying attention, and she could see the weight he was carrying, then he would look up and immediately put a smile on his face, hoping she hadn't noticed. Everyone else was fooled by the jokes and the charm, but not her.

Rita continued driving to the sound of snoring until they reached his office. She parked a little off of the curb to give her room to help him out of the car. She jogged around to the passenger side and opened the door. At some point, Silver had shifted his position and was back to leaning against the door, so when Rita opened it, his seatbelt was the only thing keeping him from hitting the pavement. The feeling of falling startled him awake.

"Shit, I'm sorry, Cliff. I didn't know you were leaning against the door," she said as she repositioned him in his seat.

"Where are we?" asked Silver groggily.

"We're at your office." Rita reached across him and undid his seatbelt. "Come on, let's get you upstairs."

Silver's nap helped him sober up slightly, so he was a lit-tle more steady on his feet than at the bar. He grunted and groaned as he stood from the car, and Rita held out her hand for him to steady himself, but he waved her off. He walked slowly, but he didn't look like he would fall over, so Rita closed the car door and just walked behind him.

"I can take it from here," said Silver as he pulled his keys from his pocket.

"I know. I just want to make sure you don't fall on the stairs and split your head open," said Rita. "Plus, I want to see what you've done with the place."

He looked at her and cocked his eye. "You know, if you wanted to get in my pants, we should've gone to your place. It smells better."

"Like you care how it smells."

"True." Silver shrugged. He unlocked the door, and they both walked in. Silver looked at the stairs, and in his current state, it felt like they were never-ending.

"You ok?" asked Rita when he stared at the stairs instead of climbing them.

"Yeah, that's just a lot of stairs."

"Well, let's get it over with." She grabbed his hand. "One step at a time."

Silver took his other hand and grabbed the rail, and then the two of them slowly walked up the stairs until they reached his office door at the top. He put his key into the door, but when he went to turn it, the knob twisted, and the door opened. He must have forgotten to lock it when he rushed out. He pushed the door open, and they entered. Silver shuffled his feet across his waiting room with Rita trailing behind him. They stepped around Lucy's desk and into his office, where Silver immediately slipped off his shoes. He took off his jacket and tried to hang it on the coat rack in the corner, but it hit the ground with a thud when he missed it entirely. Rita walked over and picked it up while he flopped onto his couch. She hung it on the rack properly, then reached into his pockets to grab his wallet, phone, and keys. She placed his things on his desk and then pulled one of the chairs over to the couch.

"How are you feeling?" she asked after she took a seat.

Silver's eyes were shut, but he still responded, "The room is spinning a little, but I'm fine. Thanks for the ride, partner."

"Cliff, I can't keep doing this."

"Can't keep doing what?"

"Carrying you out of bars. I have a life too, which doesn't include sitting around waiting for you to need a designated driver."

Silver opened his eyes to look at her. "I'm sorry, Rita. I didn't tell Sean to call you, I swear."

"I know, Cliff, but maybe it's time to stop."

"Ok, fine. Next time I'll make sure he calls someone else."

"That's not what I mean." She paused while Silver tried to catch on to what she was talking about. "Maybe it's time to stop drinking."

"Oh god, you sound like Tonya."

"So, I'm not the only one that's worried about you."

"I'm fine," said Silver sharply.

"You're not fine," she rebutted. "Cliff, it's time to admit you're not fine."

Silver rolled over, turning his back to her and signaling that he was done with the conversation. Rita waited a moment before she stood and returned the chair to its rightful position. She gave him one last long look before she headed towards the exit.

"Rita," she heard just as she was about to close his office door.

"Yes, Cliff," she said without turning around.

"Thank you for taking care of me. I know I've been a burden lately, and I hear what you're saying."

Rita turned to face him. "You're not a burden, Cliff. I just hate seeing you like this."

"Look, Rita," said Silver pensively. "There are some things I'm struggling with, things that I'm not ready to talk about. I promise when I am, you'll be the first person I come to but please be patient. Please don't give up on me."

Rita stepped back into the office and walked over to him. She bent over and gave him a kiss on the forehead. They looked each other in the eyes and held it for a moment.

"I'll call you in the morning," she said before leaving him to sleep it off.

CHAPTER 4

Silver and Lucy had been surveilling Richard Lindsey for five days, and so far, the only cheating they caught him doing was on his diet. He had a pretty normal routine. Started each morning bright and early with a workout, which led to him going to the same Starbucks every morning for his pre-work coffee. Lindsey worked in an office building downtown and usually worked until about six in the evening on weekdays. He ordered lunch to be delivered every day so he wouldn't have to leave until he went to his apartment in the city for the night. The nice thing about this job is that they got the weekend off; that's the only time he went home to Sara, so there was no chance they would catch him cheating then. Silver and Lucy surveilled him in shifts. Silver watched him overnight and up until it was time to pick Chrissy up from school; at that time, Lucy would take over until about eight in the evening. Then they would watch for a couple of hours together, exchanging notes or any details that seemed important before Lucy would head home for the night to get some rest before her classes in the morning. There was no way to see inside his apartment from the street, but it was a door-manned building, and all visitors had to sign in. Lucy bribed the doorman of his building to give them a call if he had any visitors. She also bribed the doorman of the building across from his to give them roof access, which gave them a direct line of sight into his apartment. Every night, they set up two chairs on the roof with their camera positioned to see directly into his place so they wouldn't miss their shot when the time came.

Every day, Silver called Sara with a progress report. He felt it was important to do so, for one, to let Sara know that they were not sitting on their asses running up her tab and also to allow her to call them off if she was satisfied that her husband wasn't cheating on her.

Silver opened the door to the rooftop and could see Lucy staring at her phone screen while sitting next to a tripod that held a camera. He stepped onto the roof, feeling the gravel shift beneath his feet, and asked, "Anything new to report?"

"Nope," said Lucy. "Our doorman hasn't called about anyone coming up, and Lindsey's just been sitting in his living room since he came home. You think maybe the doorman would pocket our money and still not tell us?"

"That's always a possibility, but even if he does, we would still catch the woman in his apartment from here. Did you take any pictures today?"

"Yes, but I still don't see the point of taking pictures of him not doing anything."

"The point is she paid us to find proof. So whether he's cheating or not, she'll want proof to go with it. We aren't on anyone's side; our job is just to report."

"Fair enough," Lucy said as she shrugged. "You want some fries?"

Silver looked down at the takeout she was pointing to. "No, I'm good. I ate on the way." He sat in the empty chair to the right of Lucy. "I would hate to have to tell Sara that he's not cheating on her. He just doesn't want to be around her."

"That's definitely what it looks like."

"Their marriage doesn't make sense to me," Silver said with a puzzled look on his face.

"Yeah, their age difference is ridiculous."

"Yes, but I've heard that story before." He could see Lucy was confused. "What I mean is usually with a story like this, whoever married for money isn't going to be working a good job in the city. They're out spending the money they laid down for, but this guy goes to work and just goes home, and from what we can tell, he has his own money. So, if he didn't marry her for her money, I would think he married for love, but he doesn't seem interested in even being around her."

"Maybe he's going to quit his job after he divorces her," Lucy rebutted.

"Maybe, but if you're just a greedy monster who wants her money, once you're married and have access to the money, why keep the job?"

"These are good questions, boss, but do they matter for what we're doing?"

"No, but they don't sit right with me." Silver pondered that thought but shrugged his shoulders. "Maybe that's just the last trace of the cop in me talking."

"You don't talk about that a lot."

"Talk about what?"

"When you were a cop," said Lucy, causing Silver to look up at her. "And why you aren't one anymore."

Silver studied Lucy for a couple of seconds. "There's not much to talk about. I was a cop, and now I'm not."

"You seem to have some really hard feelings about it," Lucy pressed on.

"Let's just say that I was accused of something I didn't do, but instead of prosecuting me and dragging me and my family through the mud, as well as embarrassing the city, I was given the option to disappear. Out of sight, out of mind."

Lucy could see on his face that whatever happened still weighed on him. "What did they accuse you of?"

"Being too damn fine," Silver said with a grin, making Lucy laugh. "Don't worry, Luce; I'm fine with the way things turned out."

"Liar," said Lucy, giving him a slight shove.

"You should get out of here," said Silver as he checked the time. "I can take it from here."

"Yeah, you're right. It's getting late." Lucy gathered her things. "Call me if you need me."

"I'm sure I'm gonna have a real difficult time watching this boring ass dude sleep."

Lucy gave him a hug and made her way off the rooftop. Silver knew her intentions were pure, but he wished she didn't want to open old wounds. It wasn't her fault. After all, her curiosity was the reason she wanted to be an investigator and the reason he'd taken an interest in her. Still, it's not easy being a "disgraced" cop, to want something your entire life just to have it ripped away from you, and to have men you respect then look at you with disgust. Silver dealt with the whispers and murmurs about him being dirty. How he did it for the money. How he disgraced the badge. He had wanted to stay and fight, but what if he had lost? He could've gotten locked up, and there was no way he would have lived in a world where Chrissy would have to visit him in jail. He had walked away from the job, from the badge, and from Rita for Chrissy, but to everyone, it was an admission of guilt. He wanted to confide in Lucy, but she was the only person in his life that still looked up to him besides his daughter, and it wasn't a coincidence that they were the only two people in his life that don't know the whole story. What if he had told her and she lost respect for him? What if she had walked away? Silver couldn't lose anyone else because of that shit.

"Fuck, I could use some whiskey," Silver said to himself as he stood and started to pace the roof. It had been a couple of hours since Lucy left, and Mr. Lindsey was still on his couch. Silver was pretty sure the man had fallen asleep watching tv, which was what Silver wished he could be doing at that moment. Instead, Silver was thinking that he had another long and boring night to look forward to when his phone began to ring.

"This is Silver."

"Oh, I'm sorry, I was looking for Lucy," said a nervous male voice on the other line.

"I'm her employer. Is there a message I can pass along to her?"

"Well, she gave me this number and told me to call when someone signed in to go to Mr. Lindsey's apartment."

"You're Bob, the doorman," Silver said excitedly.

"Uh, yeah, but if she's not available, that's fine. I can actually lose my job for this." Bob was about to hang up the phone.

"No, wait!" Silver shouted, hoping to keep him on the line. "She gave you my number because I'm the one who sent her to you."

"Oh … well … yeah, a woman is on her way up to him now."

"Is she someone who's been here before?"

"I didn't recognize her, but she also wore a large pair of sunglasses, so I didn't get a good look at her face."

"Thank you, Bob, you've been a lot of help." Silver hung up the phone and then snatched up his camera. Mr. Lindsey was still sitting on his couch, but Silver could see something drawing his attention to the door. He walked to the door and opened it, revealing a young woman matching the doorman's description. She wore a long coat with oversized sunglasses and had black hair that appeared to be a wig. Her attempts to disguise herself gave Silver the impression that she was a pro, which would make sense considering neither he nor Lucy had observed him chatting with anyone in the week that they had been surveilling him. Silver made sure to snap a picture of her entering the apartment. The woman walked into the living room and turned her back to the window. She dropped her coat, revealing that she was wearing nothing under it except lingerie. Mr. Lindsey walked to her and put his hands on her waist to pull her in for a kiss. Seeing this brought a frown to Silver's face; he could not believe anyone would kiss a prostitute on the mouth, but he made sure to get a clear picture of Lindsey's face before, during, and after the kiss. Don't want him denying that it was him when these pictures were thrown in his face later.

Mr. Lindsey grabbed her hand and led her to the bedroom. Silver shifted his focus to the bedroom window, but the light was still off, so he couldn't see anything. When it was turned on, the woman stood again with her back to the window. She started to give Mr. Lindsey a show, first taking off her bra and then slowly removing her panties. Silver thought that if Sara didn't want these pictures, he would be happy to keep them. That was until Mr. Lindsey started to undress. Silver made sure to get a few more shots of them embracing before they climbed into the bed and out of view.

That was all he needed. No need to stay on that roof. Silver knew how that story ended. He packed up his camera and folded up his chairs to make his way back to the ground. He threw the chairs in the car trunk and sat the camera on the passenger side seat when he returned to his car. He thought about going home but decided to head back to the office and go through the pictures he had gathered. That way, he could call Sara and give her the bad news as early as possible. Of course, this was what she expected, but it's still hard to break that kind of news to someone, and it's best to rip it off like a Band-Aid.

Silver began the long drive back to his office. He thought about calling Lucy and telling her that he got the money shot, but it was already pretty late. If she wasn't already asleep, she would insist on coming in and looking at the pictures, and he wouldn't want to keep her up all night. It would be nice to have some company but dealing with Lucy without her getting her eight hours was no picnic. Maybe he could call Rita? He hadn't seen her since the night she helped him home from Sean's. Between surveillance and sleeping, he hadn't had much free time. He also limited his drinking while working a job, so there was no reason to babysit him. He grabbed his phone and called her.

"Hello," she said in a groggy voice when she answered.

"You want to come over and look at some dirty pictures with me?" he responded.

"What the fuck is wrong with you!" Silver had to move the phone away from his ear from how loud she shouted. "Do you see what time it is?"

"Yes."

"So why are you bothering me?"

"Well, in my experience, this is the best time of night to look at dirty pictures."

"Cliff, stop playing on my phone."

"I'm not playing," said Silver, chuckling. "I caught my client's husband with his pants down, and I'm on my way to my office to process the photos."

"Why would I want to join you for that?"

"It could be romantic. You can bring a bottle of wine, and I'll dim the lights, and we can see where the night takes us."

"You must be desperate to get me in bed if you are trying to use someone else's pictures to turn me on."

"Well, if you don't like their pictures, we can always take some of our own." Silver could hear her trying to contain her smile through the phone.

"If I wanted to look at pictures of myself naked, I'd just go to my camera roll."

Silver's jaw and phone dropped to the floor. He reached down to recover it and could hear Rita asking if he was still there. "Yeah, I'm here. Just lost track of where I was for a moment."

"You ok?" she asked, thoroughly enjoying the thought of him getting all flustered.

Her trick definitely worked, but Silver recovered quickly. "You know, as a private investigator, I take a lot of pictures. If you want, I can take a look at yours and tell you what I think."

"Just take my word for it; they're perfect," Rita teased.

"Fair enough, guess I'll just have to critique the real thing." Silver let that simmer and waited for a response.

"Dammit," she responded after a moment. "Fine, you win."

"Victory!" Silver gloated. "In all seriousness, my case is over, and I've missed you. Figured why wait to see you."

Silver could hear her sit up in her bed. "You've missed me?" she asked softly.

"Yeah, I do," he answered in the same tone. "You know I can't go too long without some Rita in my life." For a minute, the line went silent, and all Silver could hear was the sound of traffic outside the car as he drove. It was so quiet Silver thought the call had dropped. "Rita? You still with me?"

"Yeah, I'm here." She paused for another moment. "Let me get dressed, and I'll meet you there."

"Great," said Silver excitedly.

"Shouldn't take me too long ..." Rita paused as if something distracted her. "Let me put you on hold for a minute. I'm getting another call."

"Ok," said Silver, right before the line went silent for real this time.

Silver could feel his nerves building in his gut. Rita had come to hang out in his office plenty of times, but for some reason, this felt different. Something more than just two friends getting together.

No, he must have been overthinking this. Flirting was one thing, but the two of them were just friends. If she came over and he made a move on her, things would never be the same between them. Silver could not live with himself if he did anything to ruin what they had. Silver pushed the thought of him and Rita out of his head just in time before hearing Rita's voice come back on the other end.

"Sorry, Cliff," she said. "I'm going to have to take a rain check on the nudey photos. A body just dropped."

"Oh, that's alright. I understand." Silver tried to hide his disappointment. "Could you use a consultant?"

"As much as I would appreciate your assistance, Ford would have my badge if I brought you to a crime scene."

"If he fires you, you can come work for me."

"I may take you up on that one day," she said with a laugh. "How about I come see you sometime tomorrow?"

"Sounds good to me." Silver parked in front of his office. "Maybe we could get lunch."

"You don't want me to come to your office anymore?"

"I figured with you having a new case, you won't have time for much, but you have to eat," Silver said this with a chuckle, but really, he just didn't want to admit that he wasn't sure he could be alone with her at the moment.

"Yeah, that's true," she responded. "I probably will want to dive into the case."

"Ok, perfect. I'll see you tomorrow."

"See you." Rita hung up the phone.

Silver slipped his phone into his pocket and grabbed his camera from the passenger seat. He told himself he would get the tripod and chairs tomorrow because he didn't feel like carrying everything upstairs. He lumbered up to his office, sat at his desk, and booted up his laptop. Once it was on and ready, he plugged in his camera so he could save the photos. He always took more pictures than he needed, just in case some didn't come out very well. He would only pick three or four shots to show to his client. It was crushing enough to be shown proof of your spouse's infidelity, so he didn't like to add insult to injury by showing the really revealing photos. His photos would get the point across and still be somewhat tasteful. He chose his pictures and printed them, then grabbed an empty manila envelope and put them into it. The envelope wasn't completely necessary, but it was his guilty pleasure to hand over the envelope like it contained confidential files.

Silver leaned back in his chair once everything was complete. He was happy to be done with this case and not have to spend another night on that roof. His eyes drifted to his desk drawer, where he kept his whiskey. He had replaced the bottle he had finished before he started on this case and thought that now would be as good a time as any to celebrate another case closed, so he reached in and grabbed the bottle and glass. Silver poured himself a drink and took a sip, then that sip turned into a gulp, and before he knew it, his glass was empty. Nothing better than a celebratory drink after a job well done. He put the cap back on the bottle and moved over to his couch, leaving the bottle on his desk. He flopped down and thanked god again that he wasn't freezing on that rooftop. It was nice to be able to sleep on his comfortable couch instead. He turned to his side, but his phone was poking him from his pocket, so he grabbed it and sat it on the floor next to him. Once he was completely comfortable, he closed his eyes, hoping he could slip into a much-needed sleep.

Silver was in a deep sleep when he heard someone banging on his door a few hours later. He woke up and reached for his phone to check the time, but it wasn't next to him where he thought he had left it. He dragged himself off the couch and saw that it was on his desk next to his computer and an empty bottle of whiskey. One drink must not have been enough, although he didn't remember finishing the bottle. Maybe that's when he had left his phone sitting there. He was still considering how it got there when there was another loud knock on the door. He shrugged and then grabbed the phone to check the time. It was five a.m. Maybe Lucy lost her key, but why the fuck would she be here this early? He wiped the sleep from his eyes and made his way to the door.

"I'm coming," he shouted when whoever it was pounded on the door again. He undid the lock and opened the door to see Rita and Javier standing on the other side. "Kaye! Wasn't expecting to see you this early." His eyes shifted to Javier. "Or for you to bring a guest. To what do I owe the pleasure?"

"We're here about the guy whose name you had us run for you," she responded. "Richard Lindsey."

"Oh shit, did someone see me taking photos last night?"

"So, you were at his apartment last night?" she asked.

Silver could hear something in her tone that unsettled him. "I was across the street, surveilling him for my client. What is this about, Rita?"

Rita took a breath before saying, "Richard Lindsey was murdered in his apartment last night."

CHAPTER 5

Rita and Javier stepped around crime scene techs on their way to the body in the next room. After the call had come in, Javier picked her up so they could ride in together. It was going on three hours since the nine-one-one call reporting shots fired. Detectives typically like to take their time in arriving at the scene, giving everyone else a chance to do the preliminary work. When the detectives arrived, the crime scene unit and medical examiner would already have some answers for them, and the uniformed officers had already begun their canvassing to narrow the list of potential witnesses for them to question. All of this allowed the detectives to hit the ground running on the case.

"Definitely a bachelor pad," said Rita.

"No personal photos in the living room. Pretty much just a couch and a big screen," Javier responded.

"This place could definitely use a woman's touch."

"The blood all over the bedroom could be a woman's touch." Javier shrugged.

"Not exactly the touch I was referring to," said Rita with an eye roll. "This is a nice building. How much do you think a place like this set him back?"

"Definitely more than I can afford. Why, Kaye, are you thinking about moving?"

"No, I like my building; no one there has been shot in the middle of the night."

Javier chuckled to himself, then scanned the room. "Who was the first on the scene?" he asked the officers that were standing around. Two of them stepped forward. "What can you tell us?"

One of the officers spoke up. "Your vic is Richard Lindsey. He's thirty-three years old, and he owns this apartment. My partner and I were two blocks away when dispatch reported that shots were heard here, so we were on the scene pretty quickly. Upon arrival, the building's doorman and Mrs. Faulk, the vic's neighbor, were waiting for us in the lobby. The doorman used his key to let us into the unit where we found the vic in the bedroom DOA."

"Did the neighbor call it in?" asked Rita.

"Yes, ma'am," the officer responded.

"Did she witness anyone coming and going?"

"Her and the doorman both reported a young woman visiting him, but both said they saw her leaving before the shots were heard. No one else was seen entering or leaving here between the shots being fired and our arrival."

Satisfied that there was nothing else to learn from the two of them, Rita thanked them and sent them on their way. She and Javier made their way into the bedroom, where the medical examiner was looking over the body. He was attractive, or at least as attractive as a dead guy can be.

"You found him naked?" Rita asked, pointing to the pair of boxer briefs on the floor.

"Yes," said the examiner. "And he had sex right before he died."

"How do you know that?" asked Javier.

"CSU bagged a used condom by the bed."

"I'm assuming he was killed by lead poisoning," Rita said as she moved closer to the body.

"Yes, three shots, and the shooter was close to the victim when he or she pulled the trigger. Note the stippling near the wounds," he said, pointing to one of the holes in his chest. "That would only be there if this was a close contact shooting."

"Can you tell what caliber the bullets are?"

The medical examiner put a finger next to one of the wounds on the victim's chest. "Looks like nine millimeter. I'll know for sure when I get him back to the lab and dig the bullets out."

"This guy was pretty well built," Rita said after looking at the wounds. "Whoever did him in must've caught him off guard. There's no sign of struggle. I mean, the guy didn't even get out of bed." Rita waited for a response from Javier, but he didn't say anything. "Estrada? Are you listening?"

Javier stared at the victim's face. "I've seen him before."

"Where?" Rita asked.

"I can't place it." Javier continued to stare. "And his name is familiar to me too."

"Maybe you've arrested him before," suggested Rita.

"That's it!"

"He has a record?" asked Rita.

"No, but I checked to see if he had one."

"How would you know to check this guy's record before we even got here?" asked Rita with a puzzled look.

"This is the guy whose name Silver had me run. I wonder if he was watching him last night."

"Actually, he was," said Rita. "He called me last night saying he just got the pictures he needed to wrap up the job."

"When did he call?" asked Javier.

Rita pulled out her phone to check her call history. "I got his call at twelve forty-eight."

"Dispatch received the shots fired call at twelve forty-two."

"So, Silver just missed it." Rita looked out the window to the rooftop across the street. She would bet anyone that Silver would have found his way up there for the perfect view into the place.

"Didn't Silver say his wife hired him?" said Javier.

Rita thought for a moment. "Yeah, as a matter of fact, he did. No way a woman lives here."

"I don't see any signs that he was married. No wedding ring, no photos, and like you mentioned, there's no sign of a woman's touch in this apartment," said Javier as he scanned the room.

"Good eye, Estrada."

"Maybe she kicked him out. She did think he was cheating."

"Yeah, that's possible. When we talk to witnesses, we should be able to find out how long he's been living here."

"We should also give Silver a call. If he was surveilling him every day, he may have some insights on who could've done this," Javier suggested.

"Or know the identity of the woman he was with last night. I'll give him a call when we get back to the precinct. In the meantime, I'd like to talk to the doorman and the neighbor. All visitors to this building must sign in, so that may be a quick way to ID her, and maybe there's a chance she's a frequent visitor, and he knows her already."

They left the bedroom and asked the officer they spoke with to take them to the neighbor, Mrs. Faulk. The three of them left the apartment and walked directly across the hall, and the officer knocked on the door. Mrs. Faulk opened the door, wearing a bathrobe. She was white and looked to be at least sixty.

"Mrs. Faulk," said the officer. "These two detectives would like to speak with you."

"Hi, Mrs. Faulk, my name is Detective Rita Kaye, and this

is Detective Javier Estrada." Rita held out her hand, and Mrs. Faulk shook it. After making the introductions, the officer excused himself and made his way back to the crime scene. "Do you mind if we come in?"

"Yes, of course," said Mrs. Faulk, and she cleared the doorway for the two of them to enter. "I was wondering when a detective would want to talk to me."

"We thank you so much for your cooperation," said Rita. "Could you please go over what you told the officer?"

"You want to know everything?"

"Yes, starting with before you heard the shots and right after."

"Okay, I can do that."

"Perfect," said Rita. "Would you mind if we had a seat?"

Mrs. Faulk nodded and then led them to her living room. She sat in an armchair while Rita and Javier sat on her couch. Once they were all situated, Rita pulled out her notepad and pen, signaling to Mrs. Faulk that she was ready to begin.

"I was sitting here reading; I don't watch a lot of tv, so I can usually hear everything going on in the hall. I heard someone knock on Richard's door, which is odd because he doesn't get a lot of visitors."

"Around what time was that?" Rita interrupted.

"Midnight, exactly."

"You seem sure about that."

"I am sure because when I heard the knock, I checked the time." She motioned to the analog clock hanging on her wall.

Rita jotted "12" into her notebook. "What happened after that?"

"I got up and went to the door to see who it was because, at first, I thought the knock was on my door." Rita and Javier glanced at each other, both internally laughing at the obvious lie to cover up her being nosy.

"Did you see anyone?"

"Yes, a woman was facing his door. She had a long black

coat on and black hair. She never turned to face my door, so I didn't see her face before Richard opened the door and let her in."

"The officer told us that you saw her leave as well."

"Yes."

"And what time was that?"

"It was a little after twelve-thirty." Rita wrote a dash after "12" and wrote "12:30."

"What did you do after you saw her leave?"

"I was tired, so I went to bed, but just five minutes later, I heard the shots. They were so loud. I grabbed my phone and dialed nine-one-one as I ran back to the door. I opened it and looked down the hall, but I didn't see anyone except for a few other people who live on this floor, wondering what the sound was. Then I knocked on Richard's door, but no one answered. After that, I went downstairs to let Bob know what happened and to wait for the police."

"Mrs. Faulk, have you noticed anyone hanging around here who doesn't belong lately? Anyone who seemed to be watching the building or asking questions about Mr. Lindsey?"

"No, I haven't noticed anything like that."

Rita added a few more notes, then flipped her pad closed. "Well, Mrs. Faulk, that's all the questions we have for now." She reached into her pocket and pulled out a card. "Here's my card. If you remember anything else that you think is important, please call."

Mrs. Faulk eagerly accepted the card, then escorted the two detectives to the door. After they said their goodbyes, they decided it was time to go talk to Bob, the doorman.

"If she's remembering those times correctly, it excludes his lady friend as our shooter," said Javier as they made it to the elevator.

Rita pushed the down button to call it up to them. "Maybe, but she could have doubled back or let the shooter into the building, so we can't exclude her just yet." The elevator doors opened, and the two of them stepped onto it together. "Either way, we should track her down and see what she has to say."

As Rita and Javier rode the elevator back down to the ground floor, she thought how glad she was about the Silver connection. Not only would he be a great witness and source of information because of his attention to detail, but honestly, after they were interrupted a few hours ago, she would use any excuse to call him. She'd never admit it to him, but she missed him too, and for the first time, their conversation felt like more than just flirty banter. Ok, there was a lot of flirty banter too, but that all changed when he said he missed her. She wasn't sure what would've happened if she had made it over there, but she was prepared for anything.

The elevator reached the bottom floor, and they went to the front desk to speak with Bob, the doorman.

"Hi, I'm Detective Rita Kaye, and this is my partner, Detective Javier Estrada. We'd like to ask you a few questions about Mr. Lindsey."

"I already answered questions," Bob responded. Rita could see that he was pretty nervous.

"I know, and I'm sorry we have to keep going over this, but we just have to make sure we have the details right." Rita paused while Bob let it sink in. Then, when he nodded, she continued, "How long has Mr. Lindsey lived here?"

"Three years."

Rita and Javier exchanged looks with each other. "Did his wife live here with him?"

"Mr. Lindsey was married?" Bob asked with a surprised look on his face.

Rita never responded to questions when conducting an interview. It was an easy way to lose control, and her job was to get answers, not give them. "Did Mr. Lindsey have any problems with his neighbors, or did his neighbors have any problems with him?"

"No. I would forget he lived here if he didn't walk past the front desk."

"Does he have any regular visitors?" Javier asked.

"Occasionally but not often. Last night was the first time he's had a visitor in weeks."

"Did she sign in?" Rita asked.

"Of course. All visitors must sign in, or they won't have access to the elevators."

"Can we take a look?" Rita asked, pointing to the sign-in sheet. Bob pushed it over to her and pointed to the name she wanted. "So, Jane Doe signed in to see him, great." Rita pushed the sign-in sheet back across the desk since it was obviously a fake name. "Did you recognize her? Had she been here before?"

"No, but she had most of her face covered with a large pair of sunglasses, and I think she was wearing a wig."

Fake name and disguise. Seems like they were looking for a prostitute. "I see she signed in right before midnight. What time did she leave?"

"I believe it was right after twelve-thirty."

Rita only asked that to corroborate what Mrs. Faulk had just told them. So far, both of their stories matched, so unless they were conspiring together, it was most likely the truth.

"Is there another way into the building?" asked Javier. Good question, Rita thought to herself. Maybe their late-night visitor had let herself back in later to give herself an alibi.

"N-Not that I, uh, know of," Bob stammered.

Rita could tell there was something he didn't want to say. "Bob, is there something you want to tell us?"

Bob sat silent. Something was making him feel guilty, and Rita was going to let the silence make him uncomfortable until he talked.

After a minute of both detectives staring at him, he finally said, "There is an entrance in the back of the building. There are no cameras back there, so sometimes staff members go back there for extra breaks or to sneak in their boyfriends and girlfriends."

"Who else besides you was on the clock at the time of the murder?" Rita asked.

Bob put his head down. "No one," he said. Again, Rita let the silence pull more information from him. "Someone paid me to let a guy in right before Mr. Lindsey was killed. Can we please keep that between us? I need this job."

"Who paid you?" Rita asked.

"I didn't get a name or see them in person. It was all over the phone," Bob said frantically. "You gotta believe me; I didn't even think he was serious until the money was put into my account."

"Do you still have the number?" Bob nodded yes. Rita passed him her notepad. "Write it down."

Bob grabbed the pad and pen, then scrolled through his recent calls to find the number.

"Did you get a look at the guy you let in?" Javier asked while he wrote the number down.

"Yeah, him and his car were parked in the alley by the door. He looked Black, but his skin was lighter. He was well over six feet tall, and he drove a black Mustang."

Rita's heart began to race. "Are you sure about that description?"

"Yes, I'm positive," said Bob as he handed her back the notepad with the number on it.

Rita looked at the number, and her heart sank. It couldn't be.

Javier walked over to her. "What's wrong?" he whispered, but Rita didn't respond. She walked away without saying anything, and Javier almost had to jog to keep up with her. She walked out and started to pace on the sidewalk outside the apartment building.

"Kaye, you're freaking me out," Javier said after watching her pace for a minute.

"Who does that description sound like?" was all she said.

"It kinda sounds like Silver."

"Silver drives a black Mustang."

"Oh." Javier understood the implication. "That doesn't mean it was him," he said, trying to be reassuring.

"This is his number," she said, holding up her notepad for Javier to see.

Javier's jaw dropped. It couldn't be a coincidence that Silver had bribed his way into the building of the man he was paid to follow right before that same man was shot to death.

Rita started walking towards their car. "There has to be an explanation for this, and we're going straight to his office so he can give us one."

"Wait, Kaye," Javier said as he ran to block her path to the car. "Let's just take a breath."

"For what? We need to get to the bottom of this."

"Are you sure we're the ones who should be questioning him?"

"You know how many cops want to lock him up, especially our captain? I'm not gonna sit back and let him be railroaded." Rita tried to step around him, but he moved to block her path again.

"And what if he did this, Kaye? Can you arrest him?"

"Haven't you heard, Estrada?" Rita leaned in. "I turned him in once, and I'll do it again if I have to. Now get in the damn car." She shoved him out of her way and got in the driver's seat. Javier stood there momentarily and took a deep breath before getting into the car with her.

They rode to Silver's office in silence. Javier could tell that she was deep in thought, and with how fired up she just was, he was scared to speak. He knew the conversation they were about to have would be an uncomfortable one.

Rita parked in front of Silver's building and started to get out of the car, but Javier stopped her.

"Maybe I should ask the questions up there," he said to her softly.

"Fuck you, I can do my job," she responded angrily.

56

"I'm not saying that you can't. I'm saying you don't have to. Silver's your partner, whether he's still a cop or not. Your instinct is to protect him, but if you ask the wrong questions and put him on the defensive, it would only look worse for him. The best way to help him right now is to treat him like any other suspect and let his answers rule him out."

Rita thought for a moment. Javier was absolutely right. She was in protection mode. "Fine, you take the lead, but promise me one thing."

"Anything."

"Whatever we find out up there stays between us until we have concrete proof that he's involved."

Javier nodded in agreement, and they both stood out of the car. They walked into the building and up the stairs to his door. Javier knocked, and they waited.

"You're gonna have to knock harder than that. I'm sure he's still asleep," said Rita after they didn't get a response.

"Why would he come in just to sleep?"

"Since his divorce, he doesn't spend a lot of time at his apartment. I think he gets pretty lonely there." Rita thought for a moment, wondering if she should say what she was thinking as Javier pounded on the door again. "There's something else about him you should probably know."

"What's that?" Javier asked, recognizing the seriousness of her tone.

"He's a drunk." Rita couldn't make eye contact with Javier. "Since he lost his job and his wife, he spends most of his nights drinking until he passes out."

"I understand," Javier said, but Rita wasn't sure he did. Sharing that felt like a betrayal to her friend. Adding to the weight on her shoulders from getting ready to question him like a suspect. Javier pounded on the door again when they heard Silver shout that he was coming. A second later, they heard the door unlock and open.

CHAPTER 6

"Murdered!" Silver said in shock. "Did you catch the guy?"

"No, that's actually why we're here," Javier said, speaking for the first time. "We're hoping you can tell us anything you may have found out about him while you were working this case."

Silver looked at Rita, but he couldn't catch her eye. "Sure, come in. I'll tell you whatever you want to know." Silver stepped to the side and allowed them to enter. "You can head to the back." Silver closed the door, and the three of them went into his office. Javier and Rita sat in the two chairs in front of his desk while he sat behind it. "How can I help?"

"Who hired you to surveil Mr. Lindsey?" Rita asked.

"His wife, Sara Lindsey. She suspected him of cheating on her and wanted me to find proof." Silver paused but was met with silence, so he continued. "My assistant and I tailed him for six days, not including the weekend, until last night when he was visited by a young lady, and you know what happened next." Silver raised his eyebrows playfully at Rita but got no response, not even a smile. He wondered what was going on with her. "I planned on calling Mrs. Lindsey to give her the bad news when I woke up."

"While you were tailing him, did he have a normal routine?" Javier asked.

"Yes, extremely normal. The guy was pretty boring. Same thing every day without ever breaking routine."

"Did he ever meet with anyone or have any altercations?" Again, it was Javier who asked, not Rita.

Rita sat there, listening to Javier question their prime suspect, who just happened to be her friend. When they told him Richard Lindsey had been killed, he seemed genuinely surprised, but she had also seen suspects give an Oscar-worthy performance of shock the night after they killed someone. She could barely look at him. She knew the second they locked eyes, he would know that something was wrong. This is definitely not what she had had in mind for the next time she visited him.

Rita couldn't believe there was any way Silver could be involved in this; yeah, he could be a jackass, but he wasn't a killer. He would never do anything that could take him away from Chrissy. What motive would he even have to kill this guy? And if Ford were to get wind that Silver was involved in this, he wouldn't stop until Silver was convicted for this murder. Silver was answering all of their questions without hesitation and seemed like his usual self, not someone who had just murdered another human being in cold blood. She noticed the empty bottle on his desk, which meant he was drinking last night, but that was not unusual. As a matter of fact, it told her that he most likely never left this room last night. When Silver caught her staring at the bottle, he quickly snatched it from the top of his desk and put it out of view.

"Wow, the newbie taking charge. Why are you so quiet over there, Kaye?" Silver asked to draw attention away from what he just did, but something about her demeanor made him feel uncomfortable.

"He needs more practice in asking questions," Rita said softly, but she could see from his face that he wasn't buying it. He tried to make eye contact with her, but she avoided it until he answered Javier's last question.

"Well, there were no altercations, and until last night when that woman visited him, who I'm pretty sure was a pro, he never met with anyone. He went to work then went home every day."

"You mentioned that you weren't tailing him on the weekend. Why is that?" asked Javier.

"He kept an apartment in the city, but on the weekend, he lived with his wife in the suburbs. So, there was no need to watch him then because he was with her."

"His wife." Javier paused to look at his notes. "Sara Lindsey?"

"Yes."

"What can you tell us about her?"

"Well, it's not much more than I've already told you. She's much older than him, and she comes from money. She came to me because she suspected him of cheating," Silver responded.

"Is that all you know about her?"

"Trust me, I tried to get more out of her, but she shut me down. Since it's not my job to know everything, I let it go."

"So, you don't know where the two of them lived when he was not at his apartment in the city."

Silver shifted in his seat. Javier's questions were starting to make him feel like the two of them knew something he didn't. "No, I didn't. She only gave me the address to the apartment. I'm assuming she didn't want us spying on her too. My job was to get her proof of what he was doing in that apartment, so that's the only address I needed to know."

"Have you been in regular contact with her?" Javier pressed forward.

"Yes, I spoke with her daily to update her on the progress

of our surveillance. That gives her a chance to call me off if she's satisfied that he was being faithful."

"Did you get the impression that she was hoping he would cheat?"

"I don't think anyone hopes to get cheated on, Estrada."

"If a divorce would be costly for her unless he cheats, then maybe she would hope for it to save the money."

"Oh, I see." Silver pretended like he didn't know why Javier had asked that question. "No, it actually seemed like that would be the worst-case scenario for her."

"So, you don't think she would've become impatient and taken matters into her own hands?" Javier leaned forward in his seat as he asked this question.

"I don't see it, but of course, it's possible. I'm sure one of the first things my former partner taught you is that anyone will kill under the right circumstances." Silver leaned back in his chair. "But like I said, she kept me on the case, so she must've thought I would catch him eventually."

"Which you did last night."

"Yes, and I have the pictures to prove it." Silver put his hand on the manila envelope with the photos he planned on showing to Sara. "And from what I can tell, she was worth every penny."

Javier's eyes widened. "She may have been the last person to see him alive, so it may be beneficial to take a look at—"

"Were you watching the two of them the entire time she was in the apartment?" Rita interjected to get the interview back on track.

Silver used his hand to block his mouth from Rita's view and mouthed to Javier that he'd get him copies. He then turned back to Rita and said, "No, as soon as I had enough photos to prove that he was cheating, I packed up and left."

"What time was that?" Javier asked, getting back on task.

"About midnight or maybe close to twelve-fifteen." Silver looked up as if he were searching his brain for the answer.

"It had to be close to twenty minutes before I called you," he said, motioning to Rita. "Then I came to the office to upload the photos. I finished around two and then passed out on the couch."

"Can anyone vouch for that?"

"No, I didn't know I would be needing an alibi, so I was completely alone."

"We're not accusing you of anything, Mr. Silver. We're just—"

"Crossing your Ts and dotting your Is," Silver interrupted. "I've been in your shoes before, Estrada; don't worry, I understand."

"Where did you take the pictures from?" Javier asked.

"I was on a rooftop across from his building with a view into his apartment," said Silver, confirming Rita's earlier assumption.

"So, you never actually stepped foot into the building?"

"No." If Silver hadn't already been suspicious of why they were there, that question would have raised a red flag in his head. Why was Estrada trying to place him in the apartment of a murder victim? Were they looking at him like he was a suspect?

"Well, we have some other leads to follow up on, so we'll let you go back to sleep," Rita interrupted as if she could read his mind. "Can you give us the contact info for Mrs. Lindsey, and we will need a copy of those photos to try to ID the girl." She stood to leave, and Javier begrudgingly followed her lead.

"No problem. I think I have an empty flash drive around here somewhere. Just give me a minute, and I'll get the photos loaded on one for you."

Silver rummaged through a couple of his desk drawers, looking for that empty flash drive while the two of them walked out into his waiting room.

"I had a couple more questions for him," Javier whispered when he was sure Silver couldn't hear them.

"I know, but he was getting suspicious. He's a great detective, and if we press too hard, he will figure out that he's our top suspect. And trust me; he was two seconds away from getting answers out of you instead of the other way around. Hell, you already answered a couple of his questions."

"He didn't ask me any questions."

"He asked them with his answers. He knows this was more than just an exchange of information and that we're not telling him everything we know."

"How could he know that?"

"He made it a point of saying he only observed from outside the building, so when you asked him, was he ever in the building, you let him know that you suspect that he might've been. That's why I stopped you. I didn't want you to show our entire hand before we're ready to."

"You sure that's why you stopped me?" Javier asked but backed down from that question when Rita gave him a look that made him feel like he would get shot next.

Silver emerged from his office with the drive in hand. "Here you go," he said, handing it to Rita. "I made sure to include every picture we took for the entire time we watched him, just in case our mystery woman appeared another day and I just didn't notice. Also, you might want to look for anyone who appeared to be watching him, besides me, of course." Silver smiled big, hoping to get a reaction from Rita, but she still avoided looking at him. "I don't know how much luck you'll have with these if you're trying to identify the prostitute."

"Why is that?" she asked.

"Well, she was clearly trying to disguise herself. She wore a bad wig and big sunglasses, so there's no clear picture of her face."

"She never took the glasses off?" Javier asked.

"She did, but her back was always to the window, and honestly, my focus was making sure his face was in the pictures, not hers. Her identity didn't matter all that much to me. I'll text you Sara's contact info, and I promise I'll hold off on getting in touch with her until you two talk to her first. I know you would prefer to give her the news yourself."

"Thanks for this, Silver. We'll be in touch if we need anything else," said Rita. Javier opened the door for them to leave, but Silver grabbed her hand before she could walk out.

"Can I talk to you for a moment?" he asked.

All she wanted to do was get out of there, but she knew that would make things worse, so she gave Javier a nod to let him know it was ok, and he told her he would meet her in the car. Then she turned towards Silver and looked him in the eye for the first time.

"I know you can't share anything about an ongoing investigation, but is everything ok, Rita?"

Rita thought for a moment. "Yeah, everything's fine."

"You sure? You don't seem like yourself. Is this about me inviting you over last night? I'm sorry if I made you feel awkward or anything."

He was obviously searching for answers, but what should she say? Should she tell him to run? That someone was framing him again? Should she hug him? Or should she ask for a confession? No! There was no way he did this, and she didn't care if that was her heart talking. She refused to believe that he was capable of taking someone's life in cold blood. No matter what it took, she was going to prove that he was innocent.

"Cliff, I promise I'm fine." Silver held her hand for a moment while they held eye contact. In that moment, Silver's eyes told her that she could tell him anything, and her eyes told him that she would when she could. She gave him a smile while he squeezed her hand, both actions telling each other all they needed to know without anything needing to be said. Then she walked out the door to find who was trying to frame him for this murder.

When she got downstairs, Javier was leaning against the car, smoking a cigarette. He threw it on the ground and put it out with his foot when he saw her.

"Get in the car. We got work to do," she said without breaking stride.

"Where are we headed?" Javier asked as he got into the car.

"The precinct. I want to dive deeper into Richard Lindsey's life. I want to know his wife's whereabouts during the time of death."

"That's if he was married at all."

"What do you mean? Silver said his wife hired him."

"There was no sign in that apartment that he was married. According to Silver, they were happily married for five years, but he's lived at that place for three. Do you believe that his wife never once came to visit him at his apartment? And if living in the city was more convenient for him, what was stopping her from just living there with him? Doesn't seem like money would be an issue at all."

Javier had just made a very good point. That didn't sound like the lives of two happily married people. "Then we need to find out who Silver met with," said Rita. Javier didn't respond, but his silence spoke volumes. "He's not lying."

"Kaye, he could be."

"For what reason?"

"I don't know but shouldn't that be what we're trying to find out? And even if our vic had an estranged wife that no one knew about, that doesn't prove Silver is innocent."

"How come it doesn't?"

"Silver has a drinking problem and is running a struggling business." Rita shot darts at him with her eyes, but Javier didn't back down. "It's possible that a rich client offered him a lot of money to murder her husband to prevent him from taking her to the cleaners in a divorce settlement."

"It's not fucking possible!" Rita spat back at him.

"Aren't you the one who taught me that anyone is capable of murder under the right circumstances?" said Javier calmly. "Kaye, I know what he means to you, but you have to remain impartial."

"The only thing you have connecting him to the inside of

that building is a man admitting to taking a bribe to let him in. I trust Cliff over the word of an admittedly corrupt doorman who conveniently let the supposed murderer into a door that isn't covered by cameras, so no one can corroborate his story. Isn't it possible that Bob could've also taken a bribe to lie on Cliff?"

"Yes, that's possible, but why would the doorman make up a story that could not only lose him his job but could make him an accessory to murder? Couldn't he have made up a lie that didn't make him just as responsible for the murder?"

"Did Bob the Doorman seem like a scholar to you? Why are you trying to convict him?"

"I'm not." Javier sat up in his seat. "I'm just playing devil's advocate. We have to stay open to every possibility until all the facts are in. You taught me that."

Rita could not argue with that. He was absolutely right. She was sure Silver hadn't done this, but the way to prove that was to go on about the case like she usually would. Instead of trying to steer the investigation away from him, she had to collect the facts and trust that they would exonerate him. The key will be to run the investigation on two fronts. First, they had to look into who would want Richard Lindsey dead. And if Richard Lindsey was just a victim of opportunity, then who would kill an innocent man just to frame Silver?

"I get your point, Estrada. I promise to keep an open mind but for now, let's ride in silence before I punch you."

"I'll be quiet, but not because I'm scared of you, I just have nothing else to say."

CHAPTER 7

"He was murdered!" said Lucy. She had just arrived at the office when Silver gave her the news. "Of course, you get to see all of the action."

"I didn't actually witness him getting killed," Silver responded.

"So, how do you know?"

"Rita and her new partner stopped by the office this morning to question me about it."

"Why did they want to question you?"

"I had them run his name for me, and they look for people connected to him when someone is killed. So, since we were surveilling him, we are an excellent source of information."

"What makes us a good source?"

Silver loved Lucy's thirst for knowledge. "Whenever someone is killed, you look for motive, means, and opportunity. Motive, as you know, is who would want them dead. Once you have that list, you look for means, which ties in cause of death and a murder weapon, if there is one. You want to be able to connect someone with motive to a murder weapon by proving they owned it or through fingerprints and DNA. Once you have those two, you need to be able to tie them to the crime scene. If they say they've never been there before, but you find their prints or DNA at the scene, you got them. If they claim to have been there before but weren't there during the time of death window, it would be nice to have a witness to place them there. Private investigators are a great source of information because we can testify as to who was around the victim. Also, we would know his routine and if he strayed from that routine at all, which is another red flag," he explained as Lucy listened intently. "For instance, our boring guy broke pattern last night when a prostitute visited his apartment."

"Whoa! So, you caught him?"

"Sure did." Silver handed her the envelope.

"She's hot," Lucy said as she flipped through the photos. "How do you know she's a hooker?"

"I don't. It's just an assumption."

"Based on?"

"The doorman didn't recognize her, which means she's never been there before. The obvious wig and large glasses make it hard to ID her or pick her out of a lineup."

"What if she has been there before and she just concealed her identity from the doorman so that when she killed him, the doorman would say it was someone he had never seen before?"

That was actually something Silver hadn't yet considered. "That's an interesting thought, although there would be no need to keep the disguise on once she got to the apartment."

"The way she's keeping her back to the window almost makes you feel like she knew you were there."

And there it was. Lucy said what had been plaguing his mind since the detectives visited him this morning. What if the disguise was so that he specifically couldn't ID her? But how would she know he was even there?

"Yeah, that's possible," he said. "If I do know her, there's no way I can tell from those photos. There's nothing significant about her. Hell, slap a blonde wig on her, and she could be you."

"Right, my evil alter ego who honey traps and kills random men," Lucy joked.

"They say we all have a doppelganger out there some-where. Maybe yours is closer than you think."

"Trust me, there's no one walking around that looks as good as me," said Lucy confidently. "How did he die?" she asked after she finished flipping through the photos.

"Getting that info was a little tricky since detectives don't usually share those details with suspects, but I made some calls."

"Wait, you're a suspect?"

"Everyone is at first. And I was technically at the scene of the crime. So, they wouldn't want to give me too much detail because if I know exactly what they're looking for, I can get rid of it."

"But if you shoot or stab a guy, wouldn't you get rid of the murder weapon immediately?" Lucy asked.

"Not always, and it's not always that simple," Silver ex-plained. "Not all murder weapons can be easily disposed of, and if a killer kills with something they're known to have, it could raise a red flag that it's suddenly gone missing. What makes it not as simple as finding the murder weapon goes back to what I said earlier; you want the trifecta: motive, means, and opportunity. So you can find the murder weapon in someone's possession, but if you can't place them at the crime scene, it still doesn't guarantee a conviction. Let's say that while com-mitting the murder, a piece of the murderer's shoe falls off at the crime scene. When detectives have a suspect, they'll get a warrant for their shoes. When they initially question them, if they ask about shoes, then the killer will know to get rid of the shoes he was wearing, so detectives will purposely hold back

PARIS WILLIAMS

that detail until they have enough evidence to get a warrant."

"But if they have the murder weapon, doesn't that tie them to the crime scene?"

"Not necessarily."

"Oh, come on," Lucy exclaimed. "Have you ever found the murder weapon in someone's possession, and they weren't the one who actually did it?"

"Yeah, you can say that." Silver put his head down to avoid making eye contact with Lucy.

"What happened in that situation?"

Silver grew silent, not knowing how to answer that question. He lifted his head to look at Lucy. "Just know that Hargrave didn't do it. Don't you want to know how Lindsey died?" Lucy silently nodded, recognizing that it was a touchy subject. "I had to make a few calls, but I found out he was shot. Took three to the chest right after midnight while he was sleeping in his bed."

"Sounds like the hooker put him to sleep in more ways than one."

"That's one possibility."

"You don't think that's what happened?"

"When you're trained in homicide, you're taught to consider a wide range of possibilities, letting the evidence narrow your focus. If you start the investigation with a narrow focus, you run the risk of spending too much time on a scenario that could become a dead end."

"One thing you're forgetting," she said, causing Silver to look at her quizzically. "You're not a homicide detective anymore."

She was right. Silver didn't have to investigate anything. He fulfilled his obligation to Sara by finding the proof she wanted, although that no longer mattered, and to Rita by answering all of her questions. He could just go on with his day and forget about all of this, so why wasn't he? Did he miss his former life and the rush that came from solving a mystery? Or was it something else? Something in his gut was telling him that his role, in this case, wasn't done yet.

"So, what's next, boss?" asked Lucy, breaking his train of thought.

"Next, we wait for the police to notify Sara. I told them I would wait until they spoke with her before reaching out. I'm sorry her husband is dead, but we still need to get paid."

"Damn straight," Lucy said as she got up to leave his office.

Silver checked his phone. It was almost one, plenty of time for Rita to have reached out to Sara. He decided to give her a call.

Rita picked up after one ring, startling Silver. "Damn girl, you never pick up that fast when I call."

"I was actually just about to call you," Rita responded.

"Oh, ok. Do you need to ask me more questions?"

"Yes, about Sara Lindsey."

"That's actually why I'm calling. If you've already notified her, I would love to reach out and get the rest of my pay." Rita went silent. "Kaye, are you still with me?"

"Are you sure you told us everything you know about Sara Lindsey?"

"Yes," Silver said in an annoyed tone. "You know that I know better than to hold back information in a murder investigation. Do you have reason to doubt me?"

"Cliff, as far as we can tell, Sara Lindsey does not exist."

"What the fuck do you mean she doesn't exist!" he shouted.

"Silver, I don't know what to tell you. There's no marriage license with his name on it, and there's only one Sara Lindsey that lives in Illinois, and she doesn't fit the description," Rita responded.

"Are you sure?" Silver said more calmly.

"I'm positive."

"So, I'm just not gonna get paid, dirty bitch."

"Silver, this is not the time for jokes."

"I'm not joking. I need that fucking money."

"Silver, there's more." Silver could hear the seriousness in her tone.

"More like what?" he asked.

"At the scene, we questioned a doorman named Bob."

"I know Bob the Doorman. I talked to him last night."

"So you did have him let you into the building?"

"Hell no." Silver sat up in his chair. "Did that fat piece of shit tell you that?"

"He said that he was bribed to let you into the building."

"Lucy gave him a hundred bucks to call me and let me know when someone signed in to see Mr. Lindsey. Last night he called me when that prostitute showed up."

"Well, Bob is saying that he was bribed to let a tall, light skin, Black male into the building minutes before the shots were heard." Rita paused, but Silver didn't say anything. "He also mentioned this guy was driving a black Mustang. Cliff, I know you didn't kill him, but if you had Bob let you into the building for any reason, it'd be easier for me to explain this to everyone."

"Rita, listen to me," he said in an angry hushed tone. "I've never stepped foot into that fucking building. The closest I ever got was the rooftop across the street."

"He had an incoming call from your phone number right before the victim was killed."

Silver immediately checked his recent calls list. His last three calls were an incoming call from Bob and two outgoing calls to Rita. "I don't have an outgoing call to him."

"Is it possible that someone used your phone to call him, then deleted it from your recent calls list?"

Silver thought for a moment. "I don't think so. I slept in my locked office last night with my phone next to ..." Silver stopped that train of thought.

"Silver, you still there?" Rita asked when he went silent for too long.

"I could've sworn I went to sleep with my phone next to

me, but when you guys woke me up, it was on my desk." Silver's mind was racing. "I just assumed I was so tired I was mistaken."

"Any signs of forced entry?" Rita asked, but Silver was already on his way to check the door. He opened the door checking for any signs that the lock had been picked.

"What are you doing?" Lucy asked, looking up from her phone.

"I'm checking for signs that my office was broken into last night."

"Why?" Lucy asked.

"Because we think that someone besides me used my phone last night."

"Who is we?" Silver didn't answer this question. Now was not the time for Lucy's smart-ass comments about Rita.

"No signs of forced entry," said Silver, speaking back with Rita. "No scratches on the lock and no signs the door had been pried open."

"Who has access to your office besides you?" asked Rita.

"Just Lucy." Silver looked over at Lucy, still sitting at her desk. "Hey, Luce, did you stop by the office last night or before you went to class this morning?"

"No, I went straight home last night, and I barely woke up in time for class this morning," Lucy said without looking up from her social media.

Silver walked back into his office and shut the door. He scanned the room, thinking maybe someone had gotten in through the window, but both windows were locked, and there were no signs that they had been tampered with.

"Kaye, I don't see any signs that someone was in here," he said as he sat back in his chair. "What did the CSU report say?"

"They found a second set of prints in his apartment, but we didn't get a match when we ran them. Also, there was a used condom in his room. They're going to run it for DNA, but you know that'll take a couple of days."

"Well, I definitely didn't fuck him, so at least you know the DNA won't match," he said, making Rita laugh so hard she snorted. "And my prints are in the system, so I can't be connected to the inside of the apartment."

"Right. That buys you some time before you can be charged."

"Rita, we both know that I'll be charged when Ford finds out about my connection to this case. Whether the evidence is circumstantial or not."

Rita didn't respond, but she knew he was right. The investigation would start and stop with Silver, and with the evidence already pointing at him, he wouldn't stand a chance. Also, they don't know how far this goes; depending on who's trying to frame him, there's no telling how much evidence against him has been planted that they just haven't found yet.

"So, what's our next move, partner?" asked Silver.

"There's no 'our.' You're not a cop, remember."

"No way in hell I'm just gonna sit here and wait for someone to frame me for murder."

"You don't trust me?"

"Kaye, I trust you with my life, but someone is going out of their way to implicate me in a murder. I'm going to fight back."

Rita thought for a moment. "If we do this, you have to promise to do as I say and make no moves without letting me know first."

"Of course," Silver said eagerly.

"I'm serious, Silver, or I'll lock you up myself."

"Now, Kaye, when have I ever not listened to you?" That question was met with silence. "Fair enough, but I promise this time."

"Yeah, sure," she said sarcastically. "First thing we need to do is figure out who Sara Lindsey really is."

"Yeah, so that bitch can give me my money."

"Cliff."

"Yeah?"

"You're not getting that money."

74

Silver sighed exaggeratedly. "I know."

"I have to go back and give Estrada an excuse for disappearing. Can I meet you at your office?"

"Yeah, that'll be fine. I just have to pick up Chrissy and take her home. Can you give me two hours?"

"Sounds good. See you soon." Rita hung up the phone, and Silver grabbed his keys.

"What a fucking day," he said to himself as he stood to leave. He opened his office door but doubled back. He walked around his desk and kneeled under it to open his safe. He reached in and pulled out his Glock. He normally didn't carry now unless he was on a job that may get violent, but at the moment, he thought better safe than sorry. If this frame-up didn't work, whoever was behind this may try to take him out another way, and he should be ready. He walked to the coat rack in the corner of his office where his holster was hanging and put it on, then he holstered his gun. He also grabbed a jacket to conceal it; he couldn't just walk around flashing a gun to everyone.

"So you're packing today," said Lucy. Silver didn't notice her standing in the doorway.

"Fuck, Luce, you can't sneak up on me like that."

"Why? Will you shoot me?"

"I might," he said as he walked past her. "Why are you being all stealthy?"

"Because something's up, and I want to know what."

"Nothing that I can't handle." He kept walking towards the door.

"Oh really? Then what were you shouting about someone not being married?" Lucy walked ahead of him and blocked his path to the door.

"Lucy, I need to get Chrissy." He reached for the doorknob, but she slapped his hand.

"I'm your partner. So, whatever it is, you won't have to go through alone."

"Ok, there is something going on, but I don't want to worry you. Also, I'm not alone." This time, Silver successfully maneuvered around her and opened the door.

"Oh, I see. You don't want me to help because Rita's gonna be involved."

"No, I don't want you involved because I don't know how deep this goes or how dangerous it could get. I would never forgive myself if something happened to you."

"You know I could say the same about you."

"Don't worry, Luce." He gave her a hug. "Only the good die young, so I'm gonna live forever."

"Hey, Daddy!" Chrissy shouted when she jumped into the car.

"Hey, princess." Silver leaned over to give her a hug and a kiss. "You have a good day at school?"

"Yes. Look what I made." Chrissy reached into her bookbag and pulled out a picture she had drawn.

Silver let out an exaggerated gasp. "You did that?"

"Yes."

"You sure? That picture looks like you stole it from a museum."

Chrissy giggled. "No, Daddy, I made it myself."

"Oh, my god. My daughter is the best artist in the world."

Chrissy giggled again, and then she began to tell her dad about her entire day like she usually did. Under normal circumstances, Silver would have listened to every word, but today his mind was elsewhere. He had to figure out who was trying to set him up. His first thought was someone on the force, but he couldn't imagine a cop doing this, especially given that "breaking the law" was why many of them hated him in the first place. His next thought was that maybe it was someone he had arrested while still on the force. Rita should look at his old arrest and see if anyone has been released from prison recently.

He looked over at Chrissy. She was his entire world, and someone was trying to take him away from her. Whoever it is, better be ready for the fight of their life because if he was going down, he was going down swinging.

"Daddy, is everything ok?" Chrissy asked when she noticed Silver wasn't paying attention.

Silver looked at her sweet face. "Yes, sweetie, I'm ok. Thank you for asking."

There was nothing like the love from a daughter. In her eyes, there was nothing he could do to make her stop loving him. It was truly pure and unconditional, and it kept him from going off the deep end. If it weren't for her, he'd be living in a box somewhere, but his biggest fear was being a disappointment in her eyes. Chrissy was going to be proud to call him Dad.

They sang along with the radio for the rest of the ride. When they arrived at Tonya's, she was standing at her usual spot waiting for them.

"You're actually on time," she said after checking the time on her phone.

"Hey, Ma," shouted Chrissy as she ran into the house.

"We have a future artist in the family." Silver was holding up Chrissy's drawing.

"That's definitely going on the fridge."

"I promised her a museum." They laughed like old times.

"Is everything ok, Cliff?"

"Yeah, why do you ask?"

"Because I've never seen you bring a gun to pick up your daughter." Tonya lifted his jacket to reveal the Glock.

Silver looked at her trying to think of a lie she would believe. "I'm in trouble, T." He never could lie to her.

She didn't say anything. She just reached out her hand. Silver took it, and she walked him into the house. Chrissy sat on the couch watching her after-school cartoons. So, Tonya led him past her and down the hall into the kitchen. They sat at the kitchen table, and she silently waited for him to speak.

"Do you remember that client I told you about last week?" he asked. "The man I was paid to follow was killed last night."

"I'm sorry to hear that," she said softly. "Do you think someone is after you for witnessing it?"

"I didn't witness anything. I was asleep in my office when he was killed."

"Then why the hell are you walking around with a gun?"

"Because the doorman of his building lied and told Rita that I bribed him to let me into the building right before the time of death."

"You sure you weren't in his place?"

"Of course, I'm sure, T. What kind of question is that?"

"I'm just saying, sometimes you blackout, so maybe ..."

"I said I wasn't there!" Silver said sharply.

"Calm down," Tonya whispered. "Don't let her hear you."

"I'm sorry." Silver brought his voice back down to a whisper. "I promise I was asleep when this happened."

"So, you didn't have anything to drink last night?" asked Tonya. Silver didn't respond but concentrated on not making eye contact with her. "How much?"

"How much what?" he asked, pretending he didn't understand the question.

"How much did you have to drink last night?"

This was another question that had been tormenting him since his talk with Rita. He looked Tonya in her eyes and said, "I don't know."

"What the fuck do you mean you don't know?"

"I swear I only had one glass before I went to bed, but the entire bottle was gone when I woke up this morning."

"Maybe that one glass emptied the bottle, and you just didn't realize it," Tonya suggested.

"It was full." Silver's face filled with shame. "I broke the seal last night."

Tonya wanted to scold him, but nothing she could say would

punish him more than he was already punishing himself.

"Ok, what did your client have to say?" she asked after a moment of silence had passed.

"I tried calling her on my way to pick up Chrissy, but her phone number is disconnected, and Rita can't find proof that she even existed."

This time Tonya couldn't hide her disappointment. "Cliff, please tell me you looked into her before you took the case."

"Business has not been great, T. I'm barely keeping my head above water, and this woman was offering some really good money."

"I get that, but how would looking into her affect the money you were being paid?" she asked. "Admit it, Cliff; your drinking has made you sloppy. I can tell that you were hungover before you went to meet her. You knew that if you looked into her and she wasn't who she claimed to be, it would take away from your alcohol budget."

She wasn't wrong. The night before he had met Sara, or whatever the fuck her name was, he was blackout drunk. It had already dawned on him that maybe he hadn't been thinking clearly when he met her. He always checked clients for the same reason he checked who he was hired to follow. You don't want any surprises. What Rita had told him about his client shouldn't have been his first time hearing it, he shouldn't have gone anywhere near that apartment building, and he shouldn't be in this predicament.

He looked back up at Tonya. "You're right, T. I fucked up. What do I do now?"

"You fix this shit. That little girl in there needs her father so fix it."

They held eye contact with each other. Tonya could always see right through him, even the thoughts he was hiding from himself. It's what had made him fall in love with her. It was why he still loved her. Without saying anything, he leaned forward and gave her a tender kiss on her forehead. A kiss that said I hear you, and I love you. Then he stood and walked into the living room.

"Hey, princess, I'm leaving."

"Ok, bye, Daddy. I'll see you tomorrow."

Silver knelt down so he could look his daughter in the eye. "I won't be able to pick you up tomorrow, princess."

"Why not, Daddy?"

Silver spoke to Chrissy but looked at Tonya. "I have to help a friend fix something, but I promise I'll be back."

He kept his eyes on Tonya while he gave Chrissy a hug. Tonya nodded to him to let him know that she understood, then he kissed his daughter and walked out the door.

CHAPTER 8

"You said two hours," said Rita as she leaned on her car in front of his building. "It's been three."

"Sorry, there was traffic." Silver walked briskly to meet her at the door. "And T wanted to talk for a minute."

"Does she know what's going on?" asked Rita.

"Yeah. I told her."

"You sure that was a good idea?"

"I wanted her to know the truth, just in case something goes terribly wrong." Silver looked at Rita, and she could see the worry in his eyes. "Are you planning to dust my office for prints?" Silver motioned towards the case Rita was carrying.

"Yeah, I borrowed this from CSU. I figured we could see if she left any prints behind, then maybe we'll get lucky, and our mystery woman is in the system."

"Why did you wait outside? Lucy is up there. She would've let you in."

"Are you sure about that?"

"Why wouldn't she?"

"Because she's the assistant from hell, who also seems to hate me."

"She doesn't hate you," he reassured her, but Rita's look showed that she didn't believe him. "Ok, she does, but I don't know why."

"Obviously, your little assistant wants to fuck you."

"Even if that was true, why would that make her hate you?"

"She thinks me and you are fucking, and she's jealous."

"You know I may be going to jail soon, so maybe we—"

"Stay focused, perv," Rita said to cut him off.

"Right, clear my name, then we can celebrate naked." Silver opened the door and went inside. Rita shook her head and followed him.

"Oh great, Rita's here," said Lucy when they stepped into the office.

"Always nice to see you too, Lucy," Rita responded.

Silver chuckled. "Play nice, ladies. Rita's here to pull some prints."

"Whose prints are you looking for?" asked Lucy.

"Our last client's."

"Sara?"

"Turns out Sara isn't her name."

Lucy's jaw dropped. "Then what was her name?"

"That's what we're hoping to find out," said Rita.

Lucy looked at Rita suspiciously. "That info came from her?"

"Yes, it did," said Rita. She took a step toward Lucy. "Is that a problem?"

"It is a problem. You can't be trusted." Lucy took a step towards Rita.

"Who the fuck do you think you are?" Rita shouted.

"That's enough," said Silver as he stepped between them. "This petty shit isn't going to get us anywhere, so cut it out."

Rita shook her head and walked over to Lucy's desk. She sat the case on top of it and started to unpack. Lucy grabbed his hand and pulled him over to the door, where she felt like Rita couldn't hear her.

"You can't trust her, Cliff," she whispered.

"Yes, I can."

"If someone's trying to frame you, then the last person you need to be with is someone you know won't have your back."

"Lucy, take the rest of the day off."

Lucy took a step back from him and pleaded with her eyes for him to let her stay, but he wasn't going to budge. So, she stomped away to her desk and snatched her phone and purse before slamming the door on her way out.

"It was great seeing you again, Lucy," Rita shouted after her.

"Sorry about that," said Silver after he locked the door behind Lucy.

"So, I'm not to be trusted," Rita said as she unpacked her case.

"You know I trust you."

"She doesn't know the entire story, does she?"

"The entire story isn't any of her business."

"If you say so," she said as she handed him a pair of latex gloves. "Remember, if anyone asks, I printed your office on my own. Chain of custody and all."

Silver took the gloves and put them on. "Lucy cleans this side of the office pretty often, so I doubt we'll find anything here. My office is another story."

"Yeah, I bet you're a pig."

Silver gave her the finger. "Just to be thorough, she was sitting in that chair when I walked in." Silver pointed to the chair near Lucy's desk. "And I'll check this side of Lucy's desk just in case she leaned on it."

They both grabbed some printing powder and brushes and went to work. The chair had varnished wooden arms, which is an excellent surface to print. Rita applied the fine powder to the arms of the chair, but nothing showed up. Then she applied it to the underside of the arm, thinking that maybe her fingers wrapped around it and left some prints, but that side had been wiped down too.

"No luck here," she said when she was satisfied she wouldn't find anything. "How's her desk?"

"Nothing here either," he said, "She really is a neat freak." They were moving on to his office when Rita received a text.

"I called in a few favors and had that DNA from the condom moved to the top of the list," she said, reading the results. "There was the DNA of a white female found on the outside of the condom. They ran it through CODIS but didn't get a match."

"So, if she is a prostitute, she's a prostitute without a record," said Silver after she finished reading.

"What if she's not a prostitute?"

"You mean someone who showed up at that apartment to get me off that rooftop? The thought has already crossed my mind."

"This mystery woman that hired you must've had a really good fake ID if it fooled you," said Rita, but Silver didn't say anything. "You did check her ID, right?"

"It may have slipped my mind," said Silver. He was too embarrassed to look her way.

"Really, Cliff?"

"You don't have to say it. I know I fucked up. My head was pounding that morning, and I don't think I was thinking straight."

Rita could see that he was beating himself up and saw no point in kicking him while he was down. "We're going to figure this out, Cliff. I promise."

They worked silently for the next couple of minutes, repeating the same tasks from the room before, and they found nothing.

"Damn, I guess that's a dead end on the prints," said Silver as he plopped down in his chair.

"This doesn't make sense." Rita was pacing the room.

"It was over a week ago that she was here."

"It hasn't been over a week since you've been here. So where are your prints?"

Silver looked around the room. "Yeah, where are my prints?"

"You spend every night here. No way your prints should not be in this office." She stopped pacing when Silver pulled out his phone and called someone. "Who are you calling?"

"Hey, Lucy, I have a quick question."

"Go ahead," Lucy responded over the speaker.

"Were you in my office today?"

"Yeah. When I get bored, sometimes I clean your office for you. Lord knows you're not going to do it."

"Thanks, Luce. That's all I needed." Silver hung up the phone and tossed it on his desk.

"So this is a dead end," said Rita as she sat on his couch.

"Sorry, I hire way too well."

They both sat there silently, contemplating their next move. They not only had to identify Silver's client, but they had to prove she was in his office, or else it would be her word against his when they found her. Fingerprints would have been the easiest way to place her there.

"Do you have cameras in here?" Rita asked after a moment of thinking.

"Unfortunately not. This business is about discretion. I put cameras up, and clients won't trust me."

"What about outside the building?"

"Not outside my office, but my neighbor definitely has them."

"If they keep the footage—"

"Then maybe they caught her on camera coming and going," he said, finishing her thought.

"Not just her but her car," said Rita.

"A license plate could lead us right to her," he added. The two of them did not notice that they had stood and moved towards each other while they were talking. With each new thought, they moved a step closer to each other until they were close enough for him to smell her shampoo again.

"Is that lavender?" he asked.

"What?"

"Your shampoo, is that lavender?"

"Yes, it is. Why are you smelling my hair?"

"Whenever I'm this close to you, all I can smell is your hair. It's right beneath my nose."

"Well, maybe you shouldn't stand this close to me," she said, but she didn't move away.

"Yeah, maybe I shouldn't." His heart raced as he inched a little closer to her.

Silver began to lean his face closer to hers, but she moved away right before their lips touched. "We should head next door and ask about those cameras," she said, then she turned and walked away, leaving him standing there. She had to get out of that office, but something made her pause as she walked through the door.

"Hey, Rita, I'm sorry if I crossed ..."

"Don't worry about it," she said hurriedly. Then, she pointed at the door. "Is this door always open?"

"I only close it when I'm sleeping in here or if I'm speaking with a client."

"So, it was closed the day she was here?"

"Yes, it would've been."

"Did you let her out, or did she let herself out?"

Silver could see where her thinking was going. "She let herself out. As a matter of fact, I stopped her as she was leaving, and she stood there with her hand resting on the handle."

Rita pushed the door closed and grabbed the printing dust. Since it was a lever and not a knob, it was a nice flat surface, making it easy to apply the dust. Some partials and one clear full print became visible at the end of the handle where a person's thumb would rest. Rita went back to her kit and grabbed the tape and what looked like small index cards. Rita took some tape and pressed it along the length of the door handle. She then pulled the tape off, lifting all of the visible prints, and taped it to an index card.

"I'm sure most of these prints will be yours, but maybe we'll get lucky," she said as she repacked her case.

Silver pulled off his gloves and tossed them in the trash by his desk. "Well, I'm feeling lucky."

"Keep that energy when we ask for that camera footage without a warrant."

"I wouldn't worry about that." Silver was smiling ear to ear. "I got that covered."

Silver held the door open for Rita at the pawn shop next door to his office. They walked past the random merchandise toward the back of the store, where a heavy-set, middle-aged Black woman sat behind the counter, playing on her phone.

"My beautiful Patrice. How are you doing today?" said Silver.

Patrice lifted her head from her phone and beamed when she saw Silver. Then, she stood up and came around the counter to give him a hug.

"What brings your fine ass in here today?" she said as she wrapped her arms around him.

"I need a favor, sweetheart," he said, but Patrice's focus was on Rita.

"And who might you be?" she asked Rita.

"I'm Detective Rita Kaye." Rita held out her hand for Patrice to shake it, but Patrice just stared.

"Clifford Silver, are you trying to make me jealous?" she said, bringing her attention back to Silver.

"No, my love, she's actually helping me out too."

Patrice looked Rita over. "I don't normally do threesomes,

but she's cute, I guess."

"I'm flattered," Rita said sarcastically.

Silver chuckled. "No, she's helping me look for someone."

"And how can I help, baby?"

"Can we take a look at your security footage?" asked Silver. Patrice's eyes went over to Rita again. "You can trust her, sweetheart, I promise."

"I believe you, Clifford. The only problem is someone smashed my camera last night."

"Around what time?" asked Rita.

"I checked the footage to see the motherfucker who did it, and the last recording was a little after ten."

"Did you see the motherfucker who did it?" Silver chimed in.

"No, baby, whoever did it was in the camera's blind spot."

Silver and Rita made eye contact and agreed that Patrice's camera getting smashed was related to the case without saying a word.

"What time did you notice it was broken?" Rita pulled out her notebook so she could jot down the details.

"When I was leaving late last night at about three thirty."

"Why were you here so late?"

"I wanted to take inventory before I went home for the night, and it took longer than I expected. I was gonna see if someone was up for some late-night fun." Patrice ran her finger across Silver's chest. "But I had just missed you."

"What do you mean?" asked Silver.

"I saw you sitting in your car with the door open and went out to talk to you, but you shut the door and pulled off when I came outside," said Patrice.

"No, Patrice, I was upstairs asleep in my office."

"You must've been hitting the sauce again."

Silver could barely contain himself as he processed what Patrice had just said. He looked for a reaction from Rita and could see that the news had shaken her as well. Why would someone take his car just to bring it right back?

"You know what, Patrice, you're right. I went home last night. I must be thinking about another night." Silver tried not to let Patrice see how shaken he was. "How long do you keep the footage from your camera?"

"The footage uploads to the cloud. I only delete when I run out of storage."

"What about nine days ago?"

"I should still have that."

"You think we can take a look?" asked Silver, but Patrice hesitated. "I have a client who's trying not to pay me. If I can get a picture of her, my friend here can run her through facial recognition and get her address for me."

"Let's find this bitch." Patrice began to walk, and they followed. She led them to a room in the back corner of her shop and opened the door, revealing a small office containing just an alarm panel, a computer, and a freestanding safe. Opening the door caused the alarm to beep rapidly, but she punched in the code to disarm it. The two of them stood in the doorway while she sat at the computer, pulling up the footage.

"What day do you need to look at?" she asked after she logged into her cloud storage.

"Last Tuesday," Silver responded.

"Time?"

"Can you pull up two p.m.? We can scan through it from there."

Patrice changed the date and time and waited for the new footage to load. Once the video was ready to go, she stood to leave.

"I have to watch the front of the store, but you two take as much time as you need." They cleared the doorway, giving her space to walk out. "I do have to lock you in because my safe is in here, so just give me a shout when you're ready."

Silver and Rita stepped into the office so that Patrice could close the door, and they heard the deadbolt lock them in afterward.

"Why do the women that want you hate me so much?" Rita said quietly.

"Maybe they just don't like your ass," Silver retorted. "Don't put that shit on me."

Rita playfully slapped him on the back of his head, and they shared a laugh. Silver sat at the computer and used the mouse to press play on the footage. Then he hit the fast-forward button three times to speed up the video.

"Shouldn't take too long," said Silver with his eyes trained on the computer. "She arrived at the office while I was getting Chrissy from school." Sure enough, shortly into the fast-forwarding, a car pulled up, and his client got out of the back seat. Silver pressed the play button so the video could play in real-time, and Rita leaned forward to get a better look. The picture was surprisingly clear for a storefront camera, but it would likely become more pixelated if they tried to zoom in. The camera mostly focused on the sidewalk in front of the pawn shop. So, when she walked up to his door, the best shot they could get of her was a side profile. Silver paused the video and captured a still of her before she stepped on the curb, and from that angle, he could see part of the front of her face. Then he zoomed in as much as he could without completely distorting the picture and captured another still.

"You're pretty good at this," said Rita as she watched him work.

"Most of my job is catching people doing things they shouldn't. So you have to get pretty good with a camera." Once he got the images he wanted, he began to fast forward again.

"Too bad there's no footage from last night. We could see who took your car."

"What a coincidence that her camera was destroyed hours before my car apparently was stolen."

"At least we know one thing."

"What's that?"

"Bob wasn't lying about seeing your car in the alley."

"But he did lie," said Silver, doing nothing to hide the irritation in his voice.

"I'm confused. Why would they take your car if it wasn't for him to see it?"

Silver paused the footage. "Think about the timeline. He claimed that he let me in right before the shots were heard, but I was in my car on my way to the office at that time." Silver let that realization sink in for Rita. "So even if he did see that car, he's lying about me driving it, and I'm thinking that someone took my car just long enough for Patrice to assume I left and didn't come back. When you guys questioned me, I told you that my alibi was that I was in my office all night, but if you questioned her as a witness, it would look like I lied."

"Maybe that's how we can rule you out. We can check traffic cam footage that shows you nowhere near the building at the time of the shooting." Rita was attempting to pull something optimistic out of this situation.

"Traffic cam footage will probably lock me in as a suspect." Rita could feel that optimism dim down a little. "I called you about fifteen to twenty minutes after I left, which was right after the shots were fired, so traffic cam footage would show me still in the vicinity of the crime scene."

Now Rita's excitement was dampened entirely. Silver was absolutely correct. The traffic cam footage, as well as Bob's statement, would confirm him as the primary suspect.

"Whoever this is was smart to get a ride. A license plate on a car registered to her would lead us straight to her front door," Rita said to break the tension that was filling that tiny room.

"I was thinking that, but someone had to come pick her up, and from this angle, we should be able to get a clear picture of their plates. We can run down that person and get them to tell us where they dropped her off."

"Good thinking, Silver."

"You're not the only great detective in the room."

"Yeah, yeah, whatever. Pay attention, 'Detective.' She just came back out."

Again, Silver pressed play on the video so they could watch it in real time. His client stepped onto the sidewalk and pulled her phone out of her purse. She typed on it for a moment, slipped it back into her bag, and waited.

"She must've just ordered a ride," said Silver. It didn't take long for a car to pull up to the curb, and it was different from the one that dropped her off. She opened the door and climbed into the back seat. Once her door was shut, the car began to pull away from the curb, and Silver paused the video. The vehicle was angled away from the curb with its back left tire still touching. This angle gave them a clear picture of the car's license plate.

"Got it."

CHAPTER 9

Silver sat in the passenger seat of Rita's car, looking over the pictures he printed from Patrice's security footage. They were on their way downtown to her precinct to track down the owner of the vehicle that picked up his client. Rita wanted to leave Silver at his office, but he insisted on coming along. He didn't want to waste valuable time by having her drive back and forth, so they agreed she would park a block away from the station, and he would wait in the car. The last place anyone looking for him would think to search would be in a detective's car.

"I hope we can get an ID from these pictures of her," said Silver. "The clear picture is pretty far away, and the close-up is pretty grainy."

"Don't worry, someone will recognize her." Rita was trying her best to reassure him. However, from the moment they had left Patrice's shop, she could see the flirty class clown facade begin to chip away.

"I don't know. I could barely recognize her from these photos."

"You only saw her once, Cliff. I'm sure you didn't remember what she looked like at all until you saw that picture."

"I guess," he said, not convinced by her reasoning.

"How about you put those pictures down and talk about what's really on your mind."

He sat the pictures in his lap. "How could I fuck up this bad, Rita?"

"What do you mean?"

"How did I end up in this position?" he reiterated. Rita let him vent. "I sat back and watched while someone snatched my career away from me, but that wasn't enough. Now they've come back for my life. I need to be here for Chrissy."

"You will, Cliff."

"I'm not so sure anymore."

"You can't think like that." She reached over and held his hand. "I will not rest until I find whoever is trying to do this to you."

"Thanks, Rita."

She gave his hand a squeeze and then put it back on the steering wheel. It was going to take both of them to figure this out, so she needed to keep him focused. If she could keep his mind on solving the mystery, it wouldn't wander to all the possible negative outcomes.

"Do you have any idea who could be behind all of this?" she asked.

"No. No one comes to mind."

Rita could hear in his voice that there was something he wanted to say. "You sure there's no one who hates you enough to go to these extremes?"

Silver stared out the window. "That list is too long."

They drove in silence the rest of the way. Rita parked a block away from the precinct like they had agreed, and Silver laid his seat flat so he wouldn't be seen if someone from the precinct just happened to walk past.

Rita made the short walk over to the station and took the

elevator up to homicide. Javier rushed over to her as soon as she stepped into the bullpen.

"Where the hell have you been?" he asked in a hushed voice.

"I had some personal business to take care of. What's going on around here?" There was a different energy in the bullpen from when she had left.

"Ford is on to Silver."

Rita grabbed Javier by the wrist and pulled him to the side where they wouldn't be heard. "How is he on to him?"

"He received an anonymous call saying that Silver committed the murder." Javier paused as someone walked past. "After the call, he had us check traffic cam footage, and Silver's car was seen in the area immediately after the shots were heard."

"Fuck," said Rita. They had less time than she thought. The walls were going to start closing in on Silver very soon. "Does he know about the doorman's statement?"

"No, I didn't want to mention it until after I spoke with you."

Rita thought for a moment. "Go ahead and tell him. If he finds out you withheld evidence, you'll get in a lot of trouble. Just tell him that you didn't put it together that the description matched Silver until after the tip came in."

"Copy that, but Kaye, there's something else," said Javier. Rita could sense that this was about to be bad news. "The medical examiner pulled the slugs from the body. They determined the bullets were shot from a Glock nineteen. Silver has a Glock nineteen registered in his name."

Rita's legs disappeared from under her. "How long before they have the warrant?"

"Any minute now. You might want to tell Silver to turn himself in. It would be easier that way."

"Estrada, I need you to trust me, I'm working with Silver to find who's behind this, but if he gets locked up, it's over."

"I got your back, partner," he responded. "What do you

need me to do?"

"Work the case like you would any other. Dive into Richard Lindsey's life. Right now, the best thing we have working for us is that Silver had no motive to want him dead, so find someone who does. While you do that, Silver and I will work from the angle of who has motive to frame him."

"That's a good plan."

"I do need one favor from you to help us get started."

"Name it."

"Thank you so much. We're trying to track down the woman who hired him to follow Richard Lindsey." She reached into her pocket and pulled out the fingerprints they had collected. "We pulled these prints from his office. Can you have someone in the lab run them for me?"

"Of course." Javier took the prints from her.

"We also took some stills from a security camera on his block of the car that picked her up. We believe it's a rideshare company, but if we can get in touch with the driver, he may remember where he dropped her off." She showed him the picture of the plate. "Can you run this plate for me and get me a name?"

She handed him the picture. "How did you get security cam footage without a warrant?" he asked.

"Apparently, Silver has fans," she said with an eye roll.

"You know what, I don't even want to know. Cap is looking for you. I'll run this while you're in his office."

Javier rushed to his desk while Rita walked to Captain Ford's office. Rita would much rather sneak out of the precinct without being seen, but she knew it would be good to find out how locked in Ford was on Silver. He was sitting at his desk, completing paperwork. Rita knocked and peeked her head into his office.

"You looking for me, sir?" she asked.

"Close the door and have a seat," he said without looking up from his work. Rita obeyed and softly shut his office door before taking a seat across from him. "Did Estrada fill you in?"

"Uh yeah, he says we have a suspect."

Ford looked at her over his glasses. "A damn good suspect."

"Sir, I can't imagine him doing this."

"Why not?"

"Because I know him, sir."

"Kaye, I don't think you should work this case." Ford put down his pen and sat back in his chair.

"Sir ..."

"Rita, I know how you feel about him, but it does not look good. I have the utmost faith in your ability to do your job, and I know that if it came down to it, you would slap the cuffs on him yourself. But that would destroy you, and I can't sit back and watch that happen."

"Sir, I can do this. When he was in trouble before, I was the one who turned him in, remember."

"Rita, we both know why you turned him in, and it wasn't because you thought he was guilty." Ford gave her a chance to respond, but Rita didn't say anything. "You both knew that there wasn't enough to charge him with anything, and turning him in meant that they were less likely to call you his accomplice."

He was right. Once the accusation came, Silver knew he was done and that no one would believe that his partner didn't know. Even if he beat the case, he would be handcuffed to a desk for the rest of his career, hidden away in the darkest basement the department could find to hide their embarrassment, and she would never be trusted again. So it was Silver's idea for her to report him to internal affairs.

"Kaye, you know how I feel about him, but I need you to trust me. Right now, the evidence is pointing his way whether you believe it or not, and our job is to follow the evidence. Go home, Rita. You don't need to be here for this."

Rita knew this was a battle she wasn't going to win. "Thank you, sir. I'm going to take your advice and use some vacation time." She left his office and walked over to Javier's desk. "He's benching me."

"Maybe that's for the best," said Javier. "It'll be easier for you and Silver to investigate without you having to report your movements."

"Yeah, you're right, and I definitely need to stay attached to Silver's hip to make sure he doesn't do anything stupid," said Rita. "He's not going to take this lying down, and I need to have his back."

"Well, in that case, please get some rest in your time off," he said loud enough for everyone in the bullpen to hear, sliding her a folded sheet of paper simultaneously.

"Thank you, and call me if you need anything." She grabbed it and headed to the elevator.

Daryl Watkins lived at 4709 South Drexel, and the car that had picked up Silver's client was registered to him. Silver and Rita drove straight to the address after leaving the precinct. When they arrived at the apartment building, they found his name listed on the doorbells and buzzed his apartment. No answer. His car wasn't on the street, so they figured he must've been out working. Javier had also slipped Rita Daryl's DMV photo when he gave her Watkins' name and address, so the two of them decided to sit on his place until he returned home.

"You've been quiet," said Silver after they settled back into the car.

"I've been trying to get my thoughts together," said Rita.

"Care to share?"

"Ford knows you're connected to this, so he took me off the case."

"Fuck, I'm sorry, Kaye. You know I don't want to get in the way of your career. I could work on my own from here to keep your hands clean."

"You already fell on your sword for me once. I'm not going to sit on the sidelines again. It's not looking good, Cliff."

"Have they found more evidence against me?"

"Ford received an anonymous call naming you as the shooter. After that, he had traffic cam footage pulled and has your car leaving the vicinity of the murder just minutes after it was committed."

"Well, that's just fucking fantastic."

"Just wait. There's more."

"Well, this is starting to sound like the world's worst infomercial."

"That's a Glock nineteen you're carrying, isn't it?"

Silver clutched his gun in its holster. "Yeah, why?"

"Do you always carry?"

"No, I keep it in a gun safe until I feel like I need it." Silver's anxiety began to rise. "What are you getting at?"

"Did you have it on you last night?"

"No, I didn't take it out until today. Please just tell me what you know."

"The slugs they pulled from the victim were shot from a Glock nineteen. Ford knows you own the same type of gun, and with your car being seen near the crime scene, they have probable cause for a warrant to take possession of your gun and run it for ballistics."

Silver immediately pulled his gun out of its holster and smelled the chamber. The last time Silver had discharged his weapon was two weeks ago at the range, and he cleaned it regularly, so the smell of burned gunpowder indicated that it had been fired within the last day or two. He ejected the clip, and three bullets were missing. Silver felt as if he had just hit a brick wall. How could he not have noticed?

Rita sat there in silence. She knew there were no words that could help him at that moment. The second Javier told her about the weapon, she had known Richard Lindsey was killed with Silver's gun.

"So, someone took more than just my car, it looks like," said Silver after ten minutes of silence. "I need to run."

"You are not running," said Rita sternly.

"I don't think I can win this one." Silver felt a lump grow in his throat. "Even if we find out who's behind this, the evidence points to me only. No way I beat this in court, and Chrissy is not going to visit me in prison."

"They still don't have motive. The evidence may still point at you but proving someone out there has a vendetta against you and was capable of pulling this off is reasonable doubt. Run, and you'll never see Chrissy again. Run, and everyone is going to say it's because you were guilty. Run, and Chrissy will grow up being the daughter of a cold-blooded killer."

Silver knew in his heart that Rita was right. If he ran, he would be running for the rest of his life. He would be abandoning Chrissy.

"They will be searching my office and apartment soon if they aren't already," he said, snapping back into focus. "After that, they'll reach out to Lucy and Tonya, trying to find me. With the gun missing and no one close to me knowing where to find me, Ford will label me a fugitive, so we have to move fast."

"Time is definitely not on our side, but the one advantage we have is their not pursuing this line of investigation. It's going to take them a while to thoroughly search your place and office, so that reduces the chances of crossing paths with them. It should give us just enough time to find this person."

"If we can't find her, we need to get me off the streets."

"We'll cross that bridge when we get to it." Rita wanted to focus on one issue at a time. No need to get too far ahead of themselves.

Their stakeout lasted hours and went late into the night. Under normal circumstances, since this guy was not a danger to anyone, they would've gone home and come back in the morning, but by the morning, the entire Chicago Police Department would be looking for Silver.

Silver's stomach growled and made him think they should've stopped for snacks. He hadn't noticed the growl was loud enough for Rita to hear, and now she was staring at him.

"What?" he asked innocently.

"Was that your stomach or your ass?" she asked.

"What if it was my ass?"

"Then I'm putting you out of my car. I don't care if you get arrested."

"Damn, you wouldn't even take me home first?"

"Nope. Your ass can walk." They laughed with each other for the first time in hours. For Rita, it was nice to see him laugh again.

"Speaking of home," he said after the laughter died down. "I can't go back there tonight."

"Yeah, that wouldn't be a great idea," said Rita in agreement.

"I couldn't, even if it was a great idea. My keys to my apartment are in my car."

"Why would you leave your keys in your car?"

"Since I don't go home often, I barely use them. I kept forgetting where they were, so I started leaving them in my car so I'd always know where to find them."

"I guess that makes sense," Rita said with a shrug.

"I would stay at Tonya's, but that would be the first place they look."

"What about Lucy?" Rita suggested.

"No. Can't go there," he said dismissively.

"I know she was pissed at you earlier, but she wouldn't turn you away."

"It's not that." Rita gave him a look urging him to explain. "If my ex-wife would be the first place they look, then my assistant would be the second."

"Maybe you're right, but it seems like you have another reason in mind."

"Well, I also don't know where she lives," said Silver, shrugging his shoulders.

"You've never been to her place?"

"No, why would I?" he asked, but Rita looked straight ahead and tapped her steering wheel. "I've never slept with her."

"Mhmm, sure. She's just protective of you because she loves you as a boss."

"Is that so hard to believe?"

"I'm just saying she's young and attractive. She clearly adores you. Why else would she put up with you?"

"That's actually a question I've been asking myself lately," said Silver jokingly.

"You could stay the night with me," said Rita sheepishly. Silver cocked his eye at her. "Not like that, perv. I mean on my couch."

"Rita Kaye, are you trying to use this moment of vulnerability to get in my pants?" Silver covered his mouth as if he was shocked.

"You know what, sleep in a box for all I care."

Silver laughed. "Kaye, I honestly appreciate the offer, but I can't have you harboring a fugitive."

"You're technically not a fugitive yet, and the last place they'll look is the apartment of the partner who turned you in before."

Silver thought for a moment. "They know we're still friends."

"But like Lucy said, I'm not to be trusted," she said. Silver was warming up to the idea when a car matching the one from the video drove past them.

"Is that our guy?" asked Rita.

"Plates match. Let's go." Silver opened his door, but Rita stopped him. "What's wrong?"

"Stay here," she said.

"Why?"

"Because we aren't supposed to be together, and I don't want him to be able to ID you." Rita slid out of the car, and Silver closed his door, conceding that she had a good point.

"Daryl Watkins?" said Rita as she approached.

"Who's asking?" he asked as he turned to face her. He was stocky and Black. His driver's license had him as twenty-two years old, although Rita would have guessed that he was younger.

Rita held up her badge. "I'm Detective Rita Kaye."

"Am I in trouble?" Daryl asked apprehensively.

"Not at all, Mr. Watkins. I'm trying to locate someone, and I believe you can help me."

"How?" he asked, baffled.

Rita held up the photo of Silver's client getting into Daryl's car and shined her flashlight on it to give him a good look. "Is this your car this woman is getting into?"

Daryl leaned forward to get a good look at the photo. "Yes, that's my car."

"This was last Tuesday. Do you remember anything about this passenger?"

Rita made sure to hold up the close-up photo as well. "Not really, but I give a lot of people rides," said Daryl.

"You picked her up from an office in the Bridgeview area." Rita was trying to jog his memory.

"Did you say Bridgeview?" he asked, and Rita nodded yes. "I actually do remember her. I almost declined that fare because of how far she had to travel, but she tipped very well."

"Do you remember her name?"

Daryl looked up as if he were trying to literally look into his brain. "I think it started with a V, but I can't be too sure."

Rita wrote "V?" into her notebook. "Do you remember where you dropped her off?"

"That I do remember. It was a pretty long drive to the south suburbs. Some trailers near Blue Island off of 135th street. With what she was wearing, she definitely didn't belong there."

"I'm assuming you don't remember an exact address?"

"No. I didn't drop her off at an exact address."

"What do you mean?"

"I never actually drove into the trailer park. She stopped me before I could and walked the rest of the way."

Rita wrote, "Trailer park near 135th?" "Thank you for your time, Mr. Watkins. This was a lot of help."

"No problem. I didn't help her escape from a crime scene or anything, did I? I swear I never met her before that day."

"No, we just have some questions for her."

"Are you sure? Because she talked with someone on the phone, and it sounded pretty sketchy."

"Do you remember what she talked about?" Rita asked eagerly.

"She mentioned someone named Silver. I remember because I thought that was a cool name."

"What about Silver?" said Rita, trying to hurry him along.

"Well, I couldn't hear what the other person was saying, but this lady was talking about how he fell for it and that they were going to take everything from him. Just like he did to her."

CHAPTER 10

"That has to narrow the suspect list down," said Rita as she poured herself a glass of wine.

They had just made it back to her apartment after questioning Daryl Watkins. On the way, Rita filled him in on everything she had learned, including the conversation Daryl overheard.

"You would think so," said Silver. "But I can't think of anyone."

"So, no suspects fall off the list?" asked Rita.

"That's not it at all, actually. It wiped the list clean."

"It has to be someone that comes to mind."

"No woman whose name starts with a V. And if I really took everything from her, I think I would recognize her sitting across from me."

"You're being too literal," she said as she joined him on the couch. "Maybe you didn't do anything to her directly."

"Then that leaves everyone." Silver leaned forward and rubbed his forehead. "Too many for us to check on our own."

Rita pushed herself closer to him and placed a hand on her shoulder. "Why don't we take our minds off the case for a little while."

Silver stood from the couch abruptly. "Rita, I'm running out of time. We should've gone there tonight."

"And did what, Cliff? Randomly knock on doors in the middle of the night?"

"That's better than sitting on our asses doing nothing," he said as he started pacing.

"I promise we'll get up first thing in the morning and track her down." Rita sat down her wine and stood up with him. "For now, let's just relax. You're no good if you're run down."

"How can I relax right now?" he said more calmly.

"You can start by showering." She frowned her face at him. "I didn't wanna say anything, but you're smelling a little ripe."

Silver sniffed his armpit, and his eyes teared up. "Damn, you're right. Wait, is that why we stopped at a store on the way here?"

"You didn't think your funky ass was gonna stink up my couch, did you?" She grabbed a bag from her counter and handed it to him. "I bought you a change of clothes and deodorant."

"You didn't have to do this, Rita."

"Like I said, I did it for my couch."

"I could've given you the money for this."

"What money? You're broke as fuck."

"Very true," he said with a smile. "Thanks."

"It's really not a big deal. I bought you the cheapest clothes they had."

"Not just for the clothes. For everything." Silver didn't need to say anything else. Rita had become his lifeline, risking her career to help him and keep him calm and under control. Silver wasn't sure how all of this would end, but either way, he wanted her to know how thankful he was, and from how she looked at him, she did.

"Don't go getting soft on me, big guy," she said, nudging

him with her fist. "Now go wash your ass."

Silver threw his hands up in surrender before making his way toward the bathroom, when they heard a knock on the door. Silver and Rita looked at each other and had one of their famous non-verbal conversations.

With his eyes, Silver asked, "Are you expecting anyone?" Rita shook her head, then both of their eyes shot back to the door. There was a small hallway leading to it; her kitchen was the nearest room, so Silver kneeled in its entryway and peeked around the corner. Once he was out of sight, Rita approached the door.

There was another knock on the door just as she reached it. "Who is it?" she shouted through the door.

"Ford," a booming voice shouted back.

Rita looked back at Silver to motion him to get out of sight, but he was already gone. She waited until she heard her bedroom door close before she opened the door for Captain Ford.

"Sorry to keep you waiting, sir," she said once the door was fully open.

"No worries, may I come in?" he asked.

"Of course." Rita cleared the doorway for the captain to enter.

He walked into the living room but did not sit. Instead, he turned to Rita and said, "We should talk."

"Is everything ok?" she asked.

"I know I sent you home, but I still want to keep you updated with the investigation."

"Thanks, sir. Would you like to sit down?"

"No, thank you," he said, waving her off. "This won't take long." Rita sat on the arm of her couch and gave him her full attention. "We searched his apartment and his office. His apartment looks like he hasn't been there in weeks, so it wasn't a shock that we didn't find anything there. At his office, we found a small gun safe under his desk. We took possession of it, and they're going to crack it open tomorrow. If the gun is there and ballistics match, there will be an arrest warrant put out for him."

Rita sat silently while he spoke, but in her mind, she was glad that Silver decided to carry today. Without matching ballistics, there's no way a judge will sign an arrest warrant, and that bought them a little time. She quickly scanned the room with her eyes, hoping that Silver hadn't taken his holster off and sat it somewhere in plain sight.

"Do you know if he has another vehicle?" asked Ford.

"No, why do you ask?" Rita responded.

"In the morning, we're going to put out a BOLO for him, and I wanted to include a vehicle."

"Why not his Mustang?"

"It's parked at his office, and since he's nowhere to be found, I'm assuming he has another way to get around."

"That doesn't make sense."

"What do you mean?" Ford looked confused.

"Sir, Silver is a former homicide detective. If he had access to another car that isn't registered to him, why would he drive his car to commit a murder?" Rita paused to let that sink in. "And why would he use a gun that leads us back to him? Doesn't this evidence seem too convenient?"

"I hear you, Kaye, but we have to investigate. We can't exclude a suspect because the evidence against him is too 'convenient.'"

"I'm just saying, the last thing the department needs is another scandal involving planted or fabricated evidence leading to someone being falsely imprisoned."

"At least this time, it wouldn't be a cop," said Ford harshly.

"Sir, there's more to this story," she implored.

"If there is, we will find it."

Rita knew that with time she could convince him that something didn't add up, but with Silver in the other room, the sooner she got Ford out of there, the better, so she stopped trying to plead Silver's case.

"I have eyes on his office and apartment," Ford said as he turned to leave. "I also have someone watching his ex-wife's place in case he visits his kid. I wanted to put a unit on your building, but Estrada assured me that you would call it in if he shows up here. Is he right?"

"Of course he is." Rita made a mental note to thank Javier later.

"It's pretty late. I'm gonna get out of your hair. Sorry for barging in."

"No need to apologize, sir. I appreciate the update."

Rita walked him out and waited at the door until she couldn't hear his footsteps anymore. Once she was sure he wouldn't double back, she rushed to her bedroom to give Silver the all-clear. He was sitting on the corner of her bed when she opened the door.

"Thank god he's gone," he said. "I was two seconds away from looking for your porn collection."

"So, we're going to pretend like you didn't have your ear to the door?"

"Well, I was the topic of conversation. By the way, I see Ford still lacks basic common sense."

"He's not that bad once you get to know him."

"Oh please, he's a bureaucrat, not a cop," said Silver dismissively. "But I appreciate your attempt to educate him."

"He's smarter than you're giving him credit for, he could've called and passed along that information, but he showed up to subtly make sure you weren't here."

Even Silver had to admit that if that indeed was the point of Ford's visit, then maybe he had slightly more common sense than he thought.

"Well, it's a good thing I hadn't taken my holster off yet," he said, patting his gun. "That would have been game over."

"Very true. I don't think I could've lied my way out of that one."

"There's something that's really been bothering me." Silver

waited until he had Rita's full attention. "I'm not buying the whole 'anonymous' caller putting Ford onto me."

"Then how else would he have gotten on to you?" Rita raised an eyebrow. "You don't think I told him, do you?"

"Of course not, but you aren't the only one who knew of my connection."

Rita could see what Silver was implying. "It wasn't Estrada. When I got to the precinct, he still hadn't told Ford about Bob's statement."

"So he says."

"Why would he lie to me?"

"Look, I wouldn't blame him if he did. It's a lot to ask him to stick his neck out for someone he doesn't know. You know that I would never do this, but to him, it looks like a man is dead, and the evidence points towards me."

"He's my partner. He has my back."

"And that's why he would lie. He wouldn't want to betray your partnership," said Silver. Rita shook her head, dismissing Silver's suspicions. "I'm not telling you not to trust him. I'm just saying that I wouldn't blame him if he chose himself over me."

"I guess you're right," she said reluctantly.

"Until we figure this out, we should be careful with what we share." He walked past her out of her room. "I'm going to take that shower now."

"Towels are in the hallway closet next to the bathroom," said Rita. He stopped at the closet, grabbed what he needed, and disappeared into the bathroom.

Rita could hear the shower start to run as she sat back on her couch and grabbed her glass of wine. She sipped it while she thought about the point that Silver had just made. She hadn't considered how Ford got on to him as fast as he did. Sure, the anonymous tip would have given him the initial push but the thought to check traffic cam footage was something different. Ford was a good captain because he knew how to cut through red tape and enjoyed paperwork, but old-fashioned police work was not his strong suit. The only way he could've made the Silver connection was if someone made it for him, and as far as she knew, only she and Estrada were aware of that connection. If Estrada was feeding Ford information, that would complicate things for them moving forward. She had been working under the assumption that they could stay under the radar as long as they didn't cross paths with the investigation of Silver, but if Estrada was telling everything he knew, then they could be leaving breadcrumbs that lead right to them.

Rita was so deep in thought that she didn't notice how much time had passed. The shower stopped, and Silver was standing in front of her, dripping wet and wearing nothing but a towel.

"Sorry, I don't mean to be dripping water all over your floor, but I forgot to take the clothes in there with me," he said.

"Um, no worries," she said softly.

"Truthfully, I'm used to showering then walking around naked to air dry." Rita could barely focus on what he was saying. "So I'm not used to taking clothes into the bathroom with me while I shower."

"Thank god you didn't take me seriously when I said to make yourself at home," she said jokingly, although she wouldn't have been mad at him if he had. But that must've been the wine talking.

"Can I get dressed in your room? It's really hot in there," he said, pointing back towards the bathroom.

"Yeah, sure," she responded. It was starting to feel hot in her living room as well.

He took the bag of clothes into her bedroom and closed the door. Rita kept her eyes on him until the door was completely shut, then she gulped down the rest of her wine. When this day had started, she would not have guessed that Clifford Silver would be standing in her living room wearing nothing but a towel. Maybe this was fate putting them together. After all, life rarely goes as expected. Or maybe she just wanted to fuck him and say it was fate. Then, just as she was about to join him in her room, the door opened, and he emerged fully dressed.

"I'm impressed." He spun in a circle, modeling the clothes she had bought him. "You got all the right sizes."

"I have a good eye." She stood and walked to the kitchen to pour herself another glass of wine. Looking back at him, she noticed a tremor in his right hand. "Are you ok?"

"Yeah," he responded. "Why do you ask?" Rita pointed at his hand. "Oh, this is nothing. Usually, around this time, I would be pouring a drink to take the edge off.

"I see," said Rita. "Would you like some wine or a beer? Just enough to stop the tremors."

"No, this actually isn't that bad, and I think I'm done drinking for a while," he said as he sat on the couch.

"Really? What made you make that decision?" She finished pouring her glass and joined him, sitting a bit closer to him than she needed.

"I think it's affecting my decision-making and my attention to detail," he said. "I was hungover the day I met this client, and I didn't verify anything she told me."

Rita didn't say anything. She could tell he had something he wanted to get off of his chest.

"This client didn't feel right from the beginning. She showed up wearing thousands of dollars in clothes and was willing to spend whatever for a low-end PI. When I asked who referred her to me, she ducked the question. I would've looked into her if I were thinking clearly. Turns out someone sent her to my front door, and I fell right into their trap."

Rita sat down her wine and took his hand into hers. They locked eyes and had another moment where they spoke without speaking. In his eyes, she could see his demons and his burdens. She could see that he'd been walking around with the weight of the world on his shoulders. In her eyes, he could see that she was there to carry that weight with him. But there was something else there as well. A passion that they'd been avoiding from the moment they had met. She began to rub her thumb across the top of his hand in a way that made his heart thump. He moved his arm closer to his body, pulling her along with it until the smell of lavender filled his nose. Only the sound of their breathing filled the room as they floated closer to each other. He took his hand and moved her hair from her face to behind her ear and held it there, caressing her cheek. When he could no longer take the anticipation, he pulled her face to his, and their lips met. They kissed each other slowly and deeply, not wanting to rush a moment they'd been longing for, but before it could go further, Rita pushed him away.

"We should get some rest." She stood quickly and walked towards her room. "There are blankets in the same closet where I keep the towels."

"Rita," he called after her as he stood from the couch.

"Goodnight, Cliff," she said before closing her door.

He slowly walked to her door and grabbed her doorknob but didn't turn it. Instead, he just held it there for a moment, considering all the possibilities waiting for him on the other side. Rita was one of the few good relationships he still had in his life. What would happen if they crossed this line? Was the reward worth the risk? While he was standing there considering all the consequences of crossing that threshold, he felt the doorknob he was still holding turn and leave his hand when it opened.

Rita was standing there staring at him. "What are you waiting for?" she asked tenderly.

Seeing her in that moment made Silver push all of his doubts to the side, and he entered her room. Their eyes were locked on each other, but with every step he took towards her, she took a step backward until she could feel her bed behind her. When her bed stopped her from moving anymore, he stopped moving in her direction. Neither of them spoke, they just stared intensely at each other, and the only sound that could be heard in the room was their hearts thumping.

Rita was the first to make any kind of move. Without breaking eye contact, she slowly began to undo her blouse. With each button, Silver could feel his heart beat a little faster. He watched intently as she unfastened the final button and let her shirt drop to the floor, with her bra following it shortly after. He wanted to move across the room and throw her on the bed, but he didn't want to lose the staring contest that had developed between them, so instead, he just removed his T-shirt so that they would be even on the amount of clothes they were wearing.

Sensing that it was her turn again, Rita undid the button of her pants, pushed them down off her waist, and kept going until they were around her ankles. She then stepped out of them and kicked them to the side. Silver again matched her by taking off his sweatpants. Rita bit her bottom lip when she saw the bulge in his boxer briefs. Then, keeping up with the game they were playing with each other, she quickly removed her panties, forcing him to reveal what his underwear was hiding.

Now they both stood there naked and admiring each other. They could feel the anticipation rising in the room, but neither was ready to break the trance they found themselves in. This was a moment that both of them had wanted, but they weren't ready to give that up just yet. The wanting and the longing for each other had been sustaining them for so long. What would happen when they finally gave in? The moment had become a game of chicken to see who would break first.

Silver couldn't take it anymore and took a step towards her, but it was almost as if she had read his mind because she made a move at the exact same time. Before they knew it, they collided with each other, locked in a deep embrace and a long kiss. Nothing was separating the two of them, but they couldn't be close enough. They kissed passionately until they fell onto the bed that Rita had been standing against. Silver was on top of her and let out a slight moan when he felt her thighs squeeze his hips. When Rita had a firm enough grip, she flipped them so she would be on top, straddling him. Their lips were still locked with each other until Silver broke it off so he could look at her.

"Are you sure you want to do this?" he asked.

Rita, however, didn't respond. Instead, she just smiled and kissed him softly. Then she made her way down to his neck, then to his chest, then to his abs until she was low enough for Silver to know that she was absolutely sure.

CHAPTER 11

Silver rolled over to put his arm around Rita, but her side of the bed was empty. He opened his eyes to locate her but was met by the sun peeking through her blinds. He sat up in the bed and wiped the sleep from his eyes. Had last night really happened? He got his answer when he looked towards her bedroom door and saw his pile of clothes where he had left them the night before. Silver threw the covers off himself and got out of bed to find where Rita was hiding. He wasn't sure how she would feel about him walking around her place ass-naked, so he stopped at the door and put his underwear back on before he stepped out of the room. He could hear the shower going in the bathroom down the hall, and the thought of seeing the water glistening on her naked body excited him enough to make him think about joining her, but first, he wanted to check his phone.

It was sitting on the coffee table beside the couch where he had thought he would have been sleeping. The first thing he did was check the time, and he saw that it was a little after five in the morning. The day before had been so exhausting that he couldn't believe he had awakened so early. There were multiple messages from Lucy demanding to know where he was and if he was ok. He began to type a response but thought better of it. The less she knew, the better. For all he knew, Ford could have been standing over her shoulder waiting for his reply, so he deleted what he had typed and sat his phone back down. His eyes found their way back towards the bathroom door, and the thought of joining Rita in there was at the top of his to-do list, but the water stopped running before he could. After a moment, Rita emerged wearing a towel.

"Good morning," he said, startling her.

"Jesus, Cliff, you scared the shit out of me," she responded.

"Sorry, I didn't mean to. I was just checking my phone."

"It's ok. I didn't wake you, did I?"

"Not at all."

"I figured we should get an early start on tracking down V. I know you had a long day yesterday, so I wasn't going to wake you until after my shower."

"I appreciate that, but I should probably take a shower too. After last night, I need one." Silver chuckled, but Rita didn't react. "I'll make it quick so we can head out."

"Ok," said Rita, then she walked past him, trying her hardest to avoid making eye contact. Silver watched as she went into her room and closed the door. He brushed off that moment and proceeded to take a shower, but it only became more and more awkward between them from there. From that point on, she avoided conversation with him, hoping to not have to address the elephant in the room. They left her apartment around six and rode silently on their way to look for V. At one point, Silver opened his mouth to try to start a conversation, but Rita turned the volume up on her radio before he could get a word out.

Did she have regrets? Since his divorce, Silver had thought about taking their relationship a step beyond just friends, but he always feared this moment. They gave in to their lust, and now she couldn't even look at him. He would give anything to know what was going through her mind, and at some point, they would need to have a conversation about what happened between them, but that will have to wait. There was still a mission that needed to be accomplished. Once it was complete, Rita would have his full undivided attention.

When they arrived at the trailer park, their plan was simple. With it being just the two of them, there was no way they could do a door-to-door search, so instead, their plan was to drive down each row of trailers. That way, they could cover more ground than on foot and still be able to stop and flash her picture when they came across someone already outside.

There weren't many people out this early in the morning, but Rita flashed her badge and the picture of V at the few they did spot. Those who did not completely dismiss them didn't recognize her, so they kept driving along. It wasn't a very large community, but it was a maze. It took them an hour to figure out how to navigate in a way that covered every street and did not have them circling the same blocks over and over. Once they figured out the best approach, they passed through the streets as discreetly as possible. Drive too slowly, and they would look suspicious; too fast, and they may miss something. They also took a risk by asking about her and showing her picture. Word could get back to her that a cop was roaming the streets looking for her, and she could run, but that may also be the only way to flush her out, so they decided it was a risk worth taking.

Another hour passed without any luck. They kept their eyes trained on opposite sides of the road. Scanning for either V or another pedestrian they hadn't already asked about her. They rode in complete silence, only speaking to point out when they spotted someone. Silver was itching to break that silence, but Rita was in no rush. She knew that once it was broken, there was only one thing to talk about, and she was not ready for that conversation.

"So ... looks like we may be doing this for a while," said Silver when he couldn't take the silence any longer.

"Yep," said Rita without taking her eyes off the road.

"You know, it's going to feel even longer as long as we're not talking."

"Really? I've been enjoying the silence."

"Oh, come on, Rita. We have to talk about it, and we're stuck in this car together, so let's just get it out of the way."

Rita pondered what he said for a moment, trying to think of a way out of having this talk, but he was right. "Ok, so what would you like to talk about?"

"I've been thinking about last night and what it could mean going forward."

"Look, Cliff, I had a little to drink, and you were feeling vulnerable. So, let's not overthink what happened."

"Oh, so this was just a drunken mistake? Not something that we have been flirting with the idea of for a while now?"

"Yes, we flirt, and we kid, but I never wanted to be just another notch on your headboard."

"Rita, I would never look at you that way."

"Cliff, I want something real. Not just some occasional booty call."

"And who says that I can't give you real?"

"Sorry, but I find that hard to believe."

"Why?" asked Silver. Rita stopped the car and made eye contact with him for the first time that morning.

"Yes, we flirted with the idea of sleeping with each other, but all that shows is that we're attracted to each other physically. That's not enough."

"I'm sorry," said Silver shamefully. "I never meant for you to feel like you have nothing to offer me except for how you look. Honestly, the reason I've never asked you out is because I agree with you. I don't know what I have to offer you."

"I never said that you have nothing to offer me."

"My life's a mess. I'm a broke and divorced drunk. Whenever I get the idea of being with you, I think that you deserve better."

"Cliff, cut it out with the self-loathing. You have plenty to offer."

"Do you want what I'm offering?"

"The thought has crossed my mind."

"If what I just said doesn't bother you, what's giving you hesitation?"

"Do I really have to say it?" She looked at him, and he gave her a nod to continue. "I don't want to be someone's consolation prize."

"Are you talking about Tonya?"

"I've always admired how faithful you are to her."

"You say that as if it's the present tense. I'm divorced, remember."

"Only on paper," she rebutted.

"What does that mean?"

"That means that your heart still belongs to her. Before last night, had you been with anyone since your divorce?"

Silver opened his mouth to say, of course, but then it occurred to him that the answer was "no." His divorce became final over a year ago, and he hadn't been with a single woman since. He looked at Rita and shook his head.

"Why do you think that is?" she asked rhetorically. "You're telling me that someone as good-looking, funny, and charming as you has been with no one in over a year? No one stands a chance with you."

Silver went silent, and Rita put the car in drive and continued their search. He hadn't realized that he was giving off the impression that he still had feelings for Tonya. They rode in silence for another twenty minutes while he tried to find the right thing to say.

"Rita," he said.

"Yes?"

"So, you think I'm handsome," he said with a sly grin.

"Really, that's what you took from everything I just said?"

"No, I also heard funny and charming."

"Focus on your side of the street," she said, trying not to laugh.

"You're the one who needs to focus. I know all this sex appeal and charm can be distracting." He gave Rita a smile that made her blush. "If you can't handle being in the car with me, I could walk."

Rita brought the car to a stop. "Ok, get out."

Silver laughed until he looked up at Rita and didn't see a smile on her face. "Wait, are you serious?"

She held her expression for about thirty seconds before she smiled. "I guess you can stay in here with me, you and your 'charm.' " This time, they both laughed as she put the car back in drive.

"All jokes aside, your concerns are extremely valid. Yes, you are beautiful, but you are also smart, caring, funny, and, overall, the best person I know. Trust me when I say that I see all of you." Hearing these words made Rita's heart flutter, but she didn't dare to interrupt him. "And let me make one thing very clear. Yes, I will always have love for Tonya because she gave me my daughter, but I am no longer in love with her. So, you're right when you say that no one has stood a chance with me, but you're wrong when you say the reason why is Tonya. Maybe I've been too stupid to see it myself until last night, but the reason no one has stood a chance with me is because no one is you." He spoke with a sincerity that Rita had never heard from him before. She had to restrain herself from pulling the car over and kissing him. "But none of this matters unless we solve this case, and I know actions mean more than words, so as soon as this is over, I promise I'm going to show you that I mean every word I'm saying. So let's table this for now and go back to being partners." He held out his hand to her. "Deal?"

"Deal," she said, and they shook on it. She could barely keep a smile off of her face.

"Ok, good," he said enthusiastically. "Now we've been at this for a few hours with no luck. Maybe we should rethink our strategy."

"The only other strategy is to go door to door," she said as she turned another corner.

"She was annoyingly smart about concealing her identity. She didn't drive, so we don't know if she owns a car that we could look out for, and she didn't let the driver know her exact address just in case we tracked him down."

"Well, let's just hope she didn't leave town."

"She wouldn't leave town," he said assuredly.

"What makes you so sure?"

"Because her motive is revenge, and what's the point of revenge if you aren't around to witness it."

"Good point."

"There's a man we haven't talked to yet." Silver pointed at an elderly man walking a small dog midway up the block.

Rita parked the car at the end of the block, and they walked over to him. They didn't want to spook him by pulling up to him in a random car.

"Excuse me, sir," said Rita when she was sure they were within earshot.

"Yeah," he said as he turned to face them.

She flashed him her badge. "I'm Detective Rita Kaye. We were hoping you could tell us if you know this woman." Rita showed him the picture of V.

"Yeah, that's Vicky," he said after only looking at the picture for a second.

"Does Vicky live near here?" asked Silver.

"Yeah, she lives right there." He pointed to the trailer on the right-hand side of the end of the block. "But she's not home right now."

"Do you know where she is?" asked Rita.

"She left over a week ago, and she ain't been back yet. This is her pup here. She asked me to watch him for her. Normally she takes the little bastard everywhere she goes."

Silver and Rita traded glances with each other. If she really was never apart from that dog, then most likely, she had no intentions of ever returning.

"Why are y'all looking for Vicky?" the old man asked.

Rita started to answer, but Silver interrupted, saying, "Her family hasn't heard from her, so we told them we'll look into it."

"Was it her niece, Tracy? That's who she left with."

Silver jumped at the chance to learn more about Vicky. "I think it was her niece, but can you describe her for me so I can be sure?"

"Well, she's about this tall." He held his hand up to measure her height. To Silver, it looked to be about five foot six. "She's thin and blonde with a pretty face. She's a sweet girl."

"Yep, that's her," said Silver.

"It's funny. I didn't even know Vicky had any family before Tracy started coming around about eight months ago. Ever since she lost her brother, this dog was the closest thing she had to family."

"What happened to her brother?" asked Silver.

"He got himself in some trouble and got locked up. Then someone stabbed him in jail. Poor Vicky took it really hard. Her and Billy were so close."

"Thank you for your time, sir," said Rita once she was sure they got all they could from him. "Here's my card. If she comes home, can you give us a call so we can let Tracy know?" He took her card and tucked it into his shirt pocket. They said their goodbyes and walked back to her car.

"Ok, so we have a name," said Silver when they were back situated.

"Do you recognize the other two names?" asked Rita.

"No. I don't know a Tracy or Billy."

"Right now, my theory is that she blames you for Billy's death," said Rita.

"And Tracy is Billy's daughter," Silver added.

"And they came together to plot against you," Rita concluded.

"You think Tracy is our mystery prostitute?" asked Silver.

"It's possible, but she could've also been an actual prostitute that has nothing to do with his murder," Rita responded.

"She vaguely fits the description."

"Yeah, but you wouldn't be able to pick her out of a lineup, and you don't know her actual hair color."

"That's true."

"Honestly, it's not much of a description. A young and skinny blonde of average height, we might as well walk downtown and find a million women that fit that description. Hell, Lucy fits that description."

"Call Estrada. I'm sure he would love that assignment."

Rita laughed. "Something tells me that sending a Hispanic man to randomly pick up white women won't go over too well."

"Right, we should narrow it down." Silver motioned towards her home. "Maybe she has a picture of her."

"Yeah, but she's not home."

"Exactly, it's the perfect time to search her place."

"Without a warrant?"

Silver rolled his eyes. "Yes, without a warrant."

"I know I'm helping you off the books, but I'm still a cop. I can't illegally search someone's home."

"That's fair, but I'm not a cop, so how about I go in alone? That way, it wouldn't be an illegal search. It'll just be illegal."

"No, Silver. When I agreed to help you, you agreed to do things my way."

"So we just sit here and do what?"

"Now that we know where she lives, we sit on her place and wait for her to come home."

"Then what," said Silver. "She has no reason to answer our questions."

"We could tail her."

"Tail her where? She's the only person we're looking for. We were hoping to find out more from her."

"I don't know, Silver. We'll figure it out, but we're not breaking into her place."

"Fine." There was no point in arguing when Rita put her foot down. "Can I at least go and take a piss, boss?"

Rita handed him an empty water bottle.

"What am I supposed to do with this?"

"Pee, I won't look."

"No fucking way I'm peeing in this bottle," he said, tossing it back at her.

"Sorry, I forgot to drive my car with the bathroom attached."

"I'll just find somewhere to go out here." He opened the door and started to get out.

"Silver, you can't just whip your dick out in broad daylight."

"I'll find somewhere private." He stood from the car and shut the door.

Rita watched him as he ducked in between two trailers and out of sight. She could appreciate his sense of urgency since it was his life on the line, but they had to do things by the book. They could pick the lock and search her place, but anything they found that was incriminating would become fruit of the poisonous tree because it was found illegally. Moments like this made Rita glad she was with him to keep him from doing anything stupid.

Just as that thought crossed her mind, she looked down the block and saw Silver sneaking around Vicky's trailer. He turned his head to look down both ends of the block to make sure no one could see him, then moved stealthily towards the door. He crouched next to the door to stay low and as out of sight as possible and pulled a small pouch from his pocket. Rita was pretty sure it was a lock-picking kit, and sure enough, he pulled something from it and started working on the door-knob.

Rita was in shock as she watched him open the door and slip into Vicky's home. She was about to drive to the trailer and drag his ass out of there but thought a car outside might draw attention. So instead, she jumped out and jogged. When she reached it, she checked her surroundings to make sure no one was watching before she opened the door and entered.

"What the fuck are you doing in here?" she asked angrily as soon as she closed the door.

Silver didn't respond. He was standing with his back to her, looking at something he was holding.

"Silver, we need to get out of here before someone calls the police." She paused, but he still didn't respond. "Are you listening? I said let's go."

Finally, Silver turned to face her, and he was holding a picture frame. "I ... I found her motive," he stammered.

"What is it?" she asked.

"I know who Billy is." He could not take his eyes off the picture.

Rita waited a moment for him to clue her in, but he just kept staring at the photo with his mouth open. "Are you going to tell me?"

Silver turned the photo towards Rita, and when she saw it, her jaw dropped too. "It's William Hargrave."

CHAPTER 12

"Cliff," said Rita after several minutes of them standing there in silence and disbelief. She waited for a response, but Silver didn't give her one. Instead, he just stood there staring at the picture of the woman they were hunting standing next to the man who had been haunting him for the last two years.

It was killing Silver that he couldn't figure out what possible motive she could have for coming after him, but now that he was staring it in the face, it hit him like a ton of bricks. The last person he would have connected to this was William Hargrave, but at the same time, he understood why Vicky wanted to see him suffer. He blamed himself too.

"Cliff!" Rita shouted this time, snapping him back to reality. Silver looked up at her, then took one more glance at the photo before placing it back where he found it.

"Ok, now that we know who we're fighting and why, we can come up with a plan on how to defend ourselves." He spoke with a sense of urgency, but his tone was calm and measured. "We should get out of here as quick as we can, but first, let's try to find a photo of Tracy."

"Right," said Rita. Seeing him take charge of the situation reminded her of when they had been partners. In a different situation, it would have made her smile, but there was work to be done.

The trailer wasn't huge, so searching it quickly wouldn't be a problem. The key for them was to search it without completely ransacking the place. When Vicky returned, they wanted it to look like no one had been there. The wall opposite the door was basically a shrine to William. It was covered from top to bottom with photos of him surrounding a table with an urn that presumably held his ashes. Rita quickly scanned through these photos, looking for anyone that could fit the description of Tracy but no luck. Silver entered her bedroom area, looking through her dresser drawers and under her bed. He was hoping to find a stash of family photos, but it looked as if every picture she had was on the wall dedicated to William.

"Do you see any kind of computer in there?" asked Rita from the other room.

"No, it looks like this lady is living off of the bare necessities," Silver responded.

"Yeah, but everyone has a computer."

"Laptops are portable. It can be on her wherever she is."

"Yeah, that's true." Rita went back to looking at all the photos on the wall. "The old man wasn't lying about her being really close to her brother."

"Do you remember him having a daughter?" asked Silver.

Rita stopped and thought for a moment. "No, I actually don't."

Silver went to join Rita near the trailer door. "I vaguely remember him having a sister, but obviously, I never spoke with her. After what happened, the least I could've done was speak to her."

Rita could see that Silver was in his head, so she reached out and held his hand. "Cliff, what happened to him was not your fault."

"That sounds so much more convincing coming from you than when I try to tell myself that."

"It's the truth. You followed where the evidence was pointing, like we were trained to do. And what happened to him doesn't justify what she's trying to do to you."

"You mean the same way the evidence is pointing at me now?" Rita didn't have a response to that point. "Let's face it, Rita. There's always a story. With William Hargrave, the story didn't add up, and I didn't pursue it like I should have. So maybe she isn't justified in the lengths she's taking to get back at me, but that doesn't mean I'm completely blameless either."

Rita knew there was nothing she could say that he hadn't already heard when it came to William Hargrave. So instead, she turned him towards her and embraced him. Rita knew how much this case weighed on him and the damage it caused to his life. She knew that her words wouldn't make anything better, but she hoped that wrapping her arms around him would at least remind him that he was not alone.

"Thank you," he whispered, confirming to her that the message was received.

The two of them stood there holding each other and forgot where they were, but they were reminded when they heard a voice say, "Why the fuck are you in my house!"

Silver took his arms from around Rita and turned to see Vicky Hargrave standing in her doorway. When she saw his face, she froze, and her eyes widened. Silver was the last person she expected to be standing in front of her brother's shrine.

"Hey there, Sara," said Silver sarcastically. "Or should I say Vicky?"

"How did you find me?" Vicky's voice cracked as she was still shocked at the sight of them.

"I guess you aren't as smart as you thought." Silver took a step towards her. "This is Detective Rita Kaye." Rita waved at Vicky with her badge in hand. "She's going to take you for a ride downtown, and you can explain to everyone that you're the one that's trying to frame me for murder."

"I'm not going any-fucking-where with you."

"You seem to be under the impression that you have a choice." Silver took another step towards her. "Either you come willingly, or I'll drag your ass there myself."

Vicky looked behind Silver and could see Rita take out her cuffs. Her eyes darted from left to right, looking for a way to escape.

"Don't even think about it," said Rita. She recognized Vicky's flight-or-fight response leaning towards flight. "Just come quietly, and no one will get hurt."

Vicky looked as if she were still weighing her options but seeing that her chances of getting away were dim, she raised her hands in surrender.

"Turn around and put your hands on your head," said Rita as she walked towards her to cuff her. Vicky complied with Rita's demand and turned her back to them with her fingers interlocked on the back of her head. Just as Rita reached to slap the cuff on her wrist, Silver heard a noise just outside the window. He looked to locate what made the sound, then tackled Rita to the ground just before the shot was fired. The bullet went into a picture of William on the wall right where Rita's head would have been.

"You hit?" asked Silver.

"No, you?"

"I'm good." Silver looked up just in time to watch Vicky dart out the door. He scrambled to his feet and ran to the doorway. He watched her jump on the passenger side of a black car that pulled off before the door could fully close. "She's getting away," Silver shouted to Rita as she got to her feet.

"Which direction?" asked Rita.

"West. They're heading for the exit. There's only one way out of here. Let's get to the car and try to cut them off." Silver knew that would be a long shot with their head start, but they had to try. Once they made it to the street, it would turn into a high-speed chase, which is the opposite of a low profile.

The car was parked on the other end of the block where Rita had left it before she followed Silver. They ran as fast as they could, not wanting the other car to get too far ahead. At least if they couldn't cut them off, they wanted to see which direction the car went after it exited so they could pursue. They reached the car, and both jumped in. Rita was pulling away from the curb before Silver could close the door entirely. Although the other vehicle had a head start, they still had an advantage because they were parked facing the exit. Their suspects had to drive in the opposite direction because turning around would've taken time, and Silver could have caught them on foot. They most likely planned on going up and around to get out, but these streets were narrow, and there was no way they could drive a high speed and still negotiate every turn without crashing. Rita made a beeline straight for the exit. There was only one turn for her to make, which would help them make up ground. Rita turned the corner and could see the entrance to the trailer community. She picked up her speed slightly, not wanting to go too fast just in case someone darted into the street at the last minute. Just as they were about to reach the opening, the black car they were pursuing sped past and into traffic.

"There!" shouted Silver as he pointed to the car that was now heading north.

Rita turned the wheel to the left, guiding them to the trailer park exit. She was careful not to dart into the street as quickly as their suspects just in case there was oncoming traffic who wouldn't have time to stop. Once she saw it was all clear, she turned on her siren and made the same right turn to continue their pursuit.

The car had put some distance between them by being less cautious. One disadvantage they had was trying to keep up with speed while also caring about the safety of other drivers and pedestrians. Rita was a master at this, always keeping the car they were pursuing in view while managing to put no one at risk. She always found opportune times to pick up her speed and make up some ground when the roads were clear, and once she closed the distance, she made sure they never gained it back.

There wasn't much traffic yet, so Rita was able to close the gap some before they reached the bridge where Western turned into Greenwood. Traffic was slightly heavier here, so Rita had to wait for drivers to realize what was happening and clear the way while Vicky and her driver weaved between each car. Silver could see Vicky turn around and look through the back window to see how close they were. Silver gave her a smile and a wave, then watched her eyes widen before she turned back around and shouted at the driver.

"Can you see the driver at all?" asked Rita as she carefully navigated through traffic.

"Not from here. I can't even tell if it's a man or woman." Silver was straining his neck, trying to catch even the slightest glimpse of the driver.

"It has to be Tracy, right?"

"That's what I would assume, but it honestly could be anyone. Any chance you can pull up next to her?"

Just as he asked that, Rita had to swerve to avoid colliding with a car that turned onto the block without seeing them. "Not on this road. They're already driving erratically, and if I press the issue, they might get even more reckless."

"Rita, we can't chase them forever. At some point, we have to make a move to put a stop to this."

"Yeah, but only when it's safe. If they crash, they could kill someone or themselves, and she can't clear your name if she's dead."

Her logic was sound, so he sat back in his seat and let her do her thing. They were approaching a red light at 127th Street. Silver and Rita watched as the car they were pursuing never slowed down. The car ignored the light, making a hard left turn into the intersection. Multiple cars had to make sudden stops to avoid slamming into them. Thankfully it wasn't rush hour, or that could have turned into a multi-car pileup. Rita slowly weaved through the stopped cars in the intersection, also turning left to keep up with the chase. She saw them making another left at the next intersection onto Western Avenue. There wasn't another close call for this turn because they had the light, and the other cars had paused to try to see what was going on. Rita still had her siren blaring, so traffic stayed still until they were clear.

By the time they made the same turn, Vicky was two blocks ahead. This street was pretty clear, so Rita could close the gap to a block before she had to slow back down. Vicky and her driver blew through the red light at York and made a right turn at Vermont, the next block down. Unlike the last red light, there was no traffic here, so Rita could follow without losing ground. Vermont is only two lanes wide, with each lane going opposite directions. Both cars sped down the street, going downhill and under a viaduct. Once they passed the viaduct, the road ahead curved to the right. This stretch of road was an industrial area, so it was free of pedestrians. Rita took this opportunity to move into the opposite lane and try to get ahead of them to cut them off. They were still turning through the curve as Rita started to make her way past them. Silver strained his neck again to try to get a look at the driver, but just as his face was about to come into view, an eighteen-wheel truck appeared in their lane, forcing Rita to quickly fall back and move back into her lane. Their suspects took advantage of this opportunity to put some distance between them. They made it to the next light and quickly made a right turn back onto 127th Street. Rita followed but again had to contend with other traffic in the way of her pursuit.

The chase continued with their suspects growing bolder and more desperate with every second. Silver and Rita knew that if they didn't end this soon, someone would get hurt. Vicky and her driver sped down the road with Rita closely following. Up ahead were some tracks whose lights flashed to indicate that a train was coming soon. Rita looked ahead and could see the train approaching from the south. Vicky's car sped up as the gate began to lower, and the train grew closer and closer. Rita and Silver held their breath as they watched their suspects attempt to race the train. The gate was almost fully lowered just as they sped past. It was so close that the gate made contact with the trunk of their car. Rita considered going after them for a split second before quickly deciding that it would have been a suicide mission. She slammed the brakes just in time to stop right before watching the train pass in front of them. They couldn't do anything but watch, only catching glimpses of their suspects driving away in between each railroad car as it passed until eventually they were gone. At least for now.

Silver and Rita hauled ass out of the area. They could already hear the local police coming to check on the commotion they had caused. When they arrived, they were going to be asking questions that the two of them weren't prepared to answer. The ride back to Rita's was utterly silent. They couldn't help but feel demoralized, being so close but going home with nothing to show for it. Rita could feel Silver's anxiety rise from his side of the car. They had lost the element of surprise, and tracking down Vicky a second time would be even more difficult now that she knew they were looking for her. She searched her mind for the right thing to say to him but was drawing a blank.

Rita continued to think of the best way to lift his mood while he silently stared at the sky outside of his window. Eventually, they made it back to Rita's and went upstairs. The walk to her door felt like an eternity. Silver stared straight ahead while Rita trailed behind him. A couple of times, she opened her mouth to speak but thought better of it. The last thing he probably wanted to hear was whatever cliche she was about to utter.

When they reached her door, she inserted her key and pushed it open to allow him to enter. He shuffled past her, barely bothering to lift his feet as he moved. She stepped in and let the door close before grabbing his hand and turning him to face her. Rita wrapped her arms around the back of his neck, pulling him down slightly while she stood on her toes to meet him halfway. She kissed him softly and held it until she felt that her message was received. After their kiss, she wrapped her arms around his waist and buried the side of her face into his chest. Silver wrapped his arms around her softly at first but held her tighter with every second they stood there. They held their embrace for about thirty seconds, but to them, it felt like a lifetime. Neither of them wanted to let go, but there was work to be done.

"What was that for?" Silver asked after they pulled away from each other.

"The hug was to remind you that you're not alone and that we're not giving up yet," said Rita with a reassuring smile. "And the kiss was a thank you for saving my life."

Silver had completely forgotten about the shot that narrowly missed Rita back at Vicky's trailer. Looking back, he could see the hole in the wall that would have been Rita's head had he not tackled her in time. Most people would have folded from coming that close to meeting their end, but not Rita. Silver couldn't believe how lucky he was to have her during this fight. Standing there looking at her, he could feel his spirit being lifted because he believed her when she said this wasn't over yet.

"I saved your life? I was just having a flashback to my high school football days. Thought you had the ball, so I took your ass down," Silver said, shrugging his shoulders. Gallows humor was one of many tools cops used to keep the dangers they faced daily from getting to them. Silver was no longer a cop, but he hadn't lost his touch. Rita laughed and gave him a light shove. She was happy to see him being himself again.

"So, what's our next move?" asked Rita once her laughter died down.

"Your guess is as good as mine." They walked to her living room and sat on her couch.

"Yeah, I don't think we're going to get lucky enough to have her walk through the front door again."

"Also, there's another person we need to try to find."

"Right, I almost forgot about Tracy."

"Not Tracy," said Silver, drawing a puzzled look from Rita. "There was a man driving that car."

"Are you sure?"

"I'm positive."

"Did you see his face?"

"No, I couldn't see any distinguishing details."

"So now we have to identify him, a prostitute, and Tracy."

"Definitely him and the prostitute. For all we know, Tracy is just a niece who visits her aunt. She may not have any involvement in this," he said.

Rita sunk into the couch cushion and took a deep breath. "You're right. Just knowing her doesn't make her guilty."

They sat silently for a moment. Both pondered the daunting task of unraveling this mystery with just the two of them and no extra support.

"Maybe we need to go on the offensive," said Silver. Rita gave him a look urging him to elaborate. "Even if we track her down, the only thing that would prove my innocence is a confession, and what incentive will she have to confess when all the evidence points towards me?"

"So, what do you suggest?" asked Rita.

"Why kill Richard Lindsey?" Silver asked rhetorically. "When she walked into my office, she already knew details about his life. Did she pull his name out of a hat, or did the plan have to involve him?"

136

"You're saying she has a motive for killing Richard Lindsey."

"Exactly! Right now, the physical evidence points toward me, but I have no motive for killing him. We can already prove her motive for framing me, and if we can prove her motive for killing Richard Lindsey, then that physical evidence will become a lot less damning."

Rita sat up once she could see where he was going with this. "And we could use that to convince Ford of your innocence. That'll get the weight of the rest of the department on our side."

"So, who is Richard Lindsey, and why would Vicky want him dead?"

"The last thing I told Estrada to do before I left yesterday was to dive into Richard Lindsey's life. Now may be a good time to call him and see what he found. That's if you trust him."

"I don't know, Rita."

"Cliff, I know him."

"You think you know him. You'd be surprised at what the people you're closest to could be hiding."

"Well, if you can't trust him, can you trust me? I wouldn't involve anyone that would put you at risk."

Rita was the only person he truly trusted. So, he chose to trust her judgment when it came to Javier.

"Call him."

CHAPTER 13

Silver, Javier, and Rita were all sitting in Rita's living room when there was a knock on the door. Rita stood to answer it but not before giving Silver one last disapproving glance. Against her better judgment, he convinced her that it would be a good idea to call Lucy and let her know everything. He told her it would be easier to have Lucy and Javier split up and pursue multiple leads, but she knew it was because he wanted someone else in the room that he trusted. Rita opened the door, and the smile Lucy was wearing immediately left her face. Rita wanted to comment on how good it made her feel that she could wipe the smile from Lucy's face, but instead, she just moved to the side and gestured for her to come inside. Lucy turned herself parallel to Rita and shuffled past, making absolutely sure there would be no contact between the two of them. Then she walked into the living room and found her smile again when she saw Silver.

"Hey, Lucy," said Silver as he stood to hug her. Lucy let him get close enough to punch him in the chest. "What the fuck was that for?"

"I asked you what was going on, and you looked me in my face and told me that you were taking care of it. Next thing I knew, this clown"—she pointed at Javier—"and the rest of his thugs are trashing our office."

"I'm sorry, Luce. I thought I could handle it, but this goes deeper than we thought."

Lucy crossed her arms. "Well, I'm listening."

"I'll explain, I promise, but we're pressed for time, and we have to make our next move," explained Silver. Lucy stood there for a moment before taking a seat on the couch.

"Estrada, what did you find out about Richard Lindsey?" said Rita once she was sure Lucy was done protesting.

Javier pulled out his notepad and flipped it open. "Richard Lindsey was thirty-three years old. He was born in Quad Cities, Iowa, before moving to Chicago, where he went to law school at DePaul. After passing the bar, he went on to work for the public defender's office, where he worked for four years before moving on to corporate law."

"Any chance he and I might have crossed paths when he was with the PD's office?" asked Silver.

"I was actually going to ask you that," responded Javier. "He never worked on any high-profile cases. As far as I can see, he mostly just helped negotiate plea deals."

"Have you already talked to friends and family?" Rita chimed in.

"I spoke to his coworkers and his family back in Iowa, and they all said the same things about him. He lived for work and didn't really have a social life. So, I asked if anyone might have known the woman who visited him the night he died, and everyone said they were pretty sure he wasn't dating anyone, so that supports her probably being a pro like we thought."

"Why did he leave the PD's office?" asked Silver.

"His coworkers said he left for the money, but when I spoke to his mother, she said there was more to it than that.

She said that he liked being a public defender and had been resisting offers to 'sell his soul,' as she put it, but something happened in his last case that shook his faith in the system."

"Do you know the details of that case?" asked Silver, even though he could see where this was heading, and from the look on Rita's face, she was on the same page.

"All his mom knew was that he had a client who swore he was innocent, but the evidence against him looked concrete, so he convinced the guy to take a plea agreement. Later it was found out that the man was innocent, but before he could be released, he was stabbed to death in prison." Javier flipped through a couple of pages in his notepad. "The client's name was—"

"William Hargrave," said Silver, finishing his sentence for him.

"Yes, William Hargrave, how did you know? Do you remember crossing paths with the victim?"

"No, I just know the case."

"Was it a big deal at the time?"

"Yeah, it's the case that forced me to retire."

Javier and Lucy both just stared at Silver. They both understood the gravity of this connection between him and Richard Lindsey, but neither wanted to speak just in case it would discourage him from elaborating. Silver looked to Rita, and she gave him one of her reassuring nods, and with that, he continued.

"A girl was found raped and strangled to death at a downtown apartment building, and Rita and I got the call. Her name was Janet Donovan, and she was only twenty-two years old. She was found in her apartment by the building's maintenance man. That man was William Hargrave."

"You said it was her apartment?" Javier interrupted. Silver nodded yes. "She could afford an apartment downtown at her age?"

"She came from money," Silver explained. "She was fresh

out of college, and her parents were paying her rent as she started her career." Silver paused for a moment to allow any other questions, but when none came, he continued, "According to William, they were friends, and every morning, they shared a coffee before she went to work. When she didn't show up that morning, he went up to her apartment to check on her, but there was no answer. Fearing the worst, he used his master key to let himself in, and that's when he found her in her living room. He claimed that when he saw her lying there, he ran to her and scooped her into his arms, hoping she was just unconscious and not dead. Once he realized there was nothing he could do for her, he called the police."

"What made you guys consider him to be a suspect?" asked Javier.

This time, Rita responded, saying, "There was no forced entry, and he admittedly had a master key that could open her door, so we explored the idea that maybe he committed the crime and came back later to discover the body as an alibi. Also, the idea of a twenty-something-year-old rich girl befriending a fifty-something-year-old maintenance man didn't ring true to us, so we asked around to confirm it. We started at the coffee shop where he told us they went every morning, and they confirmed his story about them having coffee together every morning. Once we confirmed that part of his story, it rang true to us that he would be alarmed by her not showing up for their usual date. We moved off of him as a suspect until we got the coroner's report."

"There was no physical evidence on the body except for fibers from William's clothes," Silver continued. "We were expecting to find that based on his story, but with a crime that up close and personal, we didn't think it was possible for the killer not to leave anything."

"They do a rape kit?" asked Javier.

"Yes," answered Silver. "They found spermicide, which indicated that the perp wore a condom. Uniforms canvassed her building, and no one saw anything out of the ordinary or any men there that shouldn't have been there, so that left William as our only lead. Rita and I decided to go back to the building to ask her neighbors if they knew anything about their friendship, and what we heard didn't help his case. His coworkers indicated that he might've been obsessed with her. All he did was talk about her. When we spoke to her neighbors, they didn't know anything firsthand but described him as being somewhat of a stalker. They said he seemed to linger around on her floor and was always watching her from a distance. This was a completely different description of their relationship from the one we got at the coffee shop, so we weren't sure what to do with it. Why would he have to stalk a friend? What we had to decide was which story was the truthful description of their relationship because it was entirely possible that the people within her building thought what we did at first, that there was no way they could be friends, and they mistook a friendship to be an older man's creepy obsession."

"So, what did you do?" asked Lucy, speaking for the first time since he started telling the story.

"We wanted to look into him some more, but we didn't want to spook him just in case he was our guy. So we called him in for questioning, using the excuse of trying to learn more about the victim, but when we asked him for his alibi, he caught on that we were up to something. Using her liver temp, the coroner had the time of death at approximately eight p.m. the night before. According to William, he would have been on the bus on his way home at that time. We checked his Ventra card, and it did have him getting on the bus at seven twenty, but his card only showed when he got on the bus; it didn't confirm that he actually rode it all the way to his stop. With the only physical evidence on the body coming from him, there being no forced entry with him possessing a master key, and the fact that his alibi was flimsy, we had enough to get a warrant to search his place."

"What were you searching for?" Javier again interrupted. "She was strangled, but you didn't mention any ligature marks, so I'm assuming the killer used their hands. With no murder weapon, what were you looking for?"

Silver didn't respond to that question. He just looked at Rita, and that was her cue to tell that part of the story. "When we spoke with her family, they asked if they could have her bracelet. It was a bracelet that belonged to her sister, who had been killed five years before her." Lucy and Javier were both visibly upset at the thought of those parents having to bury both of their daughters. "It was a charm bracelet with a single charm, a letter G that stood for Gina. The bracelet was not found on the body, and they assured us that she never took it off, so our search warrant listed the bracelet, with our thinking being that maybe he kept it as a trophy. We showed up at his door with the warrant, and he didn't resist. He said he had nothing to hide and wanted us to get it over with so we could stop wasting our time with him. We looked around his place, but we didn't completely turn it upside down because I don't think either of us was completely sold on him as a suspect, but when we looked under his bed, we found a small wooden box and inside the box was a charm bracelet with the G charm, so we made the arrest."

"Sounds like he was your guy," said Javier with a puzzled look on his face. "I don't understand why you were forced out because of it."

"William denied having any knowledge of how the bracelet got there," said Silver with his head held low. "He insisted that it was planted, and when we asked who would want to frame him, he pointed the finger at us. No one paid him any attention, thinking they were the desperate claims of a desperate man, but something about that case nagged me. I felt like we were missing something, but I couldn't quite put my finger on it. Weeks had passed since the murder was committed, and under the advice of his lawyer, William took a plea deal. That's when I got the call from her mom telling us that she found the bracelet and not to worry about it anymore. The only problem was that we still had the bracelet in evidence. I asked her if she was sure the bracelet belonged to her daughter, and she said she was positive it did. Janet had an infinity symbol engraved on the back of the G. I immediately checked the bracelet we had out of evidence. There was no infinity symbol on it."

"Couldn't he still be released?" Lucy chimed in.

"Yeah, but he ..." Silver tried to speak, but the lump in his throat was preventing him.

"He had already been killed by another inmate," Rita finished for him. The room fell silent for a moment while Silver collected himself. He had been hiding this guilt for so long but talking about it again brought it back to the surface.

"After talking to her mother, it dawned on me what was bothering me," he said after clearing his throat. "It was his Venture card. It only showed him getting on the bus once that night, so if he did immediately get back off the bus like we theorized, then how did he get home? We pulled his financials, and there was nothing showing that he called any kind of ride-share, and he lived across town, so he couldn't have walked. We pulled traffic cam footage for the bus stop closest to his house, and there he was, crossing the street at eight-fifteen. No way he could have killed her." Silver paused again. "He never felt right as a suspect to me. I could have pulled that footage sooner or talked to the driver on his route to see if he remembered him riding all the way to his stop, but I didn't, and now he's dead, and her killer was never found."

"You followed the evidence like you were supposed to do," said Javier.

"Well, when it was found out that the bracelet never belonged to the victim and his claims that it was planted, the department thought we might have helped the evidence along."

"If they thought you both planted it, how did only one of you lose your job?" said Lucy, pointedly in Rita's direction.

Rita looked at Silver for permission to tell what happened, and he gave her the ok. "With William dead and the real killer probably in Mexico by then, Cliff guessed that the department wouldn't want to pursue this and face public embarrassment, and that's exactly what happened. Although they reopened the case and cleared William's name, they never publicly said why. I'm still with the department because Cliff had me tell internal affairs that he was alone when the bracelet was found, and he did the same. Since the only person that could corroborate that was dead, they accepted it."

"But how did you accept it!" shouted Lucy. "You were his partner. How could you let him take the fall on his own?"

"She tried to, Lucy!" Silver shouted back before Rita could respond. "I wouldn't let her. There was no reason for us both to go down, and I was the lead detective. What happened fell on my shoulders, and I wasn't going to let it cost her her career."

The room went silent again while everyone let the tension die down. At that moment, Silver could feel all the shame that he had been desperately trying to drink away. He sat there staring at the ground, trying to avoid eye contact with anyone in the room. He felt like he had lost their respect. That's when he felt a hand on his shoulder.

"Cliff, it's alright," Rita said as she took a seat next to him. "Everyone in this room knows that what happened to William was not your fault. If you had known sooner, you would've done everything you could to save him." Silver looked up at Javier and Lucy, and both of them nodded in agreement with Rita. "I know you've been struggling with this for the last two years, and I know it may take more time, but I hope talking about this today will be the first step towards forgiving yourself."

"Thank you," said Silver as he fought back tears. He gave her hand a squeeze, then cleared his throat again. "So that brings us to the last couple of weeks." He directed his attention to Lucy. "I already told you that Sara doesn't exist. Well, what I didn't tell you is that she's trying to frame me for the murder of Richard Lindsey, and it looks like, somehow, she used my gun."

"What the fuck!" shouted Lucy.

"You never told me you thought his gun was used," Javier said to Rita.

"I didn't tell you because we thought we could track her down and make her confess, but since that didn't work, we called you here today to give you all the relevant information," Rita explained.

"Do you have any other information?" asked Javier.

"Yesterday, we spoke to the driver who picked up my client and took her home the day she was at the office," said Silver. "He didn't remember her name, but he remembered it started with a V and the area where he dropped her off. This morning we canvassed that area and found a neighbor who identified her as Vicky and showed us where she lived. After we entered her house—"

"You searched her house without a warrant?" Javier interrupted.

"Silver went in first, and I went in to make him leave," said Rita.

"So, what if he did?" Lucy barked at him.

"So that would be illegal," Javier barked back.

"Is he supposed to sit back and wait for the CPD to pull their heads out their asses and find her?"

"That's enough," said Silver, shutting down this distraction. "You guys are here to help, and arguing isn't going to help anything. Yes, Estrada, I searched her place, and that's how I found out her name is Vicky Hargrave. William's sister." Both Javier and Lucy's jaws dropped. Lucy even mouthed the word "fuck." "Obviously, she blames me for the death of her brother, and now we know she killed Richard Lindsey because she blames him for convincing him to take the deal."

"We need to have someone sit on her place until she comes home and bring her in," Javier suggested.

"We don't think she's going to be returning anytime soon," said Rita.

"Why not?"

"Because she came home while we were in her place," answered Silver. "When we went to take her in, someone took a shot at Rita through the window, which gave her time to get to a car that was waiting outside. We pursued but were cut off by a train, and they got away."

"Which is why we called you, Estrada," continued Rita. "I'm going to text you the license plate number, and I need you to run it for me and track down that car. Silver and I have to lay low for a bit. That car chase drew a lot of attention, and we don't want anyone to know about our investigation just yet."

"Why not?" asked Lucy. "Doesn't finding her prove that she's behind the frame job?"

"All we can prove right now is that she has motive," answered Rita. "We still can't prove how she got her hands on Silver's gun, and we can't place her at the scene."

"How were you able to place Cliff at the scene?" asked Lucy.

"From an eyewitness who claims to have let a man matching Silver's description in the building through a service entrance around the time of death," Javier responded. "He also gave an accurate description of Silver's car."

"So he just gave a description but did he actually identify Cliff as the man he saw?" Rita and Javier looked at each other. They never showed Bob the Doorman a picture of Silver. "Real great detective work, you two."

"Well, how do you explain Silver's phone calling him right before the shooting?" Javier responded defensively.

"Do you know how easy it is to clone a phone? Hell, if Vicky got her phone close enough while she was in the office, she could have done it then."

"Silver, give me your phone." Rita held out her hand, and Silver handed it to her. "Estrada, when you run the plates, can you also take this to tech and see if they can detect if it had been cloned by anyone?" Javier took the phone and put it in his pocket.

147

"And Lucy, can you go back to the building and find Bob and show him a picture of me to see if he still claims it was me he saw," said Silver.

"Will do, boss," Lucy responded enthusiastically.

Javier and Lucy both stood to leave and take care of the assignments they were given. They walked out together and closed the door behind them, leaving Silver and Rita to ponder their next move.

"That only leaves the gun," said Silver.

"I've been trying to think of a way they could have gotten it, but I'm lost."

"The office was empty a lot the week we tailed him, so they had plenty of opportunities to take it, but they would have had to return it when I was asleep in the office."

"Were you drinking that night?"

"I had a drink, but something weird did happen."

"Weird, how?"

"I opened a brand-new bottle, and I only remember having one drink before going to bed, but when you guys woke me the next morning, the bottle was empty on my desk. I don't remember drinking the entire bottle."

"You sure you only had one glass, Cliff?"

"I'm positive."

"So, what do you think happened?"

"Maybe they drugged me somehow. To make sure I wouldn't wake up when they were returning the gun."

"They're supposed to open your gun safe today. Maybe they'll dust it for prints too."

"I doubt someone going through this much trouble would handle the safe or the gun without gloves."

"Then what are we going to do?"

"We have to find a way to prove someone else was in my office without my knowledge."

"That's easier said than done." Rita stood and walked towards the kitchen. "In the meantime, do you want something to eat?"

"Oh, I could think of something I'd like to eat." Silver had his eyebrows raised flirtatiously.

"Food, Cliff. I'm talking about food."

CHAPTER 14

It had been three hours since Javier and Lucy left to take care of their assignments. Three hours of Silver and Rita watching the clock and checking her phone every five minutes, assuming they must have missed a call. Neither of them were very good at sitting around and waiting while working a case. Delegation is a vital tool to use while trying to solve a murder, especially if there are multiple leads to pursue. However, waiting for news while not being able to do anything themselves was torture for them. It didn't help that the sexual tension between them could be cut with a knife, but they were honoring their agreement to put things on hold until the conclusion of this case. Rita had been resisting the urge to jump him since he had saved her life back at Vicky's place, so Javier's call came at the perfect time to avoid her ultimately saying goodbye to her self-control.

"What do you have for me, Estrada?" asked Rita as she picked up the phone after just one ring.

"Sorry it took so long for me to get back to you," Javier responded. Rita put the phone on speaker. "First thing I did was take Silver's phone to tech, and they let me know that it'll take a little time for them to run a diagnostic on it, but they'll definitely be able to tell if it has been cloned or not. I also ran that plate you gave me, and it's registered to what looks to be a dummy corporation, so I don't know if that'll lead us anywhere."

"It does tell us one thing for sure," Silver chimed in. "Vicky has to be backed by someone. Someone who probably has some real money."

"Speaking of Vicky," continued Javier. "That's what took me so long to get back to you. The car thing was weird to me, based on what you told me about her, so I decided to look into her and William some more. She was the older sibling between the two, and she practically raised him after their parents died. She was eighteen at the time, and he was fourteen. After his death, she tried filing a suit against the city, but since it was never actually proven that the CPD had anything to do with framing her brother, it was found that the department was well within reason for arresting him."

"That's not what was said when they fired my ass," Silver said under his breath.

"What did she do for work?" asked Rita.

"She worked in a lunchroom at a local school up until she retired right after the death of her brother."

"Any other family besides William?"

"No, neither of them were married or had any children."

Silver and Rita immediately locked eyes with each other, "Hey, Estrada, did you say that neither of them had any kids?" asked Silver.

"Yeah. Why?"

"We talked to one of Vicky's neighbors today who said that, lately, she's been visited a lot by a niece named Tracy. Was William her only sibling?"

"He was, as far as I can tell."

"Then Tracy must've been someone just pretending to be

her niece," said Silver, speaking mainly to Rita.

"She must be involved," Rita responded. "Why else would she lie about how she knew Vicky?"

"We should find her and ask her."

"Where do you suggest we start?" asked Rita.

Silver thought for a moment, "Hey, Estrada."

"Yeah?" Javier responded.

"Have you got the prints back from the crime scene?"

"No, not yet. CSU still working through their backlog."

"What about the prints I gave you from Silver's office?" Rita added.

"I asked about them when I got back, and they won't run them until they have nothing else to do because it's off the books."

"Nope, that doesn't work for me." Rita leaned closer to her phone. "I need you to go back down there and talk to Sandra Collins. Remind her that she owes Detective Kaye a favor and get those prints moved to the top of the line."

They listened as Javier scribbled down the name she gave him. "Anything else you need me to do for you?" he asked.

"Yes," said Rita. "I know the plates on that car weren't registered to a specific person, but I still want you to put a BOLO out on it. Maybe we'll get lucky, and our mystery man will get caught behind the wheel."

"Ok, will do ..."

"Estrada!" Rita and Silver could hear Ford's booming voice come through the phone so loudly they thought he was actually in the room with them. "Is that Kaye on the phone?"

"What was that, sir?" Javier stammered, but Ford didn't repeat the question. He just snatched the phone from him.

"Kaye!"

"Yes, sir, it's me."

"I just got off the phone with the Blue Island Police. Apparently, someone just led a very dangerous high-speed chase through their town, and when they tracked it back to its origin, they found witnesses who reported a Detective Kaye and an unnamed man asking questions about a local resident."

"Sir, I can explain."

"Explain what?" Ford shouted, cutting her off. "Explain how you and that clown are out causing trouble?"

"We were just trying to get answers. He didn't do this, Cap."

"If that's true, then why is every bit of evidence pointing at him?"

"That's what we're trying to figure out, sir."

"Kaye, you need to bring him in and let the system do its job. If he's truly innocent, then he'll be just fine."

"You mean the way William Hargrave was just fine when he found himself in the system?"

Rita's response was met with silence on the other end of the phone, but she could practically see the steam shooting out of his ears in her head.

"Well, how about this," said Ford in a scarily calm voice. "Either you bring him in, or you'll be running his piece of shit PI business for him while he does twenty-five to life."

Ford hung up the phone after throwing that last haymaker. They both just stared down at it for a moment, almost as if they both expected him to come climbing out of it. They knew that Ford meant every word.

"Look, Rita—" said Silver, breaking the silence.

"No," she responded without letting him finish.

"We've already started putting some of the pieces together. Maybe if we went in with what we have now, I could beat this."

"But there's still a chance that you won't, and I can't live with that."

"And I can't live with you losing your career to protect me."

"Well, you already lost yours to protect me, so I guess that'll make us even."

"Rita, it's not the same."

"How come it's not?"

"Because I was going down either way. What I did just

made sure we both weren't thrown out on the street."

"Cliff, I am not throwing you to the wolves until I know you can properly defend yourself. That's the end of the discussion."

Rita turned her back towards him, mostly so he couldn't see the tears starting to form. Silver stood with her and placed his hand on her shoulders, giving them a light squeeze. Rita wiped away the single tear that was about to fall before turning around to meet his eye.

"Well, if we're going to save me and your career, then we need to get a move on it. There's no way you'll make it as a PI."

"Right, because you're crushing it as a PI."

"Look, it's more than just wisecracking and being a peeping Tom, although that William Hargrave comment could've given me a run for my money."

"Oh, you liked that one, huh?"

"Did I like it? It got me all hot and bothered."

"Well, I suggest you cool yourself off. Can we get back to the task at hand?" Rita steered the conversation back to the case before Silver could suggest they move things to her bedroom. "Our problem is there really isn't anything for us to do right now. We have no leads to chase down beside what Estrada was working on."

"Well, we still have Bob the Doorman. Lucy's taking her sweet-ass time to go and talk to him. Maybe we can call her off and talk to him ourselves."

"No," said Rita shaking her head. "If he is lying about seeing your face, actually seeing your face could spook him."

"Then we need to get Lucy on the phone and figure out what the fuck is taking her so long to talk to one witness."

Rita handed him her phone so he could call her, and Silver began to pace back and forth as it rang. He couldn't believe Lucy was taking so long to get back with them on something that was this important. He had been so proud of her when she had the idea to go to Bob and get a formal ID on who he saw. That could be the missing piece. Without a positive ID placing him at the crime scene, the entire case against Silver could fall apart.

The phone rang and rang and rang until it finally reached her voicemail. Silver could feel his anxiety rise slightly when he heard it. Lucy always answers her phone. They hadn't sent her into a dangerous situation, had they? Just as he was about to call her again, Rita's phone began to ring, and it was Lucy's number on the caller ID

"Where the hell have you been?" shouted Silver before Lucy could say anything.

"Hi, Cliff; nice to hear from you too," Lucy responded sarcastically.

"Ford just called. He's on to us, and we need to make a move. Bob is our last lead, and we're stuck twiddling our thumbs waiting for you."

"I'm sorry, I already went to his job, but he wasn't there."

"Was it his day off?"

"No, he admitted to taking a bribe to let someone in the building, and one of their tenants was killed, so they fired his ass."

"Can't argue with that reasoning. Why didn't you tell us? We could've had Estrada get his home address."

"I already have it. They gave it to me with no problem."

"Is it far away or something?"

"No, it's not far at all."

"So, let's double back to my original question. What's taking you so long?"

"Your original question was actually 'where the hell have you been?'"

"Lucy, do you really think this is the time for jokes?"

"I had something to do, Cliff?" This was met by silence from Silver. It was often a technique used to get a suspect to talk, an uncomfortable silence compelling them to tell on themselves. "I had a lunch date, ok."

"So, you went on a date instead of tracking down the man

who could clear me on a murder charge?"

"I didn't think I was up against a clock. Once I went to his job, and he wasn't there, I thought I had time to do both, but don't worry. I'm on my way to him now."

"No, text us the address and stand down. We'll take it from here."

"Cliff, you can trust me with this."

"Obviously, I can't because you don't recognize the urgency of the situation. Just go home, Lucy."

Silver hung up the phone before she could plead her case again. A moment later, a text came to Rita's phone from Lucy of an address for Bob's place. He stayed on the south side of the city, but it wasn't too far, as Lucy had mentioned. With any luck, he could be off the hook for this within the hour.

"You were a little hard on her, don't you think?" said Rita.

"I would've thought you would've enjoyed that."

"Don't get me wrong, I did, but I think you have to keep in mind that she's still pretty young. Her priorities aren't all the way there yet."

"She'll be better for it. She has to learn that when you do this type of work, you're always up against the clock."

"I guess you're right."

"Sometimes tough love is the best motivation."

"You ever think that maybe that's why Ford has always been so hard on you?"

"Threatening me with twenty-five to life sounds like a little bit more than tough love."

"Well, obviously, it's not tough love anymore," Rita admitted. "But you guys bumped heads long before you left the force. Sometimes I get the sense that it's not hate he feels when it comes to you, it's disappointment."

Silver thought about that for a second. There was a chance that maybe Rita could have been right, but that didn't change the fact that it felt like he was out for blood now. "Well, let's get over to Bob's so I can disappoint him again by clearing my name."

Silver and Rita made the fairly short ride over to Bob's place as quickly as possible. They were hoping that his getting fired could work to their advantage. Maybe he would want to help as much as possible to get back at the people who sent him to the unemployment line. He lived on the second floor of a three-story apartment building. It looked like ordinarily the front door of the building would have been locked, and they would need to be buzzed in, but lucky for them, whoever entered last ignored the handwritten sign that said, 'PLEASE CLOSE DOOR COMPLETELY TO MAKE SURE IT LOCKS.' Instead, it was left slightly ajar, so they pulled it open and let themselves in.

Bob lived in apartment 2B, so they made their way upstairs once inside. They reached the second-floor landing, and the door immediately to their left read 2A. Both of their eyes went to the only other door on that floor, and they looked at each other when they noticed it had been left slightly ajar. Their guns were holstered under their jackets, but they both cleared any obstructions to their weapons. They approached his door cautiously. Rita braced herself against the banister while Silver held his back against the opposite wall. They didn't know what was on the other side of that door, but they wanted to stay out of the middle of the frame just in case someone decided to open fire. From Rita's side of the door, she could see through the slight opening, so she knelt down and tried to peer within.

"Can you see anything?" said Silver in a hushed tone.

"I think I see blood," Rita whispered back. Silver nodded, and they both unholstered their guns. "Bob, it's Detective Kaye from the crime scene yesterday. Are you home?" Rita yelled into the apartment, but there was no response.

Silver and Rita made eye contact and gave each other a silent three-count before she pushed the door completely open, and Silver quickly slithered inside, with Rita following closely behind. Bob's apartment wasn't large. To the left of the door was the living room area, and to the right was a solid wall that didn't have an opening until his kitchen.

"I have a body on the couch," said Silver as he moved through the living room.

"Copy that," responded Rita as she made it to the kitchen. She quickly moved through it, making sure it was clear, before coming out of the other side to meet Silver at the opening of the hallway. The hall wasn't very long and had three closed doors. Silver gave Rita a nod for her to cover him, and when her gun was pointed towards the dark hall, he inched forward. He flipped a light switch on the wall at the beginning of the hallway, which illuminated the space. He walked to the first door on his right. And braced himself against the wall next to it. Then he gave Rita the ok for her to come and open it for him. The door swung open into the hall, so Rita reached across to grab the knob. Before she opened it, they gave each other another silent three count, then she swung the door open, clearing the way for Silver to sweep the room. It turned out to be a bathroom closet, so they closed it and moved on to the next door. They repeated this same process for the bathroom and again for his bedroom. Both rooms were clear of any potential intruders, so they turned their attention back to the yet-to-be-inspected body on the couch.

Rita was right about the blood she had thought she saw from outside the apartment. His living room was a tiny area that consisted of just a single couch, a coffee table, and a flat-screen television. The man on the couch was doubled over. He had a gunshot wound in the back of his head. The blood that Rita saw had begun to pool directly under where his head came to a final resting spot. Rita walked around the couch, careful not to step in any of the blood, and knelt to look at the victim's face.

"Do I even have to guess who that is?" asked Silver, barely masking his disappointment.

"Yeah, that's definitely Bob."

CHAPTER 15

Silver sat quietly on the passenger side of Lucy's car. He hadn't said two words since she picked him up from Bob's place, but surprisingly, his silence didn't come from frustration. Instead, it was a combination of sadness for Bob, who lost his life, then relief because Bob's murder could be used as proof of his innocence, which turned into guilt for feeling relieved that a man had died. Silver knew that the only person to blame for the murders of Bob and Richard was whoever pulled the trigger, but the fact that they were killed in pursuit of him made the guilt manifest itself, nonetheless. The key for Silver was to make Vicky, and whoever else was helping her, pay for the guilt they made him feel.

"Take me to Sean's," he said, finally breaking the silence.

"Look, Cliff, I know finding Bob like that was rough but do you think now is the time to have a drink?" said Lucy with concern on her face. "You should keep a clear head."

"I don't want a drink. I need somewhere to lay low until I can meet back up with Rita, and we agreed that Sean's would be perfect."

"Oh, I'm sorry. I didn't mean to assume ..."

"No worries, your concerns are fair," he shrugged. "I'm sober, and I plan on staying that way."

"Wow." Lucy was genuinely shocked to hear this. "Should've framed you for murder a long time ago."

Silver burst out laughing. "Alright now, keep talking like that, and you're going to move to the top of the suspect list."

She chuckled, "You'll never take me alive."

"I wouldn't be so sure about that," he said, still laughing to himself.

"Did you find out anything from the crime scene?" she asked once he stopped laughing.

"No."

"No one saw anything?"

"I don't know."

"So, there were no witnesses or anything?"

"As far as I know, no one knew he was dead before we got there." He turned to face her. "What's with the third degree?"

"Umm ... You know me ... just curious," she responded.

Something about Lucy at that moment made Silver feel uneasy. She was always naturally curious, but this time her questions felt like something else, but he couldn't quite put his finger on what. Was it urgency? Was the gravity of his situation starting to weigh on her?

"Right." He accepted her answer for the moment. "Well, there wasn't much time to inspect the crime scene, and the techs are going to do a much better job than we would've, so it made more sense to just call them in. And after what happened this morning, it wouldn't have been a good idea to have me questioning witnesses again."

"So now we're just going to sit and wait for Rita," she said as more of a statement than a question.

"Yes, that's all we can do. When Rita gets the chance, she will meet us at Sean's to give us an update. Knowing Rita, she'll have this case basically solved by then."

"Great," said Lucy through her teeth.

Lucy's curiosity seemed subdued for the rest of the ride to Sean's bar. They fell back into the same silence they had shared at the beginning of the ride, which only heightened the uneasiness Silver felt from Lucy's vibe. Something was definitely off with her. He wanted to press the issue but decided not to. Whatever was going on with her would pass, and he had enough to worry about.

When they arrived, Lucy parked in the alley to the side of the bar where Silver often left his car on nights when he was too drunk to drive. Sean's was open for business, but it was still pretty early, so they weren't surprised to see the place mostly empty when they walked in. They went and sat in a corner booth where Silver would have a bird's eye view of the entire room and everyone who came in and out of the bar. They weren't sitting there for long before Sean made his way over.

"Just the man I've been looking for," he said. "Where you been?"

"Just been working a case." Silver had no intention of divulging everything that was going on to Sean. He wanted to give his friend plausible deniability.

"That's what's up, bro. I told you things would start picking up." Sean's eyes drifted to Lucy and flashed her a flirty smile. "Who's your friend?"

"I'm Lucy," she said, holding out her hand for Sean to shake it. "I'm his assistant."

"Assistant?" Sean feigned shock. "How come I've never met your assistant buddy?"

"Because part of my job is to protect her from predators." Silver put his arm across Lucy, literally shielding her from his advances.

"Haha, very funny. I really have been looking for you. Is your phone off? I've been trying to call you."

"My bad, man. I lost my phone last night."

"Tonya has been trying to reach you today. She called me asking if I had seen you."

"Shit, really? I hope nothing is wrong with Chrissy." Silver patted his pocket by instinct, looking for his phone before remembering it was at the precinct.

Sean noticed and pulled out his own. "Here, use mine. You can call her in the back, and I'll protect your assistant from predators."

Silver grabbed Sean's phone and went to the stockroom behind the bar. He dialed her number and thought he was glad Tonya had never changed it after all of these years. The phone only rang twice before Tonya picked up on the other line.

"Hey, Sean, have you seen him?" she said. Silver could hear the extreme concern in her voice.

"It's me, T."

"Where the fuck have you been!" she shouted so loudly he had to move the phone away from his ear. "I've been worried sick."

"T, I told you I was going to solve this case."

"You didn't say you weren't going to be checking in."

"I'm sorry, things have been moving pretty fast."

"Have you found whoever is behind this?"

"We think we know who it is, but we haven't tracked them down yet."

"Does that mean you're off the hook?" she asked eagerly.

"Not quite, but we're getting close," he said, but Tonya didn't respond. "T, are you still there?"

"So, you're still a target."

"Wow, T, you almost sound like you're concerned for me."

"Don't give me that shit," she snarled. "Just because we're not married anymore doesn't mean I don't love you or worry about you."

"I know, T, I was just joking," he said to try and calm her.

"This isn't the time to fucking joke, Cliff."

"I promise you I'm ok, T. I'm not letting anyone take me

away from Chrissy. You know that, don't you?" He waited a moment for a response. "Don't you?"

"Yes, I do. But if you're not careful, that choice won't be yours to make."

"Listen to me, T. I'm not going anywhere. I promise."

Silver could hear her sigh. "I hear you, Cliff."

"Are you sure?"

"Yes." She didn't sound very confident, but he figured that was the best he would get.

"Ok, good," he said in hopes of moving on. "How is Chrissy doing today?"

"She's fine. She missed you."

"I missed her too," he said, smiling. "I'm sure she's still going to tell me all about her day when she sees me."

"Yeah, I asked her how her day was, and she told me, 'Mama, that's Daddy's job.'" They both laughed out loud with each other.

"She's right," he said after they were done laughing. "That's our after-school routine."

"I won't try to step on your territory again."

"You better not," he said, still chuckling to himself.

"So ... are you planning on telling me what all this is about?"

Silver took a beat before saying, "William Hargrave."

"You can't be serious."

"Apparently, he has a sister, and she doesn't like me very much."

"Was that the fake client?"

"Yeah, it was her." Another reminder of how stupid he was not to check into her before he took the case.

"If you know who it is, can't Rita just bring her in?"

"Because we don't know where she is, and we also don't have proof that she killed anyone. That evidence still points toward me. We thought we had a potential witness, but I just left from finding his body."

"Wait, someone else was killed?"

"Yes, but don't worry, my alibi for that murder is rock solid."

"That's not what I'm worried about," she said. Silver could hear the concern in her voice growing again. "What if she cuts her losses and comes after you if her plan doesn't work?"

That was a thought that had already crossed his mind. "There's a chance that might happen, and if it does, we won't have to work so hard to find her."

"I know you thought that would make me feel better, but it didn't."

"Look, T, I understand your concern, but I can't afford to start thinking about those things. All I can do is control what I can and make the best out of what I can't."

"I guess you're right," she resigned, but he could practically feel her roll her eyes through the phone.

"That was really hard for you to say, wasn't it?"

"Yeah, especially given how rare it is that I actually get to say it."

"Walked right into that one," he said with another laugh.

"You've always made it so easy."

"Well, now that I've given you more material for your comedy act, I should get going. I'm waiting to hear from Rita about the new crime scene."

"Alright. Please be careful, Cliff."

"I will, I promise. Give my baby girl a kiss for me." Tonya promised him she would and hung up the phone. Silver sat there for a moment to collect his thoughts. Tonya had raised a valid concern. He could eventually become a direct target. It may be a good time to send Lucy home. The longer this went on, the more likely they were to come after him, and it would be harder to properly protect himself if he had to look after her too. He made his way out of the stock room and back to their table. Sean was still there chatting up Lucy.

"Thanks for letting me see your phone, bro," said Silver as he handed it back to him.

"No problem. I also put in a burger for you. I'll bring it out with your usual drink," said Sean.

"Actually, can you make that a lemonade? I'm trying to cut back on the alcohol."

Sean was taken aback. "I am so happy to hear that, bro. Cheeseburger and lemonade coming right up."

He stood from the table and went to the kitchen to retrieve the food. Silver couldn't help but laugh to himself. You know you have a drinking problem when the person profiting from your drinking is glad to hear you stopped.

"What's funny?" asked Lucy.

"Nothing," he responded. "Just an inside thought."

"I'm really impressed that you could still smile after everything that's happened over the last couple of days."

"You can call it my gut, but something tells me things are about to break for us."

"That's good enough for me. So, what did Tonya want?"

"She was just worried when she didn't hear from me and wanted to tell me that Chrissy missed me."

"I'm sure you miss her too."

"Of course. That's why we have to wrap this up so I can buy my baby another after-school ice cream."

"Keep doing that, and you won't have to wait for whoever this is to kill you. Tonya will do it for them."

"Speaking of that." Silver shifted the tone of the conversation. "T brought up something that has me thinking it may not be a good idea to have you around me for now."

"Here we go," said Lucy with an eye roll.

"I'm serious, Luce." He looked her in the eye. "When this frame-up falls apart, they might come after me. Now, I can protect myself, but that'll be harder if I have to look after you too."

"What makes you think I can't protect myself as well?"

"I'm sure you can, but that won't stop me from worrying about you, and that could be just enough for me to lose this fight."

Lucy looked as if she wanted to protest more but could see from the look in his eye that he wasn't backing down. "Fine, but I have food coming too, so I'm not leaving until I'm fed."

"Fair enough." They shook on this compromise and began to joke with each other like their usual selves while they waited for Sean to bring their food. They didn't have to wait much longer. He and one of his waitresses made their way from the kitchen carrying two plates of food and two drinks.

"Eat up," said Sean as he set the plates in front of them. They both thanked him and then dove in. This wasn't Silver's first meal in the past two days, but it sure as hell felt like it. He was nursing a headache and couldn't tell if it came from hunger or his body craving whiskey. As he took a bite of his burger, he couldn't help but think about the things he took for granted. Before these last couple of days, he would sit night after night crawling into a bottle and wallowing in self-pity, not allowing himself to truly appreciate how lucky he was. He had a beautiful daughter who adored him, an ex-wife who still cared enough to worry about him, an assistant who would run through a wall for him, and a best friend, who would hopefully be more than that, that would ride or die for him. A moment ago, Lucy commended him on his ability to smile in the face of adversity, and he told her it was because things were about to turn around for him. He truly believed it. As long as he was surrounded by people who loved him, he knew he would be ok, no matter what was thrown his way.

Silver took the last satisfying bite of his food when Lucy's phone rang. She grabbed it out of her bag to see who it was and held it up for Silver to see that Rita was calling. He took it from her and answered it while he was still chewing.

"Hey, Rita," he said in a muffled voice.

"Are you ok, Cliff?" she replied.

Silver swallowed the last of his meal. "Yeah, sorry, I had food in my mouth. Are you done at the crime scene?"

"CSU is still working, but the body has been moved, and

we're about to head out."

"Find anything interesting?"

"Not from the scene. Based on the size of the wound, the coroner estimates that he was shot by a nine mil."

"At least we know for sure it didn't come from my gun this time." Silver chuckled but stopped when he realized Rita didn't. "Any witnesses?"

"Yeah, his neighbor came forward."

"That's great! Did they see or hear anything?"

"He claims to have heard a conversation between Bob and an unknown woman about thirty minutes before he heard us entering Bob's apartment."

"Did he hear the shot?"

"He claims that he didn't, but with the timing, we're assuming it was definitely Bob's killer he heard, if he's telling the truth."

"Yeah, that makes sense. Is he sure it was a woman he heard?"

"He says it was for sure a woman."

"Had to be Vicky." Silver could feel himself getting excited.

"We can't be sure just yet," said Rita with a flat tone.

"Oh, well, what did they say to each other?"

Rita went silent for a moment. "How about you and Lucy come down to the precinct, and we can go over everything we have?"

"I don't think Ford would be ok with that."

"Don't worry. We talked about everything, and when I explained to him everything you and I found, he agreed that there's a high possibility that you're being framed."

"I don't know, Rita. You sure he isn't just saying that to draw me out?"

"Trust me, Cliff; it isn't you that we're after, and we need your help bringing her in."

Silver got this far by trusting Rita, and he wasn't going to stop now. "Ok, I'll come in." He could see Lucy staring at him out of the corner of his eye. "Just let me send Lucy home, and I'll get a ride over."

"No, bring her too."

Silver raised an eyebrow. "You actually want her to come?"

"Yeah, it's all hands on deck if we're going to track down Vicky."

"I don't know, Rita. Bodies are piling up, and I don't want to put her in harm's way."

"I understand. Just bring her, and I promise she won't leave the precinct. There's no safer place for her to be."

Silver was still hesitant, but he couldn't argue with her logic. "Ok, we'll be right over."

"Ok, see you soon. Bye." Rita hung up the phone before he could say bye back. He looked to hand Lucy her phone back, but she still stared at him in disbelief.

"There's no fucking way you could possibly think it's a good idea for us to walk in that precinct."

"Rita says it's ok, and I trust her," he explained, but Lucy was beside herself. "Of all the people in that precinct, she's literally the last person who would walk me into a trap." Silver stood to leave, but Lucy remained in her seat. "Luce, you said you didn't want to go home, right? This way, you can keep working the case, and you'll be somewhere safe."

"I don't know, Cliff. Something doesn't feel right."

"Then I need you there to watch my back." Silver offered his hand to her, and after a moment, she took it and climbed out of the booth where they sat.

Silver and Lucy stepped off the elevator and into the homicide bullpen. He looked across the room to Rita's desk, and there she was, sitting with her head down, rubbing her temples. He led Lucy over to her desk and tapped her shoulder to let her know he was there.

Rita looked up and shot up from her desk when she realized it was him. She threw her arms around him and whispered into his ear, "I'm so sorry about this, Cliff. I really am." Then she let him go and motioned for a uniformed officer to come over to them.

"You sold me out!" Silver shouted. "Rita, how could you!"

She didn't respond. She just stood there waiting for the officer to reach them, and when he did, she looked at him and said, "Please escort her to interrogation one."

CHAPTER 16

Rita had stood outside waiting for the coroner and CSU. She and Silver had agreed it would be a good idea to call in Bob's murder. They also had decided that it wouldn't be a good idea for him to be there when everyone arrived, so they called Lucy to come and pick him up. Rita had waited until they were completely out of the area before she called Javier. They didn't want to run the risk of Silver being seen anywhere in the vicinity of the crime scene. They tried to inspect the scene as much as they could on their own, but ultimately, they weren't equipped enough to find anything pertinent. Before he left, Silver went silent. At first, Rita thought it was frustration, but the more she watched him, the more she realized it was extreme focus. Whoever did this just killed another man in his name, and Rita knew Silver didn't take that lightly. He was going to make them pay, and she was going to be there when he did.

Shortly after she got off the phone with Javier, she received a text from him saying that Captain Ford was coming to the crime scene too. So instead of trying to get answers about this murder, she was going to be stuck answering pointless questions. At least this will be another opportunity to convince Ford of Silver's innocence. She was his alibi for Bob's murder, and also, his murder only makes sense if it was done by someone who doesn't want Bob talking. There was one thought that she and Silver were kicking around before he left with Lucy. Was this just tying up loose ends, or did the suspect know they were on their way to talk to him? The coroner's van rounded the corner and pulled up in front of the building where Bob's body was waiting, temporarily giving Rita a break from her thoughts.

"The body is in apartment 2B," she said when the coroner stepped out of the van. She nodded before grabbing her bag and heading inside to inspect the body. Shortly after she disappeared upstairs, the crime scene unit and some uniformed officers showed up and began roping off the area to limit pedestrian foot traffic while they worked the crime scene. Rita assigned two officers to work crowd control and two to knock on the other doors in the building. If Bob's neighbors were home, they might've heard something, although her gut told her that wasn't the case. Odds are, if anyone heard anything significant, then Rita wouldn't have been the one to call it in.

Rita decided to stand outside and wait for Ford and Javier to arrive. Ordinarily, she wouldn't be the first on the scene, so she wanted to stay out of everyone's way and allow them to do their jobs. Rita also knew that Ford would show up ready to tear her a new one and thought it would be best not to make him have to search for her. She didn't have to wait very long. Ford's car came charging around the corner with Javier in the passenger seat, looking terrified. He pulled up going so fast that his car jumped the curb, and he tried to get out before putting the car in park, so it began to move forward while he had one foot hanging out of the door. He quickly slammed his foot back on the brakes and shoved the gear shift up. Javier sat in the car for a moment, trying to catch his breath. If the entire ride was anything like what Rita had just witnessed, then his life was probably still flashing before his eyes.

"Where the fuck is he?" Ford barked at Rita.

"He's not here," she responded as calmly as she could.

"Running from a second murder, I see."

"We don't know the time of death yet. But Silver has an alibi for this murder."

"Let me guess, his alibi is you?" he said dismissively.

Rita didn't take the bait. "As you already know, Silver was with me this morning, nowhere near this apartment. At that same time, Bob was seen alive when he was being fired from his job. Silver had been with me every minute of this day up until I came here to meet with the victim. That's when I discovered the body. If you don't believe me, you can ask Estrada." Javier had just got out of the car and went pale when he heard his name thrown into this. Rita hated throwing him under the bus but knew she needed him to fortify Silver's alibi. "A few hours ago, Javier met with Silver, his assistant, and me at my apartment to discuss the case, and he was also talking to the both of us when you jumped in on that call earlier."

Ford looked at Javier. "Is this true?"

"Yes, sir." Javier's voice cracked as he spoke. "I can vouch that there's no way Silver was involved in this murder."

"No, you can vouch that he didn't do it himself," Ford argued.

"With all due respect," said Rita. "Why would he kill Richard Lindsey himself if he had a proxy willing to commit murder for him?"

Ford didn't respond. He just stared at Rita as if he were pondering the thought, so she continued.

"And why bother to bribe Bob and let him see his face if he was just planning on killing him anyway? Sir, the only thing that makes sense is that Bob was killed to keep us from identifying who he really let into the building that night."

"But he already identified Silver."

"Actually, sir," said Javier. "It was brought to our attention that Bob never actually identified Silver as the man. He just described someone who fits Silver's description."

"Which is why I came here," said Rita, bringing Ford's attention back to her. "I wanted him to see a photo of Silver and confirm our suspicion, but I found his body instead."

"What you're saying makes sense, but it still doesn't prove he didn't call someone to do this once it was decided that you were coming to talk to him."

"Actually, sir, he couldn't have," Javier again chimed in. "We suspected his phone might've been cloned, so I took it to tech so they can have a look at it."

"You've been busy, I see," Ford glared at Javier.

"You're being a bad cop," said Rita.

"Excuse me?" Ford responded sharply.

"I said you're being a bad cop. You're so locked in on busting Cliff that you're completely ignoring all of the evidence that points to his innocence. What you're doing, sir, is unfair to him, but most importantly, it's unfair to our victims. We've proved the evidence against him is shaky, and this murder proves that there's someone else at play here, but you would rather that person get away with this than admit you're wrong about Cliff. When you let this murderer get away, I hope it's you that gets the pleasure of explaining to their families that they will never see justice because you couldn't look past your own ego long enough to do some actual police work."

Javier stood behind Ford, his eyes bulging out of his head after Rita's speech. Ford turned so red it looked as if he would combust, but he didn't immediately react to what Rita said. Instead, he just stared at her without blinking, but Rita stood her ground. She knew she was right and that it would be hard for them to get anywhere with Ford working against them, but even with confidence in her convictions, she couldn't help but think he was getting ready to drop the hammer. Then, much to her surprise, his face returned to its normal color, and his expression softened.

"You're right," he said. Rita and Javier couldn't believe their ears. "I still believe he's a suspect, but with these recent developments, there's obviously something else going on here, and it might be time to at least consider expanding the suspect list."

"Thank you, sir," said Rita. Ford did not back off entirely from Silver, but this was a good start.

"But we'll have a talk about your insubordination later," he said with a grin.

"Yes, sir," she said, smiling back at him.

"So, what do we have here?" said Ford, moving on from their shared moment.

Rita welcomed the opportunity to move on to business as usual. "Our victim is forty-two-year-old Robert Foster. He's the same man who described letting a man that matched Silver's description into Richard Lindsey's building moments before his murder. Like I said earlier, I came here today to show him a photo of Silver to confirm it was, in fact, Silver that he saw." Rita decided to omit the fact that Silver had been here too. "When I arrived, his door was ajar, and I could see a pool of blood on the floor. I called out to him and announced myself, but when there was no response, I entered and found his body."

"So you came here alone and decided to enter his apartment where you saw signs of a struggle without backup?" Ford clearly didn't believe Rita had been here alone, and he had an idea of who she had been with.

"Yes, sir, I saw the blood, but I couldn't see a body. I entered because there was a possibility that he wasn't dead and just needed immediate medical assistance."

"Fair enough," said Ford. But he definitely wasn't buying it.

Rita decided to continue before he could call her on anything. "The ME is still examining the body, but COD appears to be a gunshot to the back of the head. I could see no signs of struggle or forced entry, which would suggest that he knew his killer."

"Had to be someone tying up loose ends," said Javier.

"That's what I was thinking, but the timing seems too coincidental," responded Rita. "If someone put him up to fingering Silver for this, then for all that person knew, it was working, and everyone was looking for Silver. The only reason to kill him is to keep him from speaking with us."

"You know what doesn't make sense to me?" Ford asked rhetorically. "If someone was trying to frame Silver, then wouldn't they make sure this guy can pick him out of a lineup?"

Rita hadn't thought about that. What if Bob had doubled down on it being Silver? In that case, whoever is behind this would have welcomed them talking to him because it would have reinforced the case against Silver.

"Maybe Bob demanded more bribe money," suggested Javier. "According to him, the initial bribe was just to let someone in, and he didn't know that someone would die. That, combined with him getting fired today, could have caused him to try to pry more money from whoever paid him."

"That's plausible," Ford conceded.

"No way he already knew you were coming," said Javier. "Only the four of us knew, and we discussed that in person."

That thought had been troubling Rita. She was taught that there are no coincidences in murder cases, so the timing of Bob's murder felt like a clue more than anything. What was nagging her was that Javier was absolutely right. There was a very small list of people who knew that they planned on talking to Bob. If the killer had made his move because he knew they were on their way, they had a leak.

"Kaye, you ok?" asked Javier.

"Yeah, I'm good." Rita wasn't ready to voice her thoughts out loud. If she was wrong, there would be no coming back from that accusation.

"What were you looking for in Blue Island this morning?" asked Ford.

Rita's first instinct was to lie to her captain again, but she thought it might've been a good idea to completely clue him in on what she and Silver found and build on the goodwill she had just gained with him. So, she gave him the entire story. Starting with Vicky Hargrave coming to Silver posing as a client who was married to Richard Lindsey. How Silver was tailing Richard, thinking he was completing a job, and that he caught him sleeping with a prostitute they had yet to identify. How they tracked Vicky down and discovered she was related to William Hargrave, which led to the car chase through Blue Island. And finally, that Richard Lindsey was the public defender who represented William and convinced him to take the plea deal. The only part she decided to leave out was that they were sure Silver's gun was used to kill Richard. They were still working on a way to explain how that happened, so no point in working Ford into another frenzy.

"You're thinking Vicky is out for revenge for the death of her brother," said Ford. "First with his lawyer and now with the cop who arrested him."

"Exactly. We think her plan is to frame Silver the way that she believes he framed her brother, and what better victim to frame him for killing than the lawyer that wouldn't fight to prove her brother's innocence."

"So she has motive, but can you prove means and opportunity?"

"We haven't been able to prove that yet," answered Rita. "But when we confronted her at her place, there was another person there who took a shot at me. So we're pretty sure she's working with an accomplice.

"Our first thought was the prostitute Richard Lindsey was visited by on the night of his murder. He was killed shortly after she left, and there was no forced entry into his place. So our theory is that she left the door unlocked for the killer. Also, we spoke with a neighbor of Vicky's who told us about a niece that's been coming around lately who loosely matches the description of the woman Silver spotted with Lindsey."

"But when we looked into Vicky, there was nothing we could find that said she had any family outside of William," added Javier.

"So she has to be the co-conspirator," concluded Ford.

"One of the co-conspirators," Rita corrected him. "When we pursued them in Blue Island, Silver swore that the driver was a man."

"Do you have a description of this man?"

"No, we could never get close enough to get a good look."

"Even if we were to track her down, do you have any evidence to support her being a suspect? Right now, everything you have is just supposition."

"Yes, our evidence is circumstantial, but why else would she come up with a false identity and hire Silver to follow Lindsey? And her connection to Lindsey and Silver can't be coincidental and gives her a strong motive."

"Motive alone isn't enough."

"That's why I pulled some prints from Silver's office, and we're hoping they're a match for any prints lifted from the crime scene."

"And if they don't, then what?" asked Ford. Rita knew what he was getting at. "I'm sorry, Kaye, but with everything you have, Silver is still the best suspect. He can be placed at least near the crime scene, and all indications are that he's currently walking around with the potential murder weapon."

"I get it, sir. All I'm asking is for a little time to find the proof we need."

Ford looked at her and contemplated what she was asking of him. "Fine, but Silver can't be involved anymore."

"But, sir ..."

"No buts, even without his questionable past, his ass is on the line. Any evidence that he 'finds' will be tainted. Any decent defense attorney will rip it to shreds in court."

Rita didn't like it, but he was right. There's a reason cops aren't allowed to investigate cases where they have a personal interest. Judgment becomes cloudy, and emotions get in the way of a detective's objectivity. Rita wanted to argue for Silver to stay on, but she knew if she pushed too hard, Ford would make the case that she was too close as well. So, she nodded in agreement and let it go. Then her mind went to Silver and how she would rather be shot at again than be the one to convince Silver that this was for the best.

"Detective Kaye." Their attention was drawn by one of the officers she had sent to speak with Bob's neighbors.

"Yes, Officer McGuire," said Rita.

"I just spoke with the man who lives in 2A, and I believe you should speak with him."

"Ok, what is his name?"

Officer McGuire glanced at his notes. "Brad Thompson."

"What does he have to tell us?"

"He heard a conversation between the witness and an unknown woman approximately thirty minutes before you called in the murder."

"Ok, thank you. I'll be right up." Officer McGuire gave her a nod and returned to the building. "Would you fellas care to join?"

"You guys talk to the witness. I'll see what CSU and the ME have so far," said Javier.

"Good idea," responded Rita. They went into the building and up the stairs. Rita and Ford turned into the first apartment on the left while Javier pushed past CSU into Bob's apartment.

"Mr. Thompson," Rita called from the doorway. A Black man with darker skin and short curly hair sat on the couch in the middle of the room. When he stood to greet them, he was of medium height and regular build. Rita guessed his age to be early to mid-thirties.

"You can call me Brad," he said as he held his hand out for Rita and Ford to shake it.

"Okay, Brad, I'm Detective Rita Kaye, and this is Captain

Arthur Ford. Officer McGuire tells me you have some information you would like to share with us," said Rita.

"Yes, I am so sorry to hear what happened to Bob. I'll help in any way that I can."

"Did you know him very well?"

"Not particularly. We were cordial and spoke when passing each other in the hall."

"So, how do you think you can help us, Brad?"

"I believe I heard a conversation between Bob and whoever killed him."

Rita traded glances with Ford. "What makes you think it was whoever killed him?"

"What do you mean?"

"Just hearing a conversation between two people doesn't mean one killed the other. Did you hear any threats or a struggle?"

"No, it was nothing like that, but not even an hour after I heard them speaking, I heard you calling out to Bob, and I'm assuming he was already dead. Right?"

Rita chose not to answer that question. "Did you hear any shots fired?"

"No, is that how he was killed?"

"What was this conversation you heard?"

"Well, as you can see, these apartments aren't very large, and these walls are pretty thin, so you can really hear a lot of what's happening in other apartments and in the halls," said Brad. Rita really wanted him to get on with the story but thought it wouldn't be best to rush him. "I heard someone coming up the stairs, and I was expecting some food to be delivered around that time, so I started walking towards the door. When I got closer, I heard them knock on Bob's door. When he opened it, I heard him say, 'What are you doing here?' and she said, 'We need to talk.' "

This time Rita did choose to interrupt. "So it was a woman he spoke to?"

"Most definitely. After she said they needed to talk, he asked what about, and I heard her say, 'We need another favor,' and that's when Bob got really loud. He shouted, 'I'm not doing shit else for you people.' "

"Did you hear her say what the favor was that she wanted-ed?"

"No, because after he shouted, I heard her ask if they could talk inside of his place. I guess she didn't want any nosey neighbors like me to hear," Brad said with a chuckle, but when he saw Rita and Ford staring at him blankly, he wiped the smile from his face.

"Is that everything?"

"Yes, I believe so. Like I said, after that, the next voice I heard was you calling out his name."

"Ok, Brad." Rita reached into her pocket and pulled out one of her cards. "If you remember anything else, please don't hesitate to call, and thank you for your cooperation."

Rita and Ford left the apartment and were on their way back downstairs to wait for Javier to give them an update on what he learned from the crime scene when they heard Brad shout for their attention.

"Did you remember something else?" she asked.

"Yes, I just remembered that when he opened the door, he called her by her name."

Rita could feel the anxious energy building within her. If he says Vicky, it would be what they need to clear Silver, or maybe it was the prostitute they still haven't identified. "What was the name?"

Brad looked up as if he were searching his brain for the answer. "It started with an L. I believe it was something like Lacey ... no, wait, I remember exactly what it was." Rita could feel that energy turn into dread before he could even say it. "It was Lucy."

CHAPTER 17

Silver watched as the officer came and tried to grab Lucy by the arm. She yanked away from him and took a step behind Silver for protection, which instinctively he was inclined to provide for her. He locked eyes with Rita expecting her to avert her gaze, but instead, she didn't blink. She stared back at him, and without saying a word, she let him know that she had a very good reason for wanting Lucy in the box.

"It's ok, Lucy, you can go with him," said Silver as he stepped to the side to clear the officer's path to her.

"Cliff, I didn't do anything," Lucy proclaimed.

"Then you have nothing to worry about." He looked at her and could see the fear in her eyes. "Don't worry, just go with him, and I'll try to figure out what's going on."

The officer stepped towards Lucy again, but he didn't try to grab her arm this time. Instead, he gently placed a hand on her shoulder and held his opposite hand in the direction he wanted her to walk. Lucy looked to Silver one last time before reluctantly following the officer's lead. Silver didn't take his eyes off them until they turned a corner around a hall where he couldn't see from his angle. As soon as she was out of sight, he grabbed Rita by the hand and practically dragged her to the break room.

"Can we have the room?" Rita said to the few other cops in there enjoying their food or coffee. They all saw Silver standing with her and began to shuffle out without protest.

"Rita, what the fuck is going on?" he said in an angry hushed tone.

"I'm so sorry to blindside you like this, Cliff, but I knew that if I told you, you might have tried to protect her, and that wouldn't be a good look right now."

"I understand all of that, but I need you to tell me why you just had my assistant dragged to an interrogation room."

"Our witness reported hearing Bob open his door and refer to the woman he was talking to as Lucy." She paused for him to react, but all he did was stare at her.

"Is that all you have?" he asked when she didn't continue. "I know you don't want to question her for that alone. I know you, Rita, and you wouldn't bring her in unless you had more."

"When did you hire Lucy?"

"Like seven or eight months ago."

"So, around the same time Vicky's neighbor said her niece started coming around."

"Really, Rita. You think she's the mystery woman we've been looking for," Silver rejected the thought. "That doesn't make sense."

"He also said that her niece was about five foot six, thin, and blonde. Sound familiar?" she asked rhetorically. "The night you saw Richard Lindsey with that woman, where was Lucy?"

Silver pulled out a chair and sat down. "I sent her home."

"How long after you sent her home did the woman show up?" Silver's silence answered her question. "So, it was enough time for her to change and put on a disguise. You ever stop to think that maybe the disguise was for you and not Lindsey?

You mentioned that she always kept her back to the window, almost as if she knew you were there. The only person that knew you were there was Lucy."

"Ok, fine, let's say that her and Vicky have been plotting against me, wouldn't this plan work without her becoming my assistant? Vicky could've still come to me as a client, and Lucy could have still been used to honeytrap Lindsey without me ever having to know her. So why risk me possibly recognizing her?"

"That's something I've thought about too. Does Lucy know the combination to your gun safe?" Silver dropped his head, giving her his answer. "I think she came to work for you to figure out the best way to frame you. Gaining access to your gun linked you forensically, and just think about Vicky's role. Knowing you were underwater financially meant that they knew exactly how to get you to take the case without asking too many questions, and that's how they placed you at the scene."

When Rita mentioned the money Vicky had given him, a thought that had been nagging Silver came back to mind. He stood from his seat and paced back and forth in front of Rita, rubbing the hair on his chin.

"What's wrong?" she asked when she grew tired of waiting for him to say what was on his mind.

"Something about the day I met Vicky has been bothering me, and I couldn't quite put my finger on what until just now."

"Ok, what is it?"

"When she paid, she gave me exactly two thousand dollars upfront. She just pulled it out of her bag. She didn't have to count it or anything." Rita looked at him as if she didn't know what he was getting at. "I've never charged someone two thousand upfront, so how did she know to bring that much?" Rita's eyes widened when she finally realized what he was saying. "Lucy set that price."

The room went silent while Silver came to terms with the

fact that Lucy was a very good suspect. Everything Rita laid out for him was completely accurate, and he didn't know how he couldn't see it before. Lucy's proximity and access to him would've been perfect for Vicky to execute her plan. Still, before Silver would believe Lucy was complicit in that plan, Rita would have to prove it beyond a reasonable doubt.

"You were right to bring her down here," he said. "And I trust that you won't settle for anything less than concrete proof that she's involved, so I won't get in the way of you doing your job."

"Thank you," said Rita sincerely.

"But I also trust Lucy, so in my eyes, she's innocent until proven guilty."

"That's fair, and I promise you, Cliff, I'll make sure she is treated fairly."

He walked over to her, wrapped his arms around her, and gave her a kiss. "I know you will," he said.

Rita buried her face into his chest as she could feel the weight lift from her shoulders. There had been a pit in her gut from the moment she heard that witness say Lucy's name. She was so worried that calling her down for questioning would ruin their relationship, so hearing him say she had his trust and feeling his embrace meant the world to her. With each second they stood holding each other, the rest of the world began to melt away. They both would have given anything to be back in her living room, and for a moment, they were transported there, but they were quickly snapped back to reality when they heard Javier clear his throat.

Quickly, they released each other and put some distance between them. "You need something, Estrada?" asked Rita to deflect attention from him catching them.

"Umm, Ford wants to talk to you," he responded.

"Ok, I'll be there in a second," she said.

"No, not you. He wants to talk to Silver."

"Oh fuck," said Silver. "Do I get my last meal first?"

"Just hear him out," said Rita. "He just might surprise you."

"Well, I guess we're going to find out." Silver walked out of the breakroom to go to Ford's office.

Javier and Rita still stood there awkwardly, avoiding eye contact with each other after what he had just interrupted. He opened his mouth to speak but thought better of it when Rita gave him a look that suggested it would be better for his life expectancy if he stayed quiet.

"I'm just going to go back to my desk," he said before quickly exiting the room.

"I think that's an excellent idea," she shouted after him.

Silver approached Ford's office, where he could see the captain working diligently on a pile of paperwork. Silver had been dreading this moment, being locked inside Ford's fishbowl of an office, but knew that it had to happen at some point. He walked up to Ford's open door, gritted his teeth, and knocked on the window.

"You wanted to see me, Captain?"

Ford looked up from his work and removed his glasses. "Yes, shut the door and have a seat."

Silver stepped into the office and closed the door behind him. He sat in one of the two seats that were across the desk from Ford and waited for what undoubtedly would be an uncomfortable conversation to start. Ford leaned back in his office chair and stared at Silver as if he were trying to calculate something in his head.

"So," he started, "Kaye explained to me everything you two found out, and I have to admit, there's a chance you're innocent on this one."

"Gee, thanks," Silver responded sarcastically. "Pretty sure I could've told you that myself."

"Then why didn't you? Why have you been hiding?"

"If I thought for a moment you would've actually listened, I would've come in immediately."

"I think I deserve a little more credit than that. I know

everyone here thinks I'm just a bureaucrat, but I'm capable of interpreting evidence. What you had to say would've been heard fairly."

"You mean like you heard me when it came to William Hargrave?" Ford sat up in his seat to respond, but Silver wasn't done. "You not only didn't have my back while my career was being snatched from me, but you also helped it along. Please tell me, in what world would I trust you with my life being on the line?"

"Can you blame me? In both situations, everything points directly at you."

"Well, if you were a cop and not just a bureaucrat, you would know that sometimes the evidence doesn't tell the entire story."

"Don't give me that shit," Ford shouted, drawing eyes from the bullpen. "There's a pretty good chance that the bullets that killed Richard Lindsey came from your gun, and when it came to William fucking Hargrave, you could not have acted more guilty if you tried. You claim I didn't have your back, but I'm the reason you were allowed to retire and weren't fired for coming into work drunk."

"If I'm guilty of anything, it's not trusting my gut when it came to William," Silver shouted back at him. "I knew something was off, but the evidence was clear, so I didn't question it. Because of that, a man ended up dead. What you saw wasn't a guilty conscience because I planted evidence. It was the weight of feeling like I had failed him. A weight that I have been carrying since it happened."

Ford's office became silent except for the heavy breathing coming from the two of them after their shouting match. A shouting match that evolved into a staring contest, which Silver was determined to win. Up until this point, Silver was satisfied with letting Ford believe whatever he wanted when it came to the William Hargrave case, but he had finally reached his breaking point. Ford could either believe him or not, but he would no longer sit back and not defend his character. This time Ford would blink first, and that's exactly what happened.

"You really didn't plant that evidence?" asked Ford through his glare.

"No," said Silver, still glaring right back at him.

Ford's face softened, and he returned to his relaxed position in his chair. "Then why are you blaming yourself for what happened to him?"

Silver stood from his seat and faced the bullpen. He placed his face in the palms of his hands and slowly dragged them from his temple to his chin before taking a deep breath and turning to answer Ford's question. "I never took wearing that badge lightly. My job was to be the voice of the voiceless. William was this poor lonely man who everyone assumed was some kind of perv because he befriended a sweet young lady. He didn't have a voice because we couldn't fathom how someone like him could possibly connect with someone like her, and in the meantime, Janet's family was denied justice. Truth is, I blame the city for taking my badge from me, but I'm not sure if I would've been able to come back from that."

There it was, the truth that Silver had been denying since he was forced to leave the department. After William died, he couldn't face himself as a cop. He no longer trusted his instincts, and he climbed into a bottle to cope. Silver will never forget the day he showed up to work drunk, the day that Ford mentioned earlier. Silver was sent home immediately, and when he sobered up, he never felt lower. He actually got drunk, strapped a gun to himself, and went to work. His job was to protect and serve; he had become a danger to the citizens he had sworn an oath to protect. He had contemplated leaving the force himself, but the allegations started and gave him an easy way out. Easier than admitting that he didn't feel capable of doing the job anymore.

"Silver," said Ford gently. For a moment, Silver forgot he was still there. "I believe you."

Silver could feel the relief spread through his body. "Thank you, sir."

"We can't change the past, so let's just move forward." Ford walked around his desk to where Silver was standing and held out his hand. Silver looked down at Ford's hand and then up into his eyes and could tell that he was being sincere, so he accepted the olive branch and shook on it. Their handshake was interrupted by a knock on the door. They both looked up to see it was Rita.

"Come in," said Ford.

"I thought I was coming in to make sure you two hadn't killed each other, but I see it looks like you've made up," she said.

"We're on the same page for now," said Silver.

"Speaking of being on the same page," said Ford. "Where's your gun?"

Rita's eyes shot over to Silver, but he was prepared for this. "You know what. Now that you mention it, I haven't seen that damn thing in forever. I keep a gun safe in my office. I could run and go grab it if you need me to."

"That's funny because I happen to know for a fact that your gun safe is empty," said Ford, playing along with Silver's game.

"You've been in my safe?" asked Silver, pretending he didn't know that it was in that very building. "Well, I would ask my assistant if she knows where it is, but she's in an interrogation room at the moment."

"Just do me a favor and make sure it doesn't stay lost for too long," said Ford. "Wouldn't want it to fall into the wrong hands now, would we?"

"You're absolutely right, sir. Rita, how about you and I put together a plan to find my gun?"

"Uh ... sure," said Rita as Silver grabbed her hand and led her out of the captain's office. Ford shook his head and chuckled as he returned to his seat to get back to work.

"So, where is your gun?" asked Rita back at her desk.

"I didn't know exactly what I was walking into, so I stashed it at Sean's."

"I guess that was a good idea, although you had to know that I wasn't leading you into a trap."

"I mean, technically, you were. It just happened to be a trap for Lucy and not me."

"Fair enough."

"Speaking of Lucy, when are we going to talk to her?"

"There is no 'we.' Estrada and I will talk to her. You can watch from the observation room."

"Oh, come on, Rita, you don't think I can handle this?"

"No, I'm saying you don't have to." She put her hand on his arm. "No one should have to question a friend like they're a criminal. You're lucky I'm even letting you watch, and that's only because I know you will whether I want you to or not."

"I guess you're right," Silver conceded.

"Don't worry, Cliff. We're going to get to the bottom of this, and we're going to find out what role she plays in this."

"If she plays a role at all," Silver added.

"Another reason you can't be in the room. You're biased." She snatched up a file from her desk. "Hey Estrada, you ready?"

Javier jumped up from his seat. "Right behind you, partner."

"Never thought I'd see that day that you would choose the rookie over me," said Silver as Javier made his way over to them.

The three left the bullpen and went down the hall to the interrogation rooms. Before heading in, they all slid into the observation room, where they could observe Lucy through the two-way mirror. She was sitting at the table, fiddling with a loose thread that hung from her sweatshirt. Occasionally she would look at her reflection in the mirror, something they often saw with suspects who weren't used to being in the box. It was apparent from looking at her that she was a nervous wreck, but were those nerves because she was innocent and scared or because she hadn't thought she would get caught? After a moment of watching her, it was time for Rita to get the answer to that question.

"Let's get to it, Estrada," she said, and the two left Silver standing there alone.

As the door opened, he kept his eyes trained on Lucy, and they made their way inside. Javier walked in and leaned against the two-way mirror with his arms crossed. Rita pulled out a chair across from Lucy, slapped the file she carried on the table, and took a seat.

"Lucy," said Rita when she was seated and comfortable. "I think it's about time we talked."

CHAPTER 18

The only sound that could be heard from the interrogation room was the ticking from the clock hanging on the wall. Rita stared intently at Lucy while Lucy looked everywhere but back at her. It had only been about five minutes since Rita took her seat, but the moment's intensity made it feel like hours. Rita wanted to play on Lucy's uneasiness at that moment, using the silence to make her even more uncomfortable. It seemed to Silver that it was working. Lucy kept shifting in her seat as if she literally could not get comfortable. That was only made worse when she finally looked back at Rita for the first time and was met by Rita's steely gaze. She quickly looked away and over to Javier, who was still standing against the mirror with his arms folded. When she was met with the same judgment and disapproval from him, her eyes quickly darted to the mirror. If Silver didn't know any better, he would've sworn she knew he was standing there watching. Her eyes were begging for him to come save her, but there was nothing he could do. For that moment, she belonged to Rita.

Her eyes went to the door next, but when Silver didn't come crashing through, her eyes fell to her lap. Her shoulders slumped, and she sunk even lower into her seat, giving the overall appearance of defeat. Then, after a moment, she picked her head up and cleared her hair from her face. She took a deep breath to summon up whatever nerve she had left and looked Rita in the eye.

"Why the fuck am I in here, Rita?" she asked.

"You can call me Detective Kaye, and I'll be the one asking the questions here."

Lucy folded her arms and sat back in her seat in a show of defiance. "Then ask your fucking question. I have nothing to hide."

Without breaking her stare, Rita made a show of slowly opening the file she had in front of her and silently read through it very slowly. There wasn't much in it, but Lucy didn't know that, so she put Brad's statement on top and added some pointless papers under it to add to the thickness of the file and to make Lucy believe she had piles of evidence on her. Also, she wanted to make the point that she would start questioning Lucy when she was good and ready. They were moving on her time, not Lucy's.

After a couple of minutes, Rita closed the file and folded her hands on top of it. "How long have you known Vicky Hargrave?"

"And who the fuck said that I knew her?"

Rita leaned forward toward Lucy and talked so low it was almost a whisper. "Usually, in this room, I don't repeat myself, but as a courtesy to Cliff, I'll make this one exception. I don't answer questions; I ask them. So, I'm going to ask again, and this time you're going to show some fucking respect, watch your fucking mouth when you speak to me, and answer the fucking question." Silver could see the nerve that Lucy had mustered up leave her body. "How do you know Vicky Hargrave?"

"I don't," Lucy responded sheepishly.

"How did you know Richard Lindsey?"

"I technically didn't know him. We tailed him for a client, which I'm sure you already knew."

"Have you ever been inside Richard Lindsey's apartment?"

"I've been inside the building but not specifically in his apartment." Lucy was being careful not to draw any more of Rita's ire.

"We found a set of prints inside Mr. Lindsey's apartment that we haven't found a match for. Any chance they belong to you?"

"No way!" Lucy slightly raised her voice and sat up in her seat but calmed down when she drew a stern look from Rita.

Rita took a moment to look into Lucy's eyes to see if there was any hint of deception, then she looked at Javier and nodded. Then, without speaking, he reached into his back pocket and pulled out a pair of gloves and an evidence bag. He put the gloves on as he walked to the table and grabbed the water bottle that Lucy had been drinking out of while she waited. Lucy watched nervously as Javier put the bottle into the bag and cracked the door open. A uniformed officer was standing there, to whom Javier handed the bag before closing the door again, then he went back to lean against the mirror again with his arms folded.

"Do you want to stick with the story that you've never been inside of his apartment?" asked Rita. Lucy looked wary but still nodded her head yes. "Interesting. You're either too stupid to know that this is the time to be honest, or you truly believe that you didn't leave your prints in his apartment."

"There's a third option," Lucy spat back at her.

"Oh yeah?" Rita feigned confusion. "And what would that be?"

"That I was never in the apartment at all."

Rita pretended to think about that option. "Nah, I'm not seeing it, but I guess we'll find out, won't we?"

It had been a while since the last time Silver had gotten the chance to watch Rita during an interrogation. She was always a natural. She had this way of being intimidating without getting in a suspect's face, and the way she could control a room was second to none. How she stripped Lucy of her spirit and defiance without even raising her voice was the perfect example of her skill. The key during an interrogation was to get answers and keep the suspect from lawyering up. You wanted to lock your suspect in with yes or no answers to questions that could be fact-checked. Once Lucy said that she was never in Richard's apartment, that gave Rita something she could check, which is why she tricked Lucy into giving them her prints. If the prints matched, they'd have the leverage to question her about Richard's actual murder. Silver also would've bet that Rita planned on getting Lucy's saliva from the bottle to run her DNA and check against what was found on that condom.

"How about we move on from Mr. Lindsey, and you tell me how well you know Robert Foster." Rita was ready to play her trump card.

"I don't know who that is," responded Lucy.

"You might know him as Bob the Doorman."

"I don't know Bob."

"So, you've never talked to Bob?"

"Yeah, I've talked to him."

"But you just said you didn't know him."

"I mean ... I didn't."

"You didn't know him, but you talked to him? I'm confused, Lucy. Which one is it?"

"You already know when and why I talked to him, Detective."

"Humor me, Lucy. What interactions did you have with Robert Foster?"

"My boss, who happens to be your boyfriend"—Rita smirked but didn't fall for Lucy's bait—"had me bribe Bob to let us know if Richard had any female visitors."

"Where did you approach him with this offer?"

"At Richard Lindsey's building."

"You never saw Bob anywhere but that building?"

"No."

"Lucy, we won't get anywhere if you're going to lie to me."

"I'm not lying," argued Lucy. Rita opened the file again, pulled out a sheet of paper, and slid it across the table to Lucy. "What's this?"

"That, Lucy, is a witness statement from one of Mr. Foster's neighbors stating that he heard Mr. Foster talking to a woman moments before his death. Why don't you give it a read for me."

Lucy looked down at the statement and began reading. Her eyes bulged when she got to the part naming her as the woman, and she became very animated.

"He's fucking lying," she shouted.

"Lucy, calm down."

"No." Lucy shot up from her seat, causing her chair to fall to the ground. "I don't know what the fuck is going on, but this is a fucking lie."

When she stood from the table, Javier uncrossed his arms and stopped leaning against the mirror, preparing for the possibility that Lucy may get aggressive, but Rita didn't budge.

"Lucy, sit down," Rita said calmly.

"No! I don't know what's happening, but I had nothing to do with this. Someone is setting me up just like they set up Cliff."

"Why would someone do that, Lucy?" Lucy's eyes began to dart around the room as if she were searching for an answer to Rita's question. "How about I tell you what I know, and you tell me what conclusion you would draw? We spoke to one of Vicky's neighbors, who told us about a woman claiming to be Vicky's niece. A woman who is about your height, your build, and your hair color. This woman started coming around the same time you began working for Cliff. I know that you met Vicky before Cliff. You were speaking to her in his office before he arrived; coincidentally, she was walking around with exactly two thousand dollars cash in her purse. An amount of money that Cliff never charges and that you, in fact, set. So, how would Vicky know the amount of money she would need? The night of his death, Richard was seen, by your boss, with a woman who again matches your height and build but wore a wig to conceal her true hair color." Rita opened the file again and pulled out the pictures that Silver had taken the night of Richard's murder. "Look at these pictures, Lucy."

"I've seen them," Lucy said softly.

"Did you notice how the woman only showed her back to the window in all of these pictures? Almost as if she knew that someone was across the street watching. Someone who could've quickly identified her even with that wig on. Robert Foster was the only other person to see that woman's face that night. A man that your boss sent you to talk to, but according to you, you never made it because you went on a lunch date. A lunch date at a place that I sent Estrada to with your picture, and no one there recognized you. Your whereabouts from the time after Cliff sent you to talk to him to when we found his body can't be substantiated. And on top of all that, we have a witness who reports hearing Bob call a woman your name moments before he died. Coincidence? Ask your boss how we feel about coincidences when it comes to murder cases. So just to recap, only two people saw this woman's face in that building the night of Richard Lindsey's murder, and both of them are dead. So far, the only person involved in the case with no alibi for both murders and who has a connection to all the major players involved is you, Lucy. So please tell me, what conclusion would you draw?"

Lucy's eyes went back and forth from Rita to Javier, almost as if she were trying to figure out the best way to take them out and get out of there, but suddenly the strangest thing happened. All of the fear and cowering left Lucy's body. All emotion left her face, and she calmly picked up her chair and placed it back at the table. She took a seat, looked Rita dead in her eyes, and smirked.

"You want to know what I think, Detective Kaye? I think that everything you have is circumstantial. You have an eye-witness that heard my name but didn't see my face. Those prints you found in the apartment won't match mine, and like you said, your best two witnesses are dead. So, what I know is that you don't have shit. What I know is that I want my lawyer."

Silver couldn't believe what he had just witnessed. A switch was flipped, and the Lucy he knew was gone. The person who remained appeared to be cold and calculating, and they had no idea what she was capable of. Rita was also floored by Lucy's transformation, but she couldn't let that show. She smirked back at Lucy, collected Brad's statement from the table, and put it back into the file.

"We'll get you that lawyer right away, Ms. Beckett." Rita stood from the table and motioned to Javier that they were leaving. Javier opened the door for her to walk out, but before she did, Rita had one last thing she wanted to say to Lucy. "Nice to finally meet you."

They closed the door, and Rita instructed the nearest officer to escort Lucy to a holding cell. She was about to check on Silver when he came rushing out of the observation room.

"What the fuck just happened?" he said in an angry hushed tone.

"Yeah, that was freaky," said Javier. "It's like she has multiple personalities."

"She's definitely been hiding her true colors," Rita chimed in. "One thing's for sure; we know that she's a part of whatever is going on."

Silver was listening to them talk, but his eyes were staring toward the interrogation room as the officer emerged with

Lucy. She looked at him and gave him a wicked smile. "Let me talk to her," he said.

"No, Cliff." Rita stepped between him and the room.

"Rita, she knows something, and I know I can get it out of her."

"And why is that, Cliff? Because you know her so well?" Silver rolled his eyes at what she was implying. "Face it; we have no idea who she really is."

"So what? We just sit around and do nothing?" Silver had finally reached the end of his patience. "She's the only lead we have, and if we don't make a move soon, Vicky will be in the wind."

"We have no incentive to make her talk," said Javier. "She's right when she says that all of our evidence is circumstantial, and she probably knows that if she waits us out, she'll walk. Even if she plans on telling us everything, she'll want a deal in place first. Either way, our hands are tied until her lawyer gets here and we find out her plan."

Maybe it was the betrayal he was feeling, but Silver couldn't hear anything they were saying. His mind couldn't think past talking his way into being face-to-face with her. He honestly didn't even want to question her about the case. He shared the most important things in his life with her, and it was all so that she could turn around and use it against him. How could he be so stupid? He combed through his memories of Lucy, searching for any hint that she had a hidden agenda. Were his instincts really that bad now?

"Cliff, you can't blame yourself," said Rita, almost as if she were in his head.

"Who else should I blame? She was around my kid, Rita. I have to know what her plan was."

"And we will. We've made it this far, haven't we?" Rita asked. Silver nodded his head. "And you don't honestly think I plan on stopping here, do you?"

"No, I don't."

"So please don't lose your patience now. I know it sucks to feel like you just lost someone you trust, but you still have people in your corner."

"Yeah, bro," said Javier. "We got you."

Silver was touched by their show of support, but he couldn't help but feel like the deck was stacked against him. Just when he thought he had a firm grasp on the situation, he was hit with another bomb. At this point, he was just waiting for the other shoe to drop, which wasn't a feeling he was comfortable with. However, he was also uncomfortable with giving up, so at that moment, he decided to follow Rita's lead and keep pushing forward.

"Ok, fine. So what's our next move?" said Silver.

"Our next move is to get her lawyer up here for her," said Rita as she made a beeline toward her desk. "The sooner we get her a lawyer, the sooner we'll know her intentions."

She reached her desk and picked up the phone to make the call but before she could dial the number someone called her name.

"Yes, Officer McGuire?" she asked when she identified who it was.

"There's a woman here to speak with the lead detective on the Lindsey case. Says she has some information you may be interested in."

Rita returned the phone to the receiver. "Where is she?"

"She's standing over near the elevators. You want me to send her over?"

"Yes, please."

Officer McGuire made his way back to the elevators while they watched in anticipation of who this mystery witness was. They could see him talking to a young lady and pointing in their direction. Rita raised her hand to identify herself as the one he was pointing to and could see the young woman thank him before beginning to walk their way. She was white with bright red hair. She stood about five foot six and was very beautiful. She walked cautiously and looked over her shoulder as if she believed someone was watching her. Even the worst detective could spot a troubled woman looking for protection.

"Are you Detective Kaye?" she asked when she reached them.

"Yes, and you are?" Rita responded.

The woman nervously scanned the room again. "Do I have to give my name?"

"It would be appreciated."

"Amy," she whispered.

"Last name?" Rita prodded.

"Schultz." She looked around again to make sure no one else heard. "It's Amy Schultz, ok."

"Is someone after you, Ms. Schultz? Is that why you're here?"

"Yes ... I mean, no ... I don't know. I think so."

"Ok. Let's start over. Officer McGuire says you know something about the Richard Lindsey murder. Do you know something you think will make someone come after you?"

"Yes! That's it."

"Ok," said Rita. "What is it that you know?"

"Well, I saw that he was killed, and then I saw that the doorman to his building was killed," she rambled. "And now I'm freaking out because I think I'm next."

"Why would you be next?" asked Silver.

"Because ... I was with Richard Lindsey the night he died."

CHAPTER 19

Silver gently set the coffee Amy had requested in front of her, and she picked it up with trembling hands. They had decided to move her to a private room, where she would feel less paranoid about the wrong person hearing their conversation. The precinct had a room that was perfect for the situation, one that was often used to speak with witnesses. It had the privacy of an interrogation room without the intimidation, which was vital for the situation. They wanted her to feel safe and secure enough to speak freely about her involvement in this case. Rita thought it might've been too daunting for three of them to interview her, so she decided Javier would wait outside. She also knew that there was no way Silver would miss out on this conversation, and unlike the interrogation room, there was no two-way mirror.

Silver took his seat next to Rita, and the two of them waited while Amy got a couple of sips of coffee into her system. They were careful not to make her feel rushed or pressured. They knew that she likely held a critical piece of information and didn't want to do anything that would make her clam up. It felt as if the sound of her slurping her coffee echoed as their anticipation grew. Finally, she sat the mug back on the table. Signaling that she was ready to begin.

"Amy, do you mind if I record this conversation?" asked Rita. Amy looked hesitant to agree. "If I record you now, that would mean we don't have to keep bringing you in for you to tell this story over and over again."

"I guess it's fine," Amy said reluctantly.

Rita unlocked her phone and went to her recorder app. She pressed play and began the interview. "This is Detective Rita Kaye and consultant Clifford Silver interviewing Amy Schultz about the night of Richard Lindsey's murder," Rita announced for the recording. "Amy, how did you know Richard?"

"Nothing I say here will get me arrested, right? Even if I admit to some not-so-legal activities?" asked Amy.

"As long as you weren't directly involved in his killing, I can assure you that I won't try to jam you up for anything else."

"Ok, good, because I'm an escort."

"Was Richard paying you to visit him that night?" asked Silver.

"No ... well, I was being paid, just not by Richard."

Silver and Rita exchanged confused looks. "Then who was paying you?" asked Rita.

"His wife, Sara."

Silver could feel his heart begin to race. "Why did Sara pay you to sleep with her husband?" he asked.

"She's this rich older lady, and he was this young guy who just married her for her money." Her story sounded all too familiar to Silver. "She pretty much wanted to honeytrap him while someone was waiting with a camera to get the proof. Normally I try not to get in the middle of marital disputes, but I felt sorry for this lady. That asshole was cheating on her and was going to divorce her and take her hard-earned money. I felt I owed it to her as a woman to help her out."

"If she knew he was cheating, why did she need you to honeytrap him?" Rita interrupted. "Couldn't she have just waited until she caught him?"

"She gave me five grand, so I didn't ask or care."

"Five grand just to sleep with him?" asked Silver. Rita couldn't tell if that was shock in his voice or irritation that she got more money than he did.

"I had to do a little more than sleep with him."

"What did you have to do?" asked Rita.

"Obviously, I couldn't just show up at his door, so we had to arrange for me to meet him somewhere and have him invite me to his place."

"Where did you meet him?"

"At his gym. He worked out every morning before he went to work."

"Where was his gym located?" asked Silver. Of course, he already knew the answer, but it was important for them to ask verifiable questions. If she could answer those corrections correctly, it would add some authenticity to her story.

"It was some fancy place on State," she said. Rita glanced at Silver, and he nodded his head to confirm that was true. "I never knew the exact address because I was driven there whenever I went."

"Did you spend a lot of time with Sara?" asked Rita.

"Yeah, her and her niece, Tracy."

Rita was prepared for her to mention the mysterious Tracy. She had a folder containing two photos, and she took them out and placed them on the table in front of Amy. "Are these the people you knew as Sara and Tracy?"

"Yep, that's them," Amy just confirmed one of Rita's suspicions. One photo obviously was of Vicky, and the other was Lucy. "Her niece was usually there for emotional support, but between you and me, it was something off about that girl."

"Did you ever see where Sara lived?" asked Rita. "We haven't been able to get in touch with her."

"No, but I still have her number." She unlocked her phone and scrolled through her contacts. "Here it is."

Rita looked at the number and wrote it down but knew it was the same number she had gotten from Silver, which was disconnected. "What happened the night he was killed?" asked Rita.

"Sara had me text him, asking if I could come over. Of course, he said yeah, so she picked me up and took me to his apartment. Tracy was already there waiting for us when we got there, and they told me that someone was across the street with a camera to get the evidence they needed for the divorce. I figured this would be the case, so I brought a disguise with me. I didn't like the idea of some random guy having photos of me having sex." Silver looked away from Amy, hoping she wouldn't be able to tell that her naked photos were saved on his laptop. "They also told me to leave his door unlocked when I left. Sara wanted to confront him, but it looks like I just helped her kill him." Amy's head dropped, and tears started to fall into her lap. Silver grabbed a box of tissues and held it out for her. She thanked him as she took one and wiped her face. "You have to believe me; I never would have helped her if I had known that was her plan. No amount of money is worth someone's life. And then I heard that the doorman was dead. I don't know if it's related, but what if someone is killing everyone who was there that night? That makes me a target, right?"

Rita knew that Bob's murder was to tie up loose ends, and with Amy's part in all of this, she definitely qualified as a loose end, but the last thing she wanted to do was scare the poor girl. "We don't know exactly why Bob was killed, so we can't say for sure if the two are related. Have you heard from Sara or Tracy since that night?"

"No, when I came down from his apartment, they paid me the rest of my money, then Tracy took me home."

"Just Tracy? Sara wasn't with you two?" asked Silver.

"Yeah, it was just Tracy. Sara was on her way upstairs to confront Richard."

"Have you noticed anyone suspicious hanging around you? Do you have the feeling that you're being followed?" asked Rita.

"No, not that I noticed."

"Odds are that Bob's murder was an isolated incident and had nothing to do with Richard, but I understand your concern," said Rita. "We're going to set you up with police protection for the time being while we work on sorting everything out."

Rita stood from her chair, and Amy jumped up and gave her a bear hug. "Thank you so much, Detective."

Rita uncomfortably patted her on the back before wiggling herself loose from Amy's embrace. "You're welcome, Ms. Schultz. You can stay in here while Mr. Silver and I set up that protection for you."

"Ok."

"Here's my card. If you remember anything else, please call me."

Amy took Rita's card. "I sure will, Detective."

Silver and Rita left Amy alone in the room. She looked a lot more relaxed than when she first came to them, but after what they experienced with Lucy, they weren't going to just believe her story. Rita put an officer on the door, and they walked back to her desk.

"What are you thinking?" she asked Silver.

"I'm thinking she lowballed me with that two thousand."

"Cliff, be serious."

"I am being serious. She got five grand, and I did way more work than her, and I had to pay Lucy out of what I got."

"Cliff!"

"Alright, alright. I think that it feels like she was being honest with us, but with how this case has gone, we can't just buy everything she's saying."

"I'm right with you. On one hand, it sounds like Vicky pulled the trigger on Richard herself, and she put another nail in Lucy's coffin, but on the other hand, nothing she told us puts us closer to knowing Vicky's current whereabouts."

"We have to find her fast. Pretty soon, she will find out I'm off the hook for this, and she'll disappear," said Silver.

"What's stopping her from disappearing after our encounter with her this morning?" asked Rita.

"No way she's left already."

"What makes you so sure?"

"The same reason I'm sure she actually did kill Richard herself. Revenge is always best up close and personal. She still believes that I'm the prime suspect, and there's no way she'll want to watch my downfall from a distance."

"Let's hope you're right," said Rita as they reached her desk. "Estrada, can you come here?"

Javier quickly made his way over to them. "I thought you guys would never come out of there."

"She had a lot to say. I'll get you caught up on everything, but first, can you have an officer drive her home? Also, get in touch with her local precinct and arrange a unit to sit on her place. Tell them she's a witness, and there's a chance her life may be in danger."

"Ok, will do, but before I do, those prints you took at Silver's office finally came back while you were talking to her."

"Do they have something?" Silver asked anxiously.

"They found three sets of prints. Yours and two others that are not in the system. When we got Lucy's water bottle to them, they matched it to one of the unidentified sets of prints. They still don't know who the last set belongs to, but they could match it to a print they lifted at Richard Lindsey's apartment."

Silver let out an audible sigh of relief. If those prints belonged to Vicky Hargrave, that could be the piece of evidence that exonerated him. Rita was thinking along the same lines but knew there was still work to be done.

"Based on what Amy just told us, chances are Vicky pulled the trigger on Lindsey herself, and if that's her print, we'll be able to place her in his apartment. That gives us motive and opportunity, but we still can't link her to the murder weapon," said Rita. "Also, there's the issue of having no clue where she is."

"We have to break Lucy, or Tracy, or whatever the fuck her name is," said Silver. "No way she worked that closely with Vicky and doesn't know where she's been hiding."

"Maybe we should check her place," Javier suggested.

"We can, but I doubt she would put her at her own place," said Silver. "She wouldn't want to run the risk of me running into her there."

"I thought you said that you've never been to her place," said Rita with a raised brow.

"I haven't," Silver stammered. "I'm her boss, and it would've been extremely unprofessional for me to go to her place."

"Yeah, sure," said Rita sarcastically.

"I think you're in trouble, bro," Javier whispered to Silver.

"Don't you have to set up the protection for Amy," Silver said back to him, hoping to make him go away.

"Actually, I really should get on that. Did you get an address from her?"

"No," said Rita. "She's still waiting in the interview room."

Javier left to get the information he needed from Amy, leaving Silver awkwardly standing near Rita's desk while she pretended to ignore him. He grabbed a chair from an empty desk near hers and rolled it over to where she was sitting. Rita watched him from the corner of her eye while he made a show of wheeling the chair close enough to where its arm was touching the arm of hers. Finally, he sat down and stared at the side of her face and waited for her reaction. When he didn't get one, he tapped her on the shoulder.

"What?" she asked without turning towards him.

"You are so beautiful," he said with a smile.

"Yeah, I know," she responded flatly, which wiped the smile from his face.

"You don't think I slept with her, do you?"

"I didn't think you'd been to her place, but obviously, I was wrong about that so ..."

"No, you were right about that. I've never been to her place. I have no idea where she lives."

Rita finally turned to him with a giant grin on her face. "I know. I just like messing with you."

"That's not funny."

"It's a little funny. But I am surprised that you've never been to her place. I thought you two were close."

"Yeah, we were really close." He pushed his seat away from her. For a moment, he had forgotten the betrayal.

"I'm sorry, Cliff," she said after she realized what she had said. "I didn't mean to rub it in your face."

"It's ok. I know you didn't."

"How are you feeling about everything?"

"I'm angry, but I have to put that in the back of my mind for now."

"Sounds like a hard thing to do."

"What's the alternative?"

"We could talk about it." She moved her chair to close the distance he had created. "Right now, we're playing a bit of a waiting game. Maybe it would make you feel better to talk about it."

Silver thought about that idea for a second before it all came pouring out of him. "Just when I felt like I was back on solid ground, I had the rug pulled from under me again. She was a little sister to me. I can't believe none of it was real."

"Who's to say that none of it was real?"

"How do you grow to care for someone you're actively betraying?" Rita couldn't answer that question. "I genuinely cared for her, and I don't even know her real name. I feel like such an idiot."

"She came to you at a vulnerable time."

"Giving her the access she had put everyone I love at risk.

Being vulnerable just doesn't feel like a good enough excuse."

"I didn't say it was an excuse, but it's definitely an explanation. There's no way you could have possibly known that hiring her would turn out this way, and who wouldn't grow close to someone they see literally every day? I know you too well to tell you not to beat yourself up over it, so go ahead and have yourself a moment. Just make sure you move on. Don't turn her into another William Hargrave and drag yourself back down the hole you've worked so hard to crawl out."

Silver absorbed every word of Rita's speech and smiled. "You're amazing. You know that?"

"Yes, I do, but it's still nice to be told every once in a while."

"I'll keep that in mind," he said with a grin that made Rita blush. "You know, with Vicky still on the loose, it may not be a good idea for me to go home just yet."

"Oh, is that right?"

"Yeah, I think it might be a good idea to have someone watching my back tonight."

"I'm assuming you have someone in mind," she said, playing along with the flirty game he started.

"As a matter of fact, I do."

"Who did you have in mind?" She leaned in close to him.

He also leaned in to meet her halfway. They were so close their lips were almost touching. "Do you know if Estrada has a spare room?"

"What?"

Silver pulled back from her. "Do you know if Estrada has a spare room for me to hide out tonight?"

"Are you serious?"

"Fine, I'll just go ask him myself." He stood and took a step as if he was going to actually leave and find Javier, but Rita yanked him back into his seat.

"Stop playing with me," she said as they laughed.

"Just a little payback for earlier."

"Just for that, you're really sleeping on the couch tonight."

She turned her chair around to give him her back.

"Oh, come on, don't be like that." He tried spinning her back around, but she pressed her foot against her desk to stop her momentum. He was still trying when Javier came rushing into the room.

"Kaye!" he shouted, drawing both of their attention.

Rita turned her chair back around. "What is it, Estrada?"

"We just got a hit on the BOLO you put on that car from earlier. The plate was flagged when an officer wrote it a ticket for parking in front of a hydrant."

"That's great. We should—"

"Wait, I'm not done." Javier could barely contain his excitement. "I included Vicky's photo in the BOLO, and since the car was parked in front of a motel, the officer had the idea to show her photo to the guy working the front desk."

"And?" asked Silver.

"He positively identified her. She booked a room there sometime last week, and you'll never guess where the hotel is located."

CHAPTER 20

Silver's hand slapped the dashboard as Rita came to another sudden stop. He usually wouldn't wear a seatbelt when he was on the job, didn't want anything slowing him down if he had to pursue a suspect on foot, but with the way Rita was driving, he thought a seatbelt might be a good idea before it was his forehead that hit the dashboard next.

According to the front desk clerk at the motel, Vicky left earlier today and hadn't returned yet, and he distinctly remembered her toting multiple bags up to her room. Rita sent Javier to stake out the motel and look out for Vicky while she and Silver found a judge to sign a search warrant. Amy's statement was enough probable cause to secure a warrant, but they had to find something that would corroborate her story if they were going to be able to arrest Vicky. The only problem was that they had no clue what they were looking for. Typically a judge won't sign off on a search warrant unless you can name exactly what you want to find. Otherwise, it would look like a fishing expedition. On the warrant, Rita stated that they were looking for the murder weapon as well as any other evidence linking her to Richard Lindsey just to get her foot in the door. She neglected to mention that she knew the murder weapon was currently in Silver's holster since they stopped by Sean's to pick it up.

Rita weaved through another set of cars before making a sharp turn onto the motel's block. She came to a stop and was out of the car before Silver could even get his seatbelt off. She made a beeline for the entrance and could see Javier get out of his car and start walking to meet her there. Finding out Vicky checked into this place might end up being the break they needed, but its location filled Rita with a sense of urgency to put this case to bed. Vicky was gearing up for what they suspected was her end game all along. When Rita reached the door, she looked down the block to where she could see Silver's Mustang sitting right in front of his office building.

"Is she still gone?" Rita asked Javier when he reached her.

"I haven't seen her come back," he responded. "Is that the car you and Silver pursued this morning?"

Rita looked over to where Javier was pointing, and sure enough, it was that black car Vicky had escaped in. "Yeah, that's definitely the car."

"Do you have the warrant?"

Rita held it up for him to see, and Javier opened the door for them to enter when Silver came jogging up to them.

"We going in?" he asked.

"We're going in," said Rita pointing towards herself and Javier. "You're staying out here until we're done."

"Come on, Rita," he protested. "I can't help from out here."

"That's the point, Cliff. You agreed that you would take a backseat."

"I thought we were just saying that for Ford's benefit."

"No," said Rita with an eye roll. "If a defense attorney finds out you were involved in a search for a case where you're technically a victim, everything we find would be thrown out."

"So, I'm a victim now?"

"Come on, Cliff, you know I don't mean it like that."

"No, it's fine," he said, cutting her off. "I won't go in her room, but I think we can agree that it's probably not a good idea for me to sit out here on the curb alone and in the open."

"He's got a point," agreed Javier.

"So, how about I come up with you two, and I'll just wait in the hallway while you do your thing?"

Rita thought for a moment. "Ok fine, but if your ass takes one step into that room, I'll shoot you myself."

"You're the boss," said Silver. "Lead the way."

Rita turned and walked through the door Javier was still holding open, with Silver following closely behind.

Rita walked up to the front desk and held her badge up to the older Middle Eastern man standing behind the counter. "Hi, I'm Detective Rita Kaye, and you've already met Detective Estrada. We need you to let us into the room of the woman we asked you about earlier."

"Like I told your partner here," he responded curtly. "I can't let you into anyone's room without a warrant."

Rita slapped the warrant on the desk and slid it across to him. He picked it up and read it over before reaching under the desk and grabbing a keycard. "Follow me."

He stepped from around the counter and began walking down the hall to their right. They walked to the very end of the hall to the last room on the left. When they reached the room, he started to enter the keycard into the slot before Javier stopped him. He took the card from the clerk, then motioned for him to step to the side of the door, and Silver took it a step further by stepping in front of him.

Rita and Javier stood on opposite sides of the door and moved their jackets out of the way of their holsters. They didn't draw their weapons but wanted to make sure nothing was obstructing them in case they needed to, then Rita knocked.

"This is the Chicago Police," she shouted through the door.

"We have a warrant to search this room. If there is anyone in there, please open the door, or we will let ourselves in." She paused for a moment to give anyone a chance to respond, even though she knew the room was most likely empty. "Ok, we're coming in."

She gave Javier the nod to open the door, and he obliged. It was a tiny room, so one peek was enough to tell that it was, in fact, empty. Javier still went through the trouble of stepping into the bathroom and moving the shower curtain back, just to be certain.

Rita poked her head out of the room. "Keep an eye out for Vicky," she said to Silver.

"I got you," he responded. The front desk clerk was still standing there, trying his hardest to pretend he wasn't trying to get a peek into the room. Silver figured it would be the perfect time to ask him a few questions. "So, you were the one who checked her in?"

"Yes, it was me," he responded without looking in Silver's direction.

"How did she seem to you?"

"Like any other white woman," he said flatly.

"Did she say anything to you?"

He let out an audible sigh to show his annoyance with the questions; then he finally was kind enough to actually look in Silver's direction. "She didn't say much besides the type of room she requested."

"Which was?" Silver didn't care how annoyed this guy was; he was going to answer Silver's questions.

"She wanted a room on the first floor, near an exit, and with a view of the street. Now, is that all?" His attention was off Silver and back into the room before he could get an answer.

"Shouldn't you be watching your desk?" asked Silver in an attempt to get rid of him.

"No, it's fine," he responded dismissively.

"That was your cue to get lost," said Silver as he finally lost his patience. If looks could've killed, Rita would've been slapping her cuffs on this guy, but when his death stare had no effect, he called Silver an asshole under his breath and made his way back up front. Pot meet kettle, Silver thought to himself, but he would gladly be an asshole if it got rid of that jackass.

Silver stood there in the hall, sorting through his thoughts, and something wasn't adding up. Vicky obviously chose this motel because of its proximity to his office, and her room request suggested that she wanted to see who was coming and going and to be able to make a quick exit if necessary. Then she leaves on foot with her car in front of a hydrant, drawing attention to her presence here. On one hand, she was careful and calculating, but on the other hand, it felt like she was begging to get caught.

"Cliff," Silver was still deep in thought when he heard Rita call his name. "You should see this."

He knew it had to be bad for her to want him in there, so he braced himself before stepping in. First thing he noticed was an open suitcase on the floor and a bunch of photos spread across the bed. When he could see what was in the pictures, it made him sick to his stomach. They were surveillance photos of him and Richard Lindsay, and from what he could tell, she had been watching them for months. There were photos of him picking Chrissy up from school. Photos of him talking to Tonya in front of her house. Photos of Rita carrying him out of Sean's bar. And just when he thought that was as bad as it got, he found photos of Chrissy, Tonya, and Rita when he wasn't around. So, she wasn't just stalking him but also the people he cared about most.

"Rita, you need to send someone to keep an eye on T's place for me," he said while picking up a picture of Chrissy playing in their backyard.

"Estrada already put in the call," Rita said softly.

"We have to find her now." He put the photo back with the others and turned to look at Rita, and she could see the worry in his eyes.

"We will," she responded. "And what we found here, along with Amy's statement, should be enough to hold her while we work on getting Lucy to admit that she gave her your gun."

"I found something," said Javier, who was going through another one of Vicky's bags.

"What is it?" asked Rita.

Javier held up a cell phone. "I'm pretty sure it's the cloned version of Silver's phone."

"How can you tell?" asked Silver.

"It's not password protected, and I went through the contacts and found your ex-wife's, Lucy's, and Kaye's numbers in it."

"Bag it," said Rita. "Even if we don't get Lucy to confess about the weapon, that's enough to prove the conspiracy to set you up."

"Does this feel too easy to you?" asked Silver.

"What do you mean?" Rita responded.

"She's been covering her tracks through this entire case, and now she suddenly gets sloppy."

"They always get sloppy, bro," Javier chimed in. "That's how we catch them."

"Yes, they make mistakes, but not like this. You don't suddenly park a car you know we're looking for in front of a fire hydrant right in front of the hotel you're staying at, and if that's what she's been driving, then why is it here, and she isn't?"

"She could've ditched it," Javier offered.

"If she was going to ditch it, she would've done so right after the chase this morning, and that doesn't explain why you would ditch it here, where you've collected all the evidence pointing to your guilt in one convenient location."

"What are you thinking, Cliff?" asked Rita.

"I just don't want us to relax our guard, that's all." He

turned his focus back to the photos on the bed.

Rita could tell that there was something he wasn't saying. "Are you sure that's all that's on your mind?" Silver didn't respond to her question, and she knew he was lost in his head. "Cliff."

"We should get out of here," he said as if he had just snapped out of a trance. "Yeah, we should definitely get out of here."

"Why, bro?"

"We found the evidence we need, so let's sit on the different entrances and wait for her to return. I mean, she has to come back eventually, right?"

Rita stared at him, trying to get a read on what he was up to, but he wouldn't look her way. "You're right, that's a good idea. Estrada, collect these photos, and I want you to watch the front entrance. There's a chance she doesn't know how you look, so she might not see you coming. Silver and I will park right outside this exit. Even if she spots us, we should be able to box her in. Come on, Cliff, let's go get the car." She grabbed Silver's arm and pulled him out of the room before he could respond.

"Jesus, Rita, why are you manhandling me?"

Rita let him go when she was sure Javier couldn't hear them. "You're lying to me."

"Lying about what?"

"You thought of something in there. Now tell me what it was before I beat it out of you."

"You know as much as I do, Rita."

"Cliff," Rita softened her tone. "Please tell me what you're thinking about."

"Ok." Silver could see how concerned she was and wanted to ease her mind. "I'm scared. Seeing Tonya and Chrissy in those pictures fucked my head up."

"I get that, but don't worry. We're going to have someone watching them around the clock until we catch her."

"I know, and I appreciate that, but I think it would make

me feel a lot better if I could just see for myself that they're ok."

"Ok, I'll get a unit over here to stake out the motel with Estrada, and we can head over there."

"That's not necessary. My car is right up the block. I can be there and back before you know it."

"Absolutely not! Are you forgetting that you're a target too? You shouldn't be going anywhere without backup."

"I know, and I promise I'll be careful. Besides, I would feel much better with you here to make sure she doesn't get away this time."

"I don't like the idea of us splitting up, Cliff. I know we both picked up on the fact that her endgame is to kill you."

"Come on, Rita, you know I can take her," he said with a chuckle but stopped when he noticed she wasn't smiling.

"Do you think this is a fucking joke?"

"Of course I don't, Rita."

"Then knock it off and take this seriously. I don't want to lose you, asshole," said Rita. Silver pulled Rita into him and held her until he could feel her body relax, then he started laughing again. "Oh, I know you're not fucking laughing again."

"I'm sorry you're just the second person to call me an asshole in the last ten minutes."

"Then, obviously, it must be true."

Silver released her from his embrace and cupped her face in his hands. "I promise I'm just going to check on them and head right back here."

Before she could protest again, he pulled her face towards him and gave her a sensual kiss. "Now you're playing dirty," she said when their lips parted.

"Does that mean it worked?" he asked with a grin.

"Maybe," she responded with an eye roll. "Just promise me you'll head back here as soon as you can."

"I promise." He gave her another peck on the lips before he started walking towards the exit next to Vicky's room. "Full disclosure," he shouted back at her from the door. "I'm going to stop at my place first and take a quick shower."

He hurried and closed the door before she could yell at him, although he was pretty sure she wasn't going to yell. If he didn't know any better, he could've sworn he saw her reaching for her gun.

Silver parked in front of his apartment building and checked his surroundings. His block was pretty quiet, with no pedestrians or random cars driving past. It had been a while since he was last there, but he recognized all of his neighbors' cars and didn't see any that were unfamiliar. Still, he glanced down the block before he stepped out of the car. He reached under the seat where he kept the keys to his apartment, then quickly made his way to the door and inside. His apartment was on the third floor, and the building had an elevator, but he thought it would be better to take the stairs. He didn't like the idea of stepping off the elevator and into a sudden ambush. The entrance onto his floor from the stairs was at the end of the hall, allowing him to get a complete view of the floor. He lightly jogged up the stairs and took a beat when he made it to his level. He made sure his weapon was ready, then slowly pushed the door open just enough for him to get a good view of the entire hallway. Once he was sure he was alone, he opened the door and then jogged to his apartment, which was a third of the way down the hall. He quickly unlocked and opened the door and just as quickly closed it behind him.

Once inside, he was reminded that his place was tossed when Ford was on the hunt for his gun. It wasn't a large apartment, which was fine for Silver, considering he was hardly there, but with the mess they had made, it felt like it was no bigger than a closet. His couch cushions and pillows were on the floor, and the cabinets in his kitchen were open and emptied. Thankfully he only owned three pots, two bowls, and one plate. He entered his bedroom and saw his bed had been lifted off the rails, and clothes were dumped from their drawers. He thought to himself that he owed an apology to everyone whose homes he had searched back when he was a cop. No way did he have the energy to clean any of this up, so he grabbed a pair of underwear, a T-shirt, and jeans from the mess on the floor, then made his way to his bathroom. He turned on the shower and closed the door.

He decided to play some music while he showered, which is why he didn't hear Vicky unlock his front door. She tiptoed into his apartment and headed straight for his bathroom. She carefully stepped around the mess in his place, making sure not to alert him to her presence. When she reached the bathroom door, she checked her gun to ensure the safety was off. Then all in one motion, she opened the door and shot six rounds into his shower.

CHAPTER 21

Vicky stood there breathing heavily with smoke coming from the barrel of her gun. The shots were deafening, but she could still hear the sound of the shower and the music playing. She still had her gun pointed towards the shower when suddenly it felt heavy to her, so she let her arm drop to her side. Vicky could feel most of the strength leave her body, or maybe it was the relief of her mission being accomplished. Either way, there was one last thing she hoped she would get the chance to do. If she was lucky, none of those bullets would have killed him, and she would get the opportunity to watch him take his last breath. She stepped into the bathroom and up to his shower. She took a deep breath and pulled the curtain to the side but what she saw made her knees buckle. Before she could fully grasp what had happened, she could feel the barrel of Silver's gun press into the back of her head. In her excitement, she didn't notice him crouched on the toilet that was blocked by the door.

"Vicky, drop the gun and put your hands on your head,"

he said to her.

"How did you know?"

"I figured out that you never wanted me to go to prison. You just wanted me to experience what your brother experienced before you killed me."

"Wow, you must think you're so clever," she said sarcastically. "Did you use that cleverness when you framed my brother?"

"I didn't frame your brother. What happened to him was a tragic misunderstanding, and I'm so sorry he was taken from you. I'm even more sorry that it's taken me so long to say those words to you."

"You're sorry? Do you think those words actually mean anything to me? My brother died alone in a fucking jail cell because of you. So, save me your fucking apologies!"

"You're right. Some of the blame for what happened to William does belong to me, and I struggle with it daily, but he wouldn't want this."

"How would you know what he would've wanted?"

"I know that your brother was a kind and caring man." He could see tears start streaming down her face in his bathroom mirror. "He wouldn't have wanted his sister to kill in his name. He definitely wouldn't want his sister to be gunned down because that's what's going to happen if you don't surrender yourself to me. I'm sure my neighbors have already called the police after hearing those shots. If you surrender, I can call my partner so she can let them know you're coming out peacefully and unarmed."

"Maybe I should just let them kill me." She had defeat in her voice. "All I had was Billy. Maybe I should just join him."

"Vicky, no one else is going to die. Enough innocent blood has been spilled over this, and that ends today."

"It ends when I say it ends." Vicky spun around and attempted to raise her gun in one motion. She was able to get a shot off, but Silver deflected her arm upwards so that the bullet went into the ceiling. He then shifted his weapon to his left hand so he could grab her wrist with his right. Using his legs and body weight, he turned her to face the wall and then slammed her wrist against it, causing her to drop her weapon. He still had a grip on her right wrist, but her left arm was flailing, trying to scratch and claw at him. So, while still keeping her pressed against the wall, he slipped his gun into the back of his waistband and grabbed her left wrist. Once he secured both arms, he pulled them behind her back and cuffed her. Since her arms were subdued, she attempted to swing her head at him but instead hit the wall, which dazed her. Now that Silver had complete control, he walked her into his living room and sat her on one of the couch cushions on the floor. He took a moment to catch his breath before pulling his phone out of his pocket.

"Hey, Rita. Promise you won't be mad."

"Fuck, Rita, that hurt," shouted Silver as he rubbed his jaw where she had just punched him.

"Good!" she shouted back. "Remember that pain the next time you decide to lie to me."

Silver had just returned to the precinct after waiting at his apartment for Vicky to be picked up. Then he gave his statement on what had occurred. The second he had walked in, Rita grabbed him and pulled him into an observation room. She had told him on the phone that she would punch him when she saw him, but he didn't believe her.

"I'm sorry I lied, but can I at least explain why?" he pleaded.

She folded her arms. "I'm listening, and it better be good."

"When we were at the motel, I kept thinking that things weren't adding up. Finding that room with that evidence was too easy, almost as if it was meant for us to find so we would let our guard down, but she made a mistake in leaving those surveillance photos."

"Why was that a mistake?"

"Because it let me know that she's been watching me. If you were her and you watched me and Lindsey for months before executing this grand scheme, would you stop watching, or would you want to make sure everything is going according to plan?"

"So you think she has been following us?"

"I know she has," he said excitedly. "Think about it; what reason did she have to come to her home while we were there?" He didn't wait for an answer. "I think she showed up on purpose so we would see the car, and she could plant it at that hotel later for us to find."

"But that's risky. What if we would've caught her?"

"Was it any more risky than anything else she's done?"

"Ok, that's fair, but it doesn't explain how you knew she would try to kill you at your apartment."

"I came up with that because of a question you asked."

"What question was that?"

"Why did they steal my car the night Lindsey was killed? At first, I thought it was so I wouldn't have an alibi, but they had an 'eye witness' placing me at the scene, and even if Patrice testified that she saw my car there, it wouldn't have cleared me for the time of death."

"Ok, I'm with you so far."

"Then I thought about Patrice's smashed camera."

"Which I assumed Lucy did when she took your gun."

"That would make sense if seeing Lucy on her security camera would've raised a red flag for Patrice, but Lucy was always coming and going."

"So why do you think they smashed it?"

"Lucy was given access to pretty much every part of my life, but what is the one thing I would never let her touch?"

"Your car," said Rita as his rambling was starting to come together.

"Exactly! I don't think they intended to steal my car, but they wanted something inside of it, so they smashed the camera so they wouldn't be seen going in my car, but they didn't anticipate Patrice doing inventory that night. So when they saw her walking toward the car, they took it so she wouldn't catch them."

"But what did they want from your car?"

"Remember when I told you that I leave my keys in my car because I go long periods without going to my apartment? I keep them under my seat, so I'll always remember where to find them."

"And Vicky used a key to come into your place."

"A key she made that night." Silver beamed with pride at his crime-solving skills.

"There's one thing you still haven't explained."

"Really?" Silver was pretty sure he explained it all.

"Why did you lie to me?" Rita's face was full of disappointment. "After all we've been through and talked about the last few days, why did you shut me out?"

"I didn't want to," he tried to explain, but Rita huffed and turned away from him. "Seriously, I didn't. I knew she wouldn't come after me unless I was alone, and I also knew the walls were closing in on her, which meant she had to make a move soon. When I saw the photos of Chrissy and Tonya, I realized that she would go after my family if she couldn't get to me. I couldn't let that happen, so I baited her, and I knew if I told you, you wouldn't have let me go through with it."

"You're right, I guess, and I can understand your need to protect your family," Rita said, but her face still wore her disappointment.

"You're still upset."

"It's just that the last couple of days have been a whirlwind, and a lot has happened. Especially between the two of us, and I know we said we would try to be together when this is over, but I can't help but wonder if I'll always be on the outside looking in when it comes to your family."

"I see," Silver responded.

"I know that sounds selfish. That's your daughter and the mother of your child. They should always be a priority for you."

"Don't say that. It's not selfish at all to wonder where you would fit. I've never been in this situation before, so I don't have a straightforward answer for you. All I can say is that family comes in all different shapes and sizes, and our family isn't a closed circle. You won't be on the outside looking in if you're a part of the family."

Rita looked at him and smiled. "That was a pretty good answer. Did you just come up with that?"

"Yeah, that was good, wasn't it? Sometimes I surprise myself." They both laughed, and he reached out to hold her hand. "Now, let's really put this shit to rest."

"Oh, you can close the book on this one," said Rita triumphantly. "She was fingerprinted when she first got here, and they matched the one from your office and Lindsey's apartment. So now we can place her at the scene and corroborate your story."

"Nice." They bumped fists like they did whenever they cracked a case as partners.

"Vicky is on her way up to interrogation now." Rita opened the door for them to leave. "You coming?"

"No, I'll watch from here."

"You sure?"

"Yeah, you won't get anything from her while I'm around." As they were talking, the door to the interrogation room opened, and an officer walked Vicky in. Her shackles clanked against the table as he sat her down, then he walked out and closed the door behind him.

"I guess that's my cue." Rita gave him a wink and closed the door. A moment later, he saw her walking into the interrogation room with Vicky.

"Ms. Hargrave," Rita began. "Have you been informed of your rights, including your right to have an attorney present?"

"Yes," said Vicky softly.

"And you're electing to waive that right?"

"What do I need a lawyer for? I have nothing to say."

"If I were you, I would have a lot to say." Vicky stared at her coldly. "We have surveillance photos that you took of Richard Lindsey and Clifford Silver. We have an eyewitness who reported seeing you on your way up to Richard Lindsey's apartment moments before he died, your fingerprint in his apartment, and don't forget you attempted to kill Clifford Silver just a few hours ago."

"If you have all of that, what do you need me to say?" Vicky wasn't flinching.

"Confess to Richard Lindsey's murder, and I'll talk to the DA on your behalf."

"How sweet of you."

"We have Lucy in another room with her lawyer, working out a deal. The second she starts talking, all deals involving you will be off the table."

Vicky's eyes went dark. "Do you think I care about a deal? Do you think I expected to have a life when this was over? My life ended the day Billy's did. Now, unless you just like wasting both of our time, can you please return me to my cell?"

Rita stared at Vicky for a moment but realized that she meant every word she said. "Have it your way." She stood from the table and opened the door. "Can you please return Ms. Hargrave to the holding cell?" she said to the officer who was standing guard. He gave Rita a nod and walked over to Vicky. Rita stood there as he stood her up and led her past.

As he stepped into the hallway with her, Silver was coming out of the observation room. When Vicky saw him, a sinister smile crept onto her face. "I'll be seeing you in hell, Clifford Silver." And with that final word, Vicky was led away to await her fate.

"That's one hard woman," said Silver to Rita.

"It's like she said. She has nothing to live for."

"Were you telling the truth about Lucy?"

"Yes and no," responded Rita. "She is talking to her lawyer, but I have no clue if she's trying to cut a deal."

"You're about to find out." They didn't notice Javier approaching. "Her lawyer said she's ready to talk, but she'll only talk if Silver's in the room too."

"Oh nice, I've been waiting for this." Silver could barely contain his enthusiasm to come face to face with this new Lucy.

"Cliff, our objective is to get information," said Rita. "If you come at her, she might clam up."

"I'll behave myself." Silver raised his right hand. "I swear."

"You better," said Rita. She led the way to the interrogation room where Lucy and her lawyer were waiting.

When they entered the room, Lucy beamed at Silver. "Hey, Cliff, it's so nice to see you."

"You can call me Silver," he responded. "Cliff is for my friends."

"So, we're not friends anymore?"

"Friends don't frame friends for murder." Silver put a phony smile on his face as he sat at the table.

"You're taking this too personal, Cliff. You were just a job, but I began to see you as a friend at some point. That's why, for the small price of immunity, I'll tell you guys whatever you need to know."

"Not a fucking chance," said Rita. "Your actions led to multiple deaths. We can't just let you walk away from that."

"Rita, sweetie, I'm walking away whether you like it or not because you have practically nothing against me. I'm being nice by offering this, and I'll even give you a bonus and tell you who killed Bob the Doorman."

"So, you're going to confess to his murder?" said Silver.

"Do I have to do everything for you guys," Lucy said sarcastically. "I'm the one who gave you the idea of talking to Bob, so why would I then kill him?"

"Better question is, if your job was to frame Silver, why would you put us on to Bob?" asked Rita.

"Because I meant it when I said I like Cliff, so I tried to help you. Unfortunately, he found out, and Bob died because of it."

"Right ... thanks for the help," said Silver sarcastically.

"Who killed Bob?" Rita said to get the interview back on track.

"Now that's a question that doesn't get answered without my immunity deal."

Rita stared at her. The last thing she wanted to do was give her a deal. "I can't go to the prosecutor and ask for a deal like this without knowing what you have to say. If you give me enough to convict Richard and Bob's killers, then I'm sure we can work something out."

Lucy looked to her lawyer, and he gave her an approving nod. "Vicky killed Richard."

"How did she kill Richard?" Rita needed details.

"We paid a prostitute named Amy to sleep with him, and she left the door open for Vicky to slip in and shoot him."

"What weapon did she use?"

"She used a weapon belonging to Clifford Silver."

"How did she get Silver's gun?"

"I gave it to her after I took it from his gun safe," said Lucy as if it were nothing. Silver could feel his teeth grind as he tried to contain his anger. "I got the code from Clifford Silver while posing as his assistant."

"Don't forget to mention how you drugged me to put the gun back," said Silver.

"What are you talking about?" asked Lucy.

"The night he was killed, you drugged my whiskey and made it look like I got blackout drunk."

"Cliff, that was a brand-new bottle. You broke the seal. How could I have drugged it?" Silver stared at her blankly. "Yes, I snuck your gun back that night, but I didn't have to drug you. You're a drunk, Cliff. All I had to do was wait."

Silver had nothing to say. Rita moved on with the interview so he wouldn't have to linger in his shame.

"Who killed Robert Foster?"

"Now that gets a little more complicated because I don't actually know his name."

"Sounds like your immunity is slipping away," said Silver.

"I said I don't know his name; I didn't say I couldn't help you get him."

"And how can you do that?" asked Rita.

"We work for the same people."

"And what people do you work for?"

"Sorry, hun, that's not on the table."

Rita glared at Lucy. "You're in no position to tell me what's on the table."

"If I give them up, I might as well have you shoot me right here."

"That could be arranged," said Silver.

"All I know is, when a job isn't going exactly to plan, he's the man they send to tie up loose ends."

"Oh, I get it now," said Silver. "You're a loose end. That's the only reason you want us to find him."

Lucy's smile left her face. "That may be the case, but that just sounds like a win-win to me."

"So, you're saying this guy killed Robert Foster?" asked Rita.

"Yes, he cornered me after I left your place, and I told him you were on your way to see Bob. Next thing I knew, you were calling me to say he was dead."

"That doesn't explain why a witness placed you at the scene."

"Did this witness have dark skin and curly hair?" asked Lucy, but Rita didn't respond, so she continued, "Was he not too short but also not too tall? Was he not skinny but also not fat?" Rita didn't want Lucy to know that she described the witness perfectly. "That's his whole thing. He's this unassuming regular-ass-looking dude that you wouldn't guess was a cold-blooded killer. I'm assuming he knew that my next step would be to disappear. So, he killed Bob, posed as his neighbor, and dropped my name so you would hold me here, and I couldn't run."

"What you're saying sounds good," said Rita. "But I haven't heard how you can help us catch him."

"Well, he obviously wants to catch up with me, so how about I call him to set up a meeting where you'll be waiting to arrest him."

Silver and Rita looked at each other and, without saying anything, agreed that it wasn't a bad plan. "Call him and tell him to meet you at Silver's office."

"Bring me my phone, and I'll get it done."

Rita opened the door and whispered something to the officer standing outside. Moments later, Javier walked in and handed Rita Lucy's cell phone. Lucy unlocked it and scrolled through her contacts; when she found what she was looking for, she dialed the number and put the phone on speaker.

"Hello," said a voice on the other end that Rita recognized immediately as the witness.

"Did you hear Vicky was arrested?" asked Lucy, getting straight to the point.

"Yes, I heard. It seems like Silver is smarter than she thought."

"I was thinking we could get together and finish the job."

"Oh, is that what you were thinking?" Silver didn't like what he heard in his tone.

"Yeah, he practically lives in his office, so you meet me there, and I can let you in while he's sleeping."

"How about you just cut the shit and put Silver on the phone," he said calmly. "I know he's right there."

Lucy looked at Silver, and he saw the panic in her eyes. Then he looked at Rita before taking the phone. "This is Silver."

"It's so nice to be formally introduced. I've heard so much about you."

231

"Well, that puts me at a disadvantage. What's your name, friend?"

"You can call me Terrell."

"Ok, Terrell, Lucy tells me that there are some things we should talk about with you."

"Lucy? Is that the name she's using with you? She never was very creative."

"I'm not really much for small talk." Silver wanted to move the conversation along, "How about we get together and have a nice discussion with each other?"

"You know what, Silver, that's a great idea, and I know exactly where you can meet me."

"Where at?"

They could hear a car door open and close through the phone. "See, I promised Vicky that if she failed, I wouldn't, so how about you meet me at 21222 Vivianne Drive."

Rita covered her mouth with her hand, and Lucy went as pale as a ghost. Silver snatched the phone from the table. "If you touch them, I'll fucking kill you!"

"You don't know this about me, but I don't deal well with cursing, so I'm going to hang up the phone now. I hope to see you here."

Silver opened his mouth to say something else, but the line went dead. He jumped up from the table, knocking his chair to the floor. He practically jumped across the room to the door and swung it open. He knocked the officer standing outside to the floor on his way out. Rita had to sprint to keep up, but they both could hear Lucy shouting, "I'm so sorry, Cliff," from the interrogation room.

Silver's Mustang jumped the curb as he pulled up in front of Tonya's house. He was so frantic to get out of the car that he almost forgot to put it in park. Once he was out, he ran up to her front door, which to his dismay, was wide open. Rita struggled to keep pace behind him with how fast he was running.

"Cliff, wait!" Rita shouted after him, but if he heard her, he didn't listen. Instead, he ran straight into the house with no regard for himself. The house was pitch black, but he still knew his way around.

"T!" he shouted. "Are you here?" There was no answer. "Chrissy! Princess, it's Daddy. You can come out now."

Silver could feel a lump form in his throat as he continued to move through the house. He was moving from the living room to the kitchen when he tripped and fell over something in the hallway. His gun slid across the floor, and he scrambled to grab it; once he recovered it, he turned and pointed it at whatever took him down just as Rita made it into the house with her flashlight. When she shined her light at where he was pointing his weapon, he saw Tonya lying on the floor, covered in blood. He threw his gun to the side and frantically crawled over to her. He scooped her up in his arms and cradled her lifeless body.

"Wake up, T," he said to her as he rocked her back and forth. "Please wake up. We need you, T."

"Cliff." Rita put a hand on his shoulder.

"Come on, T. I'm here. Please don't go." Tears began to rain down his face as he tried to wipe the blood from hers.

"Cliff."

"Please, T, I'm so sorry. I'm sorry for everything. I'll make it all up to you if you wake up for me."

"Cliff, she's gone."

ACKNOWLEDGMENTS

From the moment I outlined *Silver*, I've been thinking about writing my acknowledgments. Firstly, writing this means that I've accomplished my dream of writing a novel, and secondly, I couldn't wait to thank everyone who helped me along the way. Those who supported this "pipe dream" from day one. I'm a firm believer in giving people their flowers while they're still here to receive them, so without further ado, and before the music plays me off the stage, here are the people that helped make *Silver* a reality.

First and foremost, I have to start with the two people I literally wouldn't be here without. To my mom, Tara Williams, thank you for being my sounding board. You made yourself available whenever I needed to talk through a scenario, and I wouldn't have made it to the finish line without you. To my dad, Arnold Stewart, thank you for pushing me to pursue my writing. I remember coming to you and asking about getting into real estate. You gave me the advice I was asking for, but not before telling me that you didn't see me as a real estate agent. You asked me what did I want to do, and when I told you I wanted to write, you said, "Do it." To you those were just two words, but to me, they meant the world.

I have six siblings who show me love and support in everything I do, but I would like to take this moment to especially thank my brother Brandon. I know you thought I was crazy for quitting my job to write this book, but you showed me nothing but support anyway. It's one of the many reasons I'm proud to call you my big brother. I also want to give a special shoutout to my cousin Darius. Thank you for always being there, for the reminders to stay focused, and for the encouragement to follow my purpose.

To my brothers from another, Sean and Garswah, Silver wouldn't exist with you. Garswah, a.k.a. Terrell, thank you for being my first editor. Your chapter-by-chapter analysis kept me at my best. I knew that your seal of approval meant that I was on to something special. Sean, your words of encouragement kept me going. Thank you for always being there to talk me through the tough times and reminding me that I can go as far as my imagination will take me. I love you both, and drinks on me when this book comes out. Just the first drink; after that, you're on your own.

I want to thank everyone I had the pleasure of working with at Atmosphere Press. You guys made my dream a reality, and I am forever grateful. Special shoutout to my editor, BE. I came to you as a storyteller and left as a writer.

Lastly, I want to thank everyone who has read and supported this book. I hope you enjoyed reading this as much as I did writing it, and I can't wait to bring you more of Silver's adventures in the future.

ABOUT ATMOSPHERE PRESS

Atmosphere Press is an independent, full-service publisher for excellent books in all genres and for all audiences. Learn more about what we do at atmospherepress.com.

We encourage you to check out some of Atmosphere's latest releases, which are available at Amazon.com and via order from your local bookstore:

Finding Us, by Kristin Rehkamp

The Ideological and Political System of Banselism, by Royard Halmonet Vantion (Ancheng Wang)

Unconditional: Loving and Losing an Addict, by Lizzy and Adam

Telling Tales and Sharing Secrets, by Jackie Collins, Diana Kinared, and Sally Showalter

Nursing Homes: A Missionary's Journey Through Heaven's Waiting Room, by Tim Eatman Ph.D.

Timeline of Stars, by Joe Adcock

A Boy Who Loved Me, by Wilson Semitti

The Injustice in Justice, by Charmaine Loverin

Living in the Gray, by Katie Weber

Living with Veracity, Dying with Dignity, by Alison Clay-Duboff

Noah's Rejects, by Rob Kagan

A lot of Questions (with no answers)?, by Jordan Neben

Cowboy from Prague: An Immigrant's Pursuit of the American Dream, by Charles Ota Heller

Sleeping Under the Bridge, by Melissa Baker

The Only Prayer I Ever Have to Say Is Thank You, by M. Kaya Hill

Amygdala Blue, by Paul Lomax

ABOUT THE AUTHOR

Photo: Kenyetta Johnson

Silver is Paris Williams' first novel. He was born and raised on the southside of Chicago, where from a young age, he showed a propensity for storytelling, and he fell in love with all things mystery. He hopes to continue his career as a writer, bringing you great stories, lovable characters, and of course, mysteries that will keep you guessing.

Milton Keynes UK
Ingram Content Group UK Ltd.
UKHW040737030823
426269UK00004B/292